COUNTING ON LOVE

The Taverstons of Iversley
Book 1

By Carol Coventry

DRAGONBLADE PUBLISHING, INC.

ARE YOU SIGNED UP FOR DRAGONBLADE'S BLOG?

You'll get the latest news and information on exclusive giveaways, exclusive excerpts, coming releases, sales, free books, cover reveals and more.

Check out our complete list of authors, too!

No spam, no junk. That's a promise!

Sign Up Here

www.dragonbladepublishing.com

Dearest Reader;

Thank you for your support of a small press. At Dragonblade Publishing, we strive to bring you the highest quality Historical Romance from some of the best authors in the business. Without your support, there is no 'us', so we sincerely hope you adore these stories and find some new favorite authors along the way.

Happy Reading!

CEO, Dragonblade Publishing

CHAPTER ONE

November 1812, London

THE LONDON SEASON. *The Marriage Mart.* It was said to be the most exciting time in a lady's life—the contest for which she had been preparing since birth—during which a mere few months of attending parties would determine her entire future.

Why was that not appalling? Lady Georgiana Stewart, daughter of the Duke of Hovington, turned to her cousin Alice and forced a smile. A waiting footman handed them down from the ducal carriage onto a wide, brick-paved drive. Georgiana's mother, the Duchess, preceded them, marching ahead as if into battle, nodding greetings to other arrivals. Georgiana gestured up the crowded walkway to the entrance of a blazingly lit Greek revival-style home.

"I hope you aren't nervous, Alice." If she was, Georgiana knew she would be no help, not while laboring under her own cloud of dread.

"In these clothes? Of course not," Alice replied with a jaunty twitch of her wrap.

Alice did look particularly pretty. The high-waisted, pale-yellow gown suited her dark hair and pale complexion. Its green bows brought out the color of her eyes, which were bright with amusement, not nerves.

Alice glanced ahead at her formidable aunt. "Besides, the Duchess has reassured me tonight is strictly for practice. It's not an official function."

True, the Season would not officially open until Lady Andini's ball on Thursday. Meanwhile, Mrs. Preston, the independent-minded sister of the Marquess of Waltham, had been holding this pre-Season rout annually ever since she defied expectations and married a handsome, wealthy cit. The ton may not have approved, but invitations to her parties were highly prized, especially by those young ladies about to be launched, who appreciated a tame evening of preparation. It was the unofficial start to the most exciting time of their lives.

Georgiana looped her arm through Alice's and followed her mother up the walk.

"I need this too. I'm woefully out of practice."

She regretted the callous words the minute they left her mouth. Out of practice might be true enough. At the end of the last Season, which had been calamitous, she'd fled London for the peace and quiet of her father's country house in Marbury, determined to avoid fashionable society for as long as possible. Yet equating her situation with Alice's was unjust. Mama's widowered brother's daughter was what one might call a poor relation. Her dowry was scanty, and her father possessed only proximity to a title. Whereas Georgiana's advantages still outweighed her disadvantages—that was the problem.

Alice gave her arm a pat. "Once more unto the breach, dear friend. Stiffen the sinews. Summon up the blood."

At that, Georgiana laughed. No one understood her as well as Alice.

And perhaps their situations were not so different. At nineteen years of age, they both needed to find husbands, sooner better than later. There was no other choice.

When they were young, growing up almost as sisters, they gabbled excitedly, callowly, about coming out together. But as the time approached, without ever discussing it, they realized that a dual debut would be unfair. Alice would have to compete with Georgiana for gentlemen's attention. And how could she? Whereas Alice was merely pretty, Georgiana was a renowned beauty.

The renown was largely the result of a few egregious sonnets that had made the rounds last winter, praising her strawberry-blonde hair, her Greek nose, her milk-white skin, and, daringly, her pleasing figure—a lot of fustian nonsense. She was a duke's daughter, and her dowry would be at least twenty thousand pounds. That was the true source of her beauty's renown.

At her coming out ball, she had immediately been dubbed: *the Incomparable*, a sobriquet as embarrassing as it was unoriginal. The splash she'd made had merely increased the pressure on her to make a brilliant match. It was expected of her. And she had failed.

Oh, she'd had offers. If she possessed two heads and snakes for hair, she would have had offers. Frightened, she turned them all down. Men she barely knew were asking for a lifetime of devotion! A lifetime.

The balls, the theater, the routs, the musicales, even Almack's—especially Almack's—it had all been so…boring. And here she was, preparing to go through it all again. She must. And it would be worse: having failed to pull off a triumph her first Season, she would find suitors warier. *What is wrong with Lady Georgiana?*

What was wrong was that she could not bear to commit to a lifetime of mind-numbing dullness.

And how unfair that she would still overshadow Alice, who deserved her own opportunity to shine.

They reached the open door where Mrs. Preston greeted her guests. Mama introduced Alice. Georgiana, of course, was known. Their hostess urged them to move into the music room to find the other young people and some light refreshments. The Duchess, she claimed for herself.

Georgiana steered her cousin down the hall toward the sound

of voices. It all seemed eerily similar to last year. That impression was reinforced when they entered the music room: the same piano pushed against the wall, a buzzing assembly of prettily dressed ladies and smartly attired gentlemen, the scent of cakes, punch, and perfume. She was acquainted with most of the other guests, Alice less so. She would have to smooth her cousin's path, but just looking at the gathering made her tired.

Fortunately, the first face to emerge from the mix was that of Lord Haslet. She smiled, relaxing a bit, as he approached.

"Lady Georgiana! How good to see you."

"And you, my lord. May I present my cousin, Miss Alice Fogbotham? This is Lord Haslet."

"Delighted." He bent a leg with an absurd flourish that made Alice giggle.

Viscount Haslet, Hazard to his friends, was a forty-year-old confirmed bachelor. He drank little, gambled less, and was said to be worth a fortune: a spectacular catch if one ignored rumors of hidden vice. He had approached her last year in this same room in much the same way, flirting so maladroitly that she quickly guessed he wasn't serious. In retrospect, it had been one of the few highlights of the Season. She had looked for him at other parties, but he rarely attended once he'd "done his duty and reminded people of his existence". He'd proposed to her midway through the calendar, as soon as he was certain, he'd said, that she would refuse him—only so that he could honestly inform his mother that he had.

It seemed his mother didn't like his heir, a cousin's son who she'd decided was a wastrel.

At least that proposal had been painless. And they were still friends.

"I'm pleased to make your acquaintance, my lord," Alice said. "I've heard so much about you."

That was true. Although Georgiana had seen him infrequently, he'd brightened a few of the drearier parties, and her letters to her cousin had reflected that.

"Have you? That's wonderful. Saves me the effort of explaining myself." He straightened his waistcoat. "Would you like to accompany me to the Conservatory? The foliage is supposed to be superb and there is more air to breathe. Bad form, I suppose, for me to lure away two young lovelies, but…" He lowered his voice. "I believe the company there is more congenial."

He gestured with his chin. Georgiana directed her gaze where he indicated, then dropped her eyes. Lord Dunstun. *That* proposal had been excruciating. The dullard had been convinced of his right to have her and could not believe she didn't agree. He accused her of coyness. One thing she was not, was coy. It wouldn't surprise her if he'd gone on to speak ill of her. Hazard had evidently heard something.

"Yes," she said faintly. "We'd love to see the Conservatory."

The trio walked the length of the Prestons' home. Lord Haslet exaggerated the bend of his elbows, like chicken wings, so that he could escort one woman on each side. They passed a darkened corridor where Georgiana saw two shut doors, evidently off-limits. She wondered if they could even be locked. That might be appropriate as the chaperonage was rather lax. Mrs. Preston's guest list was known to be exclusive: young ladies as yet unfamiliar with the courtship process should not fear being led into compromising situations by rakes—but Lord Dunstun was here, so the winnowing process was not foolproof.

The next corridor was lamplit and opened into a cardroom. Several couples sat clustered at tables. Likely there was low-stakes gambling taking place, something to entertain the young marrieds since there would be no dancing. The library across the hallway was open but empty. Georgiana was not tempted by it. She had taken a peek inside last year and had been unimpressed: nothing scientific or mathematical. It looked to be a collection of travelogues and fat biographies, spines intact and pages uncut. The Prestons were not readers.

They stepped into the Conservatory. Whoever the architect had been, he'd done a beautiful job. The tall gabled ceiling was all of glass, as were the walls, mostly. Small trees with broad leaves were tucked into niches, and huge flowerpots were arranged to create a maze-like arrangement across the floor. There was statuary too, toga-clad male and female figures. A few cherubic cupids. Nothing improper. None of the niches were secluded enough for couples to disappear into. Several guests wandered here and there, no doubt flirting tentatively. Practicing.

Georgiana withdrew her hand from Hazard's arm.

"If you don't mind, I'll sit on the bench there for a few minutes while you and Miss Fogbotham have a stroll. I seem to have something caught in my shoe that I need to wiggle out before I'm blistered."

"Oh dear, we can't have that," he replied, smiling. He drew Alice closer and led her off. He was the ideal guest for this sort of rout. Charming. Safe. Perhaps she should have accepted him. There were certainly worse marriages.

Georgiana took herself to the bench, a wrought iron piece that was even less comfortable than it looked. She sat, breathing in the earthy scent of potted trees, then sighed and tried to forget that Lord Dunstun was at the party. Surely he wouldn't approach her. It would be as unpleasant for him as for her. But this was another downside to a second Season. London was littered with gentlemen from last year. Most had not chosen to court her at the time. Why would they now? And of those who had been suitors, she'd rejected the ones who'd asked for her hand and would have rejected the others. Spending more time with them, Hazard excepted, would be pointless and embarrassing.

Bending over, she ran her index finger along the heel of her stocking. She hadn't been telling a tale. There was a pebble or bit of gravel in her shoe. But all she accomplished was to push it further down to torment her more. It was unfair that ladies were not permitted to swear. Or to remove their footwear at parties and shake out the dirt.

She tried to swipe her finger under her heel, but the shoe was too tight. And now, given that her stays were digging into her ribs, she emitted an unladylike grunt, just as a shadow passed over her. She sat bolt upright.

A man had approached her bench from the side—a tall, broad-shouldered, exquisitely dressed, fair-haired man with a strong, square jaw and blue eyes that were clearly laughing. She knew him. His name sat on the tip of her tongue. What was it?

"Georgie! It is you. My word. You're a young lady now! How can that be?"

Georgie? No one had ever called her that. And if she could not remember who he was, they were not so well acquainted that he could corrupt her given name in a public place.

She gave him a cold stare. "Do I know you, sir?"

He gaped, then laughed. "Well, that put me in my place!" He wagged a finger and scolded her. "Lady Georgiana, you have known me since you were in leading strings. Our fathers hunted together. Our mothers huddled in front of the fireplace discussing novels. And you…" He drew out the word, lifting his eyebrows. "You were determined to train our barn cats."

Oh, good Lord. She did know him. His father was the Earl of Iversley. He was Lord Taverston, the eldest brother in the trio known as the lords of Iversley by the ton, which—though incorrect, as they weren't all lords—still had a musical ring to it that had made the nickname stick. He was the only one of the three sons that she'd met, although it hardly counted as a meeting. She'd been seven years old, at most, when her parents had taken her to Chaumbers, the Earl's country estate, for a house party. Lord Taverston had been home from Oxford. She couldn't recall if it had been a holiday or a send-down; however, the other boys had been away at school, hadn't they? So that hinted at send-down. He'd ignored her, naturally. Maybe he'd pulled her braids once. She'd thought him a prince. For the space of a fortnight. It all came back to her now.

"Lord Taverston, of course, I remember." She relaxed her frown. "You had the most recalcitrant cats."

He chuckled. "I can't get over it." Without being invited, he sat beside her. "Mother told me to look for you here, but I was looking for a little girl with messy red hair and dirt on her nose. I might have walked right past."

She didn't correct him, although her hair was not, had never been, red, except in some light where it might be considered redd*ish*.

She wasn't sure how to respond. The little he'd said had conveyed quite a bit. Given he was attending Oxford over a decade ago, he would be nearing thirty. He was the Earl's heir. She did not recollect any recent weddings in the Taverston family. She was a duke's daughter now, of marriageable age. And his mother had told him to seek her out.

"I can't imagine how you recognized me, bent over my shoe."

"Well, *Red*." He smiled and touched her hair. Touched it! She drew back. And realized a lock had fallen from its pin while she'd been struggling with the stone.

"Oh, for Heaven's sake," she said, flushing. "Is there also dirt on my nose?"

He shook his head, looking very amused and frightfully hand-some. *He* had not a hair out of place. Then, without a by-your-leave, he reached out and tucked the lock back where it belonged. Despite the gross impropriety, she held still as he adjusted the pin—she was distracted by his cologne, which was subtly pleasant.

He leaned back. She patted her hair self-consciously and found it secure. "Have you been trained as a lady's maid?"

"Self-trained. My little sister is a hoyden. Rides to the hounds. Both my brothers and I have learned how to fix her back up before our mother sees her. It would kill her, you see, to be banned from the stables."

"How very kind of you."

His smile broadened. "Your voice has not changed. You speak to me as if you were lecturing the cats. Am I as disappointing?"

Disappointing? No. His charm was palpable.

"Well, no." She pointed to her hair. "You are evidently teachable."

"I suppose I could be. With the right instructor." Then he winced. "I'm sorry. What an aggressively flirtatious thing to say."

It was. But how was she to freeze him after his preemptive apology?

"Well." He shrugged. "I'm just so…pleased to see how you've…" He waved his hand at her but didn't finish the sentence. Yet she knew exactly what he hadn't said. His mother had ordered him to go have a squint at the Duke of Hovington's chit. And now he was delighted to discover his mother had been right. Lady Georgiana, all grown up, was a catch.

And so, too, was Lord Taverston. In fact, he must have been one of the most eligible bachelors of the ton. Which begged the question: why had they not become reacquainted last year?

They were such an obvious match that a courtship seemed superfluous. For a moment, she felt a sickening falling sensation, worse than mere dizziness. Vertigo.

To Georgiana's relief, Alice and Lord Haslet returned just in time to rescue her from having to make some sort of response. The men greeted one another chummily. Georgiana introduced her cousin and Lord Taverston pronounced himself charmed.

"Will you ladies be at Lady Andini's ball?" he asked. It was a safe question. Of course, they'd been invited and, of course, they would go.

"Yes. And will you, Lord Haslet?" Georgiana asked, hoping that he would secure the first dance with her before Lord Taverston could.

"I expect so. I really should."

"Lady Georgiana, please say you will dance the opening set with me," put in Lord Taverston, almost before Hazard had finished speaking.

Hazard gave him a wry look. He saw the obvious. And that was why Georgiana was reluctant to appear at the Season's first ball dancing the first dance with Lord Jasper Taverston. Everyone would assume the obvious. They were going to be this Season's Grand Match.

Hazard turned chivalrously to her cousin. "And I hope you will do me the same honor, Miss Fogbotham."

"I will, thank you, my lord," Alice said, blushing a little. "Though now, I suppose, you will feel obligated to attend."

"No, now I will look forward to attending."

"Lady Georgiana?" Lord Taverston pressed.

"Why, naturally, my lord." If she refused, manners dictated she could not accept any other partner the entire evening. And she had nothing against Lord Taverston—so long as he did not persist in nicknaming her *Red*—if she didn't think about the feeling of being hemmed in.

Then, he said what should not be said. Leaning close, he whispered loudly enough to include the others and make it into a joke: "Just imagine how happy it will make our mothers."

CHAPTER TWO

*L*ONDON—THE CENTER OF the world, for all intents and purposes. Or so it was said to be. The Honorable Reginald Taverston, third son of the Earl of Iversley, thought otherwise.

After four months rusticating at the family country estate and spending two more months in Bath visiting his great aunts (well, one great aunt and one great aunt's long-time companion), Reginald had returned to the city where all fashionable gentlemen belonged, for some reason that escaped him.

He ducked his head into the wet wind and willed his feet to press on, puddles be damned.

The obligatory teasing that Jasper, his eldest brother had subjected him to—*What! Newly arrived? Why are you HERE?*— would have turned to frank mockery if Jasper had guessed that it was not only filial duty bringing Reginald directly to the Earl's London townhouse, but also a lack of enthusiasm for the visit upon which he was now embarked. Any other red-blooded young man would have hied off to his neglected mistress first.

Thank God Crispin had been absent for the taunting. Their middle brother was a wild card. One never knew whose side he would take, but if he had taken Reginald's, it would have been out of pity, not fellow feeling.

Upon arriving in the city, Reginald, being himself rather than Jasper or Crispin, had gone directly to see their mother. He went to report on Father, the Earl, who had been sickly for a while, recuperating in the country. And to reassure Mother that the aunts were still well.

Also, admittedly, he'd been looking forward to a quiet homecoming. He'd arrived the day after Mrs. Preston's annual pre-Season rout by pure serendipity—a little rude-seeming, perhaps, since the whole family had missed it last year. But Jasper's teasing struck a chord, so Reginald merely answered his mother's most pressing inquiries, then took himself off for a bit of entertainment, as young men were expected to do.

The walk was not far. He made his way to Baker Street, an out-of-the-way but still toney address where well-acquainted gentlemen were likely to pass one another without acknowledgment, giving no offense. This was what passed for being discreet. Mistresses resided here.

Being twenty-three, unmarried, and possessed of an adequate allowance, his own presence on Baker Street was hardly scandalous. It was no secret that he kept company with the sought-after Miss Annie DeBelle—not her true name—who had, for a short time, been an opera singer. At least, he had been keeping company with her, beginning a year prior to his departure from London. He continued paying her bills, which were not exorbitant, even though he'd been absent for the last six months. Granted, it was a rather one-sided arrangement, but keeping a mistress on retainer, as it were, kept him from having to go through the process of finding another.

Besides, he was fond of Annie. He should be impatient to reacquaint himself with her. After all, he had not availed himself of any alternatives—a rather embarrassing fact that he would never admit to Jasper or Crispin. True, there was little opportunity in Iversley, but one would not have had to look very hard in Bath.

He hadn't bothered. Was that strange? It seemed to him it was.

Annie had been very little bother. Thankfully. And she was

lovely, which made Reginald feel more...credible. And there were other obvious benefits besides.

He crossed the narrow street and ascended the steps to the door. The house was narrow, squeezed into too small a lot, but neatly built and comfortable. Annie had chosen it with the help of her previous protector. When the gossips reported that the man's attentions had shifted to a young actress, Miss DeBelle let it be known she would welcome a new benefactor. That had caught Reginald's interest. He'd heard her sing once. At a private party, not on stage. After a few inquiries and an interview of sorts, Reginald signed a few papers, took over the lease, and it was done.

Thinking back, it had all been pleasantly uncomplicated, although it did surprise him that she'd accepted his offer over those of other bidders. Jasper had claimed to be flabbergasted, but Crispin elbowed their brother roughly and said Annie was said to be a shrewd judge. That comment, Reginald had felt, was even more mocking than Jasper's feigned shock. Thank God he'd been savvy enough not to ask: judge of what?

Although he possessed a key, he rang the bell. She must have heard that he was back in London, but he wouldn't barge in unannounced.

Dolores, Annie's girl, opened the door. "Girl" was a misnomer. The woman may well have started out as Annie's nursemaid from the look of her.

"My lord!" She bobbed a curtsy, frowning. "Come in. I'll tell Miss DeBelle that you're here."

"She may not be expecting me."

"Don't be silly." Annie's silken voice pulled his attention to the stairway in the hall. "Of course I expected you."

Of course, she would. He felt a jolt, seeing her. She was even more beautiful than he remembered. Voluptuous. Black hair. Those almond-shaped eyes and plump lips. He was suddenly quite glad he had come. She wore a pale green dress of a fabric so thin it might well have been translucent. A swath of darker green silk draped across her shoulders and around her upper arms, a pretense of modesty likely performed for his sake; he possessed an awkward streak of prudishness that he knew amused her.

"Good evening, Miss DeBelle."

"Mr. Taverston, won't you come into the parlor?" She turned to the maid. "Dolores, please take Mr. Taverston's coat and hat."

After removing the small box from the pocket of his coat and slipping it inside his jacket, he handed his outer things to the maid and followed Annie up the stairs.

A fire warmed the parlor. Light floral wallpaper made the cozy room appear larger than it was. The furnishings were unchanged except for new plush pillows decorating the davenport and chairs. The drapes were drawn, and the lamps burned low. Perhaps the flue on the fireplace wasn't drawing properly because he caught a faint whiff of smoke. He sank onto the davenport while Annie went to a sideboard displaying glasses and a decanter.

"You still prefer sherry?" she asked.

He wondered if "still" was an admonishment.

"Sherry is fine." His preference was to drink sparingly of whatever was set before him. He hated the outside-of-himself sensation of being foxed. That was another thing Jasper mocked him for. Of course, Crispin drank no spirits at all, yet he was not mocked. Even Jasper's so-called humor had limits.

She brought him a glass. He trailed his fingertips over the back of her hand as he took it from her. She smiled but stepped away rather than sitting beside him. Which was odd. She might be angry with him. As if to confirm his suspicion, she took a seat halfway across the room.

They sat a moment in silence. It occurred to him, as he struggled for opening words, that he had always relied upon her to find topics for light conversation. As if it were her responsibility to ensure his comfort. *Not as if. It was her responsibility. Her job. Part of it anyway.* The thought left a bitter taste in his mouth. She was not his lover, but his employee.

Still. They were fond of one another. They could converse companionably about something. His six months away, perhaps? But she would not be interested in his aunts, funny though he found them, and it was inappropriate to discuss his father's illness with her.

Then he remembered with relief that he'd brought her a gift, a gold bracelet set with gemstones. He'd give it to her. They'd exchange pleasant stories about Bath. He'd take her to bed and this awkwardness would dissipate.

He cleared his throat and set his drink on the end table. "Come, sit by me." He gestured. "I have something for you."

She rose and came to sit close. Her perfume was new. Something heavy. Foreign. Alluring. He leaned forward and kissed her cheek, but she held herself so stiffly he retreated. The pillows bunched behind him. Her perfume mingled with the odd, smokey odor he'd noted before, apparently emanating from the davenport.

He ignored the nagging feeling that he was missing something important. Taking the box from his jacket and handing it to her, he imagined, or hoped, it would right what had slipped askew.

Rather than open it, she set it down on the cushion. "I shouldn't accept."

"No?" Annie had never been one to demand extravagances, but she'd never before refused a present he'd brought her. So he *had* offended her. "Should I have…?"

What? He didn't know what was correct in these situations. How was a man supposed to return to his mistress after a six-month absence?

"Should I have written?"

Her eyes widened. "Darling." She laughed a little. "You are such a dear. Of course, it would have been sweet of you to write to me, but I didn't expect it. Whatever would you have said?"

"I don't know." He took a stab at it. "That I missed you."

"Ah." She shook her head, smiling, but her eyes were shiny, a bit sad. "Did you?"

He nodded, yet didn't say the words. In truth, he'd given her so little thought it was a miracle he'd remembered to buy her a gift.

"Darling, look at me."

He did.

"How do I look to you?"

His answer was automatic. "Beautiful."

"Look closer." She leaned her face close to his, but when he bent to kiss her, she put a finger to his lips. "Do you know how you appear to me?"

He drew back sharply, confused. As his back slapped against the pillows, the smoke scent wafted out and he recognized it: *Stale tobacco.*

He didn't smoke.

"You look to me like a man growing bored. A man who has outgrown his mistress."

"That isn't true." How could she surmise that from how he "looked?" He felt a bit panicked. He hadn't anticipated this. How could he have? "Let's go to bed." He'd prove *he* wasn't bored with *her.*

She shook her head and laid her hand on his. "I need to tell you something first."

First. All right. He turned his hand over, so they were palm to palm. He didn't claim to understand women, but suspected if one wanted to talk, it was best to listen. Then he would ask if she had begun smoking cigars.

No, of course, he wouldn't.

"Go on."

She hesitated a moment before squeezing his hand. Then she said, "How old do you suppose I am?"

"What?" Where on earth was she going with all of this?

"How old?"

He didn't know, but he knew better than to guess. "Not very. Older than I am. Not enough to matter."

"How much older would matter?"

He tried to joke. "Older than you are."

"I'm thirty-three."

He blinked. *Good Lord.* She was older than Jasper. He had the presence of mind to say, "That isn't old." But his voice sounded rattled, even to himself. He added, "You don't look it."

She laughed. "That is not as reassuring to hear as I'm sure you meant it to be."

"You're beautiful to me," he insisted.

"Darling, I *am* a beautiful woman. That is my stock-in-trade."

"Well then?" He wasn't understanding. She wasn't making sense. The room began to feel overly warm.

"But I'm also practical. Beauty fades. I have to face the fact that my value can only wane."

"Don't talk like that." It was distasteful. Sordid, even. "I'm drawn to you for more than your looks."

She waved off his clumsy attempt to reassure her. Thankfully. If she'd asked him to elaborate, he would have drawn a blank. He didn't have a facility for pretty compliments and would stumble over what to say. Perhaps she wouldn't have listened anyway. She seemed hellbent on pressing a point. "So I ask myself: am I to remain with a handsome young gentleman, who pleases me very much and brings me lovely gifts, until he abandons me for—"

"I'm not *that* shallow," he interrupted, impatient with her pique. He should have jotted off a few notes. Six months was a long time. Though she was correct; he couldn't imagine what he would have said.

"—a wife," she finished, giving him a long look. "Or, do I move on while I can?"

He nearly choked. "A *wife*? That's ludicrous."

Not all men put aside their mistresses when they wed. Probably most didn't. He might, prude that he was. But it was a silly thing to worry over. It was not even a given that he would take a wife. Jasper was heir to the earldom. He needed to marry and likely soon. But Reginald was twenty-three, not twenty-nine. And then it would be Crispin's turn. Third sons were not badgered to wed and set up nurseries. Why was Annie bringing up such a concern now?

"I am years from marrying."

"But that's worse, don't you see? Who will clamor for my company in five years? God forbid, in ten?"

So. It occurred to him what she was trying to tell him, and suddenly the tobacco odor made sense. Someone was clamoring for her company *now*.

"Who is it?" he asked.

Slow as he'd been, Annie evidently hadn't expected him to catch on quite yet. She tried out a succession of expressions. Confusion. Timidity. Regret. She settled on mutinous.

"Sir Plodgett."

"Gad." Plodgett was one of Annie's disappointed "suitors" a year ago. He hadn't given up. Rather, he'd waited until Reginald's back was turned. Bad ton. Poaching a man's mistress was out of bounds.

"Mr. Taverston, darling—"

"You've been with him, haven't you? Here?" Ridiculously, his jaw clenched, and his voice hitched as if he were angry. More ridiculously, he *was* angry. Annie would trade him for a baronet who was fifty years old if he was a day. Plodgett? He could hear Jasper's laughter already.

She bit her lip as if considering what to say, then she nodded. "He is not likely to tire of me."

"No. More likely you'll be wheeling him about in a chair, wrapping a shawl over his shoulders, and fetching him possets."

That was crueler than he meant to be. She eyed him, disappointed, then continued levelly. "I am prepared for that eventuality. He said he would provide me a lifetime pension. If I don't take this offer, I am unlikely to receive another so favorable."

"But you were entertaining such offers while living under my…" Protection? What a misleading euphemism. "Roof," he finished, lowering his gaze. And now he hated himself.

He cared less that she was leaving him than that she was making him look like a fool. Weak. Practically cuckolded.

Yet bubbling up alongside his humiliation was a light feeling of relief. He would have needed to disentangle himself from her eventually. Now he wouldn't have to.

She cocked her head and regarded him steadily, and he had the uncomfortable feeling she sensed his relief.

"I am sorry," she said.

"Well, no." He tried to be magnanimous. "You're in a difficult situation."

She smiled a lightly mocking smile. Once again, he'd amused her when that was not his intention. "As are you. Believe me, I understand." Her eyes danced, making her seem more like herself. "Sir Plodgett has said that, naturally, he will see to reimbursing you for your expenses."

"God!" The oath exploded from his lips. "That mercenary blackguard."

"Yes, he is crass," she admitted.

"And a coward." Reginald saw that with a sudden clarity, and it made him feel better. "He left this whole business to you to tell me?"

"I think perhaps he was leery of facing you." She shrugged, excusing Plodgett's poor behavior. It was a habit she would have to acquire. "He didn't know what to expect. You're rather a mystery, you know, compared to your brothers."

Jasper would say it was beneath him to pummel an old man. Crispin would say to hell with it and pummel him anyway. But Reginald?

"Did he think I would take his money then? Third son? Pockets to let?" Was that how Plodgett had wooed her? Implying Reginald could not afford such a desirable courtesan?

"I believe he heard a rumor you were a crack shot." Her eyebrows arched in question as if she, too, found him a bit of a mystery. Crack shot was not out of the question, but it was out of character. He was, after all, a man who wore spectacles at the theater.

"Where would he have heard that?"

She paused before saying, "At White's. He *overheard* it. Lord Taverston let it slip."

So Jasper knew. And he'd entertained himself by terrorizing the old sod. Well, it was a revenge of a sort. And Reginald would have had to face Jasper anyway. It wasn't as if such choice gossip could be muzzled.

But, the deuce. He sank against the cushion. He would never have thought *he* could be the subject of the ton's latest *on dit.* Certainly, *no one* would ever imagine such a thing. He grimaced ruefully.

"You may reassure him that I won't shoot him."

Her smile grew. She peeled the silk wrap from her shoulders and set it to her side.

"Now that's settled, shall we go to bed before we part ways?"

He flinched. She wasn't joking. That bothered him—how little she knew him. He picked up his sherry and drained the glass.

"No. You owe me nothing."

Her expression flattened. Just there, about her eyes, he could see the start of fine worry lines. Until now, her age had never concerned him enough to notice the evidence of it. Unfortunately, that had been naïve of him.

"I am not offering out of obligation," she said, peeved. "I'd like to go to bed with you."

Scratching the itch, as Crispin would put it, in his indecorous way. Reginald supposed she *did* want him to take her to bed. Annie had taught him how to give her pleasure, and he was nothing if not a careful student.

Still, he shook his head. His face felt hot, and he wondered if he was reddening.

"I see," she said quietly. Gently. Her expression reminded him of the look she'd given him the first time they'd lain together. She hadn't been his first, but close enough to it. She hadn't said anything, but she'd known.

That first time—he wished he could forget. He'd been home on break during his first year at Cambridge. His brothers had divvied up the chore of "growing him up". Jasper got him drunk. Crispin took him to a brothel, disappearing at once with a favorite—a buxom redhead who acted delighted to see him— leaving Reginald to choose between two brunettes of indeterminate age whose faces he was too embarrassed to note. That night, and the morning after, he'd sorely wished he did not have brothers.

And now he wished he'd never involved himself with Annie.

"I feel like an idiot," he admitted. How was it that he couldn't bring himself to touch Plodgett's mistress?

"Don't. Reginald Taverston, you are a good man." The worry lines appeared again. "I wish I were less practical. Or ten years younger. I'll miss you."

He leaned to kiss her cheek. Now the strong scent of her perfume—and the tobacco smoke—made him feel a bit ill. He stood. "I'll miss you, too." He suspected he might be lying. "You needn't see me out. I'll have Dolores fetch my things."

She plucked the jewelry box from the davenport and held it up for him to take.

He shook his head. "You keep it. What in God's name would I do with it?"

"No. It wouldn't feel right."

He laughed and said a Crispin-like thing. "Are you serious? *That* is what doesn't feel right?" Then he softened it. "A goodbye gift." He stepped to the door; as he moved through it he tossed over his shoulder, "Tell Plodgett I stomped out to clean my pistols."

He thought it a fair approximation of a dignified exit.

CHAPTER THREE

GEORGIANA HAD DRESSED for the eyes of the ton, not for Lord Taverston, but the poorly hidden smirks of the Duke's entire household suggested they believed otherwise. How did servants know everything? Even Jeanette, her abigail, insisted upon a more elaborate hairstyle than Georgiana preferred and then even asked if she wanted pins that fell out or pins that stayed in. Alice must have told her about the incident; Georgiana certainly had not.

Since Lady Andini's ball was the first official function of Georgiana's second London Season, she had chosen her gown with care, well before her encounter with the Earl of Iversley's son. Last year she had dutifully worn the whites, pale yellows, and light blues in modest styles becoming to a girl new to adult society. This year, Mama permitted their modiste more license. Georgiana's gown was a luscious dark-rose. It was gathered beneath her bosom to fall in soft folds to the floor. An elaborate pattern of dark braiding on the bodice emphasized the swell of her hips and breasts and gave the appearance of an impossibly narrow waist. Georgiana had asked the modiste to raise the neckline, though. She'd rather imply an ample bosom than show. She had trunks full of beautiful new clothes, but this was her favorite. As for dressing to impress Lord Taverston, she thought the effort redundant. He needed a wife, one just like her. And here she was.

No doubt his mother was thrilled that they'd met at Mrs. Preston's. Hers was. And why not? The Duchess was not a gossip, but she nevertheless had her sources. There were no black marks against Lord Jasper Taverston. He hadn't even been sent down from Oxford that long ago time when she'd seen him at Chaumbers. He'd brought home his brother, Crispin, who had been ill. Georgiana had no memory of that. The poor boy must have spent the entire two weeks in his bedchamber.

Mama also answered for Georgiana, without her asking, why her path had not crossed that of Lord Taverston during the whole of last year when Georgiana had participated in every major ton event and a good number of the minor ones. Where had he been then?

"I'm pleased the Taverstons are back in London, most of them." Mama had offered, apropos of nothing. "The Earl has been dreadfully ill. He suffered apoplexy, I believe, two summers past, and has not left Chaumbers since. Beatrice—" she paused and corrected herself—"Lady Iversley was there most of last year. And the boys took turns staying with her. And, of course, Olivia kept them company. She was supposed to come out last year. Seventeen is too young, in my opinion, but I seem to be in the minority. Eighteen is more appropriate."

Olivia. The little sister. The hoyden.

"I didn't see her at Mrs. Preston's," Georgiana mused. "And honestly, I don't remember her though we must have met at some point."

"You have. But it's been a long time. Little girl tea parties and birthdays and such."

"And at Chaumbers."

"Yes." Mama smiled. "She followed you about like a pet. But you were more interested in Lord Taverston. And those silly cats."

"I was not 'interested' in Lord Taverston. Honestly, mother. How old was I? Seven?"

"Just."

"I don't understand…"

"Hmm?"

It had been bothering her, so she asked. "If you and Father were friendly enough with Iversley to attend his house party, why…what happened?" It was a fair question in her opinion. After all, they moved in roughly the same circles. She should have known Lord Taverston and the other sons and Olivia too, on sight.

Perhaps she had been hoping for a falling out of earthshattering proportions. Something that would have caused Father to forbid Lord Taverston to call on her. At least then there would be an obstacle for them to overcome, rather than the dull going-through-the-motions. But Mama disappointed her.

"Oh, we were not so very friendly. Though I do like Lady Iversley. We might have been better friends given more opportunity. But we are not London people. And Chaumbers is a long way from Sayles or Marbury. We went that one time because your father and the Earl were working on a bill together." Mama paused, shaking her head. "It should have passed. But the good bills never do. Anyhow, after that, your father and the Earl discovered how little else they agreed upon. They belong to different clubs. Lady Iversley and I support different charities. The friendship didn't…take." Then Mama smiled, as though to reassure her. "But there is no reason it shouldn't."

And Georgiana felt that vertigo again.

All she could choose was what dress to wear. Everything else was beyond her control.

"DON'T BE DAFT, Reg." Jasper, impeccable in evening wear, shook his head in disbelief. If Reginald had not been his brother, the man would have used the dreaded quizzing glass on him. "You can't sit at home sulking."

"I'm not sulking. I'm reading."

"Same thing."

Reginald, seated in a library chair, with a loose, somewhat battered banyan thrown over his shirt and pantaloons, spectacles perched on the crown of his head, responded by putting his nose back into his book.

"My dear, odd little brother," Jasper continued. "I know you are less bothered by the whole thing than you should be. But if you don't attend this ball, people will think you are more bothered than you should be. Not only think it. They will say it."

"And I care…why?" he asked, without raising his eyes from the page.

"Because it's preposterous. And because I don't much care for Plodgett and his fat-faced gloating. Honestly, Reg. A little family pride, please."

He set the book down, frustrated. How on earth could the loss of *his* mistress be a blow to "family pride?" "What am I supposed to do? Call him out?"

"No. Don't even dignify this with the cut direct. Go right up to him. Wish him a pleasant evening. Ask him about his gout."

Reginald snorted. It *would* be gratifying.

Jasper grinned. "Besides. I'd like you to be there tonight. I'll support you if you support me."

"Support you?"

"Yes, I'm throwing myself into the breach."

Reginald raised an eyebrow. "Meaning?"

"Facing my responsibility." He looked away, his smile gone. He even paced a few steps. This was no jest. His voice dropped low. "Father may be stable, but he has ceased improving. Mother is right." He set his jaw and spoke as if chiding himself rather than explaining himself. "I've put this off for too long."

"So you're seeking your countess." Well, it was time. He felt for Jasper. Who seemed sincerely attached to his own mistress. Idiot. He should have married her instead of giving her carte blanche. But it was complicated then and impossible now. A countess should be wellborn and must be morally beyond reproach.

"No need to seek. It seems I've found her."

That made him jump. "Good Lord, Jasper! When did this happen?"

"Sunday night. At Mrs. Preston's crush."

"A debutante? Really?"

Well, why not? Crispin was the jaded one, not Jasper. Somewhere in the recesses of his mind, he heard the thud of the front door's knocker and its echo. Had Jasper formed a party to go with tonight? Or had Mother? He'd paid no attention to the arrangements. Maybe *he* had become the jaded one.

"No," Jasper said, running a hand through his hair and somehow not mussing it. He didn't even bother to look in the mirror over the mantle to check. He wasn't vain, for all he looked it. "This is her second Season, so Mother tells me."

"Her *second?*" He pretended to reel. "What's wrong with her?"

Jasper laughed. Reginald immediately felt bad for making a joke at the poor girl's expense. Was Jasper serious about this? After one brief encounter?

Jasper said, "Word at White's is she had sixteen offers last year. Sixteen! Can you imagine? I've never heard such a thing. Must be a record."

She must be heiress to a substantial sum. But Jasper didn't need money. This impetuousness worried Reginald. Sixteen offers and Jasper had already queued up to be the seventeenth? She must be a siren.

"Waiting for you, then, was she?"

"Maybe." Jasper made a face at him, a gross imitation of the concern that had popped out on his own. Then he mused, "Actually, maybe. Mother thinks it's a possibility."

"Mother said that? Yet approves?" Odder by the moment. Usually, Mother frowned upon giggling girls who set their caps for Jasper. "Who is this paragon?"

"Come to the ball and see."

He'd have to dress. *And* shave. And lose his train of thought in his book, a complex bit of philosophy he'd been following with some difficulty. Of course, that train was already lost.

"I promised Olivia I'd wait for her before jaunting about."

"That would have been an unsolicited promise, serving yourself rather than Olivia." Jasper's brow clouded. It was a disconcerting sight, since his brother had the easiest disposition of any man Reginald knew. "Mother didn't tell you then?"

"Tell me what?"

"About Olivia's latest letter? Came this morning?" Seeing Reginald's blank look, Jasper filled him in. "Olivia will not be arriving on Saturday. She has postponed coming to London for another fortnight."

Reginald swallowed something sharp in his throat. Father must not be doing as well as they'd hoped. But Olivia must be brought out. And Jasper must…

He made himself sigh. "I suppose if I don't go out in society for a fortnight, Plodgett's crowing will become insupportable. I'd best go change my clothes." He stood and dimmed the lamp he'd been using. "Give me a hint though, will you? So I don't go soliciting a waltz with the wrong girl."

Jasper laughed. "No chance of that. I'm leading her out for the first set. That will stake my claim. But to satisfy your curiosity, it's Hovington's girl. Lady Georgiana."

He nodded gravely. "Acceptable birth." An understatement that made Jasper's grin widen. She would possess all a lady's decorative accomplishments and all the training needed to run an earl's household. "I suspect she's tolerably pretty."

"Very tolerably. And she has wit."

"She sounds too good for you."

"No. I anticipate seventeen is the charm. She can't refuse us all." His smile went crooked. "It feels right, Reg. But I would like you to come and see her. Make sure I'm not missing her third eye or cork leg."

Affection for his elder brother welled in Reginald's breast. The man was such a perfect representative of the aristocrat "type," that one could miss seeing his, well, his *humanity*. Marriage was a huge undertaking. A lifelong commitment. Even Jasper's equanimity was shaken in the face of it.

And there was the chance that his brother was leaping in simply because he felt pressured. Their father was dying. Slowly, but he was dying. If this duke's daughter was wrong for Jasper, he should be reined in. Though what qualified Reginald to judge or to do the reining was beyond him.

He said, "Too bad Crispin isn't here. He can spot a third eye at fifty paces." And Crispin had always been better at reading Jasper. He rubbed his jaw. "Can I get away without shaving?"

"No, you Slavic beast, you cannot."

Unlike his fair-haired brothers, Reginald was dark. They never let him forget it.

He heard a pattering of footsteps, and the library door flew open, startling them both. Their mother stood in the doorway, a piece of paper in her hand. Her face was as white as the paper.

"Your father has had another fit."

"My God," Jasper said, paling also. Reginald could say nothing at all.

"I'm going to Chaumbers tonight." Mother's voice was tight.

Jasper said, "I'll bring you."

The journey would take hours. Seven hours in the dark. And they had to pack. No, not pack. Only ready the carriage and horses. The servants could send their things on. What if...oh, God. They weren't prepared. *He* wasn't prepared. Why hadn't he talked to Father about...anything, but pretended everything was going to be fine?

"No, Jasper, no. You go to the ball. Reginald can come with me. For Heaven's sake. You've already asked Lady Georgiana—"

"For a dance. Surely she'll understand. And if she doesn't, I wouldn't want her."

"Reginald will bring me." Mother sounded steely. As if she wanted something to control. "We'll send word back whether you need come. Or when."

"Mother—"

"Don't argue with her, Jasper." He finally found his voice. Their mother didn't need an argument. Especially when she was wrong.

Jasper turned, startled. Angry. He growled, "And I'm supposed to dance and laugh and woo while—"

"Yes," Mother said, beginning to tremble. "Olivia says he was adamant we were not to be sent for. He doesn't want us all rushing home as if, as if…"

Reginald stepped forward and put his arm around his mother's shoulders. His brothers used to mock him for being his mother's favorite. Perhaps he was. But Jasper was their father's. And Crispin was an island unto himself.

Maybe Jasper understood that it was their mother who needed support just now, more than their father, because finally, he yielded. "Send word tomorrow. If I haven't heard from you by nightfall, I'm coming anyway."

Their mother nodded, leaning so heavily against Reginald's shoulder that it frightened him. He guided her to the door. Would he have time to gather his books and notes? He'd have to grab quickly. And his valet would have to throw a few things into a bag. He looked back to see Jasper's sagging face. He didn't look like a man eager to go courting. How would this Lady Georgiana respond to so morose a wooing?

"Make sure you go to the ball. You have to give my regards to Plodgett."

Jasper smiled weakly. "Ah, yes. At least there's that."

Chapter Four

ALTHOUGH COLLOQUIALLY KNOWN as Lady Andini's ball, in fact, the event was hosted by the Earl of Atherton and his wife. Lady Andini was his sister. The title was a courtesy. She had married an Italian aristocrat, who swept her off her feet, begat his heir, and then died in a boating accident. Lady Andini spent three years with her Italian in-laws before homesickness and other things brought her home. The grandparents claimed the child, which was the saddest, cruelest thing Georgiana could imagine. Lady Andini had visited often until Bonaparte made it impossible to do so. The poor woman must be devastated.

Nevertheless, there was the ball.

Seated together in the ducal carriage, Alice glowed with anticipation, Georgiana suppressed her nervous fidgets, and the duke and duchess smiled at the girls—and each other—fondly.

"You remember our first dance," her father said, his hand on his wife's knee. They made a handsome couple even now. Mama's skin was unlined. Her figure had remained slender. Father was heavier than he looked in old family portraits but still had all of his hair. And that light in his eyes.

"Of course. You broke my toe."

Alice's eyes widened, but Georgiana laughed. She'd heard the story before. She'd heard most of their stories. She settled back to hear this one again. Their low voices murmured together, teasing, enjoying their memories. Enjoying each other.

This was what Georgiana wanted. This. Something incalculably rare in aristocratic marriages. Love. Passionate and companionate. They'd had three children together—Randolph, Georgiana, and Charles; and even after Randolph's tragic death nearly a decade ago, their bond remained unbreakable. Even after twenty-five years together, her parents still cherished one another. It was not unusual to walk into a room and find them tête-à-tête, discussing something in the newspaper, or some bill Father favored, or some improvements they wished to make at Sayles.

Even more, they kissed one another. Regularly. She suspected whatever went on between a man and wife in private still did, since unlike many couples, they shared a bedroom. And a bed.

Only once, that she could recollect, had she heard them fight. She'd been eleven years old. A terrible age to be. It was two years after Randolph's accident, and Mama was beginning, slowly, to emerge from mourning. Perhaps that was why the raised voices had made such an impression. Or perhaps it was because they had argued about her.

Looking back, it hadn't been an argument. Merely a minor disagreement. Easily settled.

Georgiana forced her thoughts back to the present. To Lord Taverston. There was nothing wrong with the man. But there was something not right about him either. None of the men who had courted her had had that something right. And she felt rather grumpily resentful of her parents for making her expect that that *something* should be there.

Their carriage rolled into the long drive. The Athertons' London home was located a short distance from St. James Square and had all the requisite flourishes to recommend it, more brick than marble, but there was some intricate plasterwork on the facade. The gardens in the back were extraordinary and would be even more beautiful when the weather warmed and Lady Atherton held her outdoor teas.

When it stopped, some distance from the steps leading to the front door, they exited the carriage and followed the line of visitors into the house. They were not early, but there was no chance she would miss the first set. There was plenty of time to visit the ladies' drawing room to take care of necessities and make sure everything was in place after being squashed into a carriage. Jeanette had been sent on ahead with Mother's Fabienne—French ladies' maids were *de rigeur*—to enter through the servants' door and wait in the drawing room with other ladies' maids. Georgiana knew they would sit and gossip, perhaps partake of cake and tea brought to them there, and wait for their mistresses to require something of them. They would be dismissed sometime after midnight.

Jeanette would be waiting at home for the girls' return. She'd help them out of their gowns, undo their hair, and see to it that the gowns were brushed, and any spots attended to. She'd be working long after her employers fell asleep and would rise before they woke. All that waiting. Imagine what Jeanette would think if she heard Georgiana complaining the ton's entertainments were dull.

After they greeted their hosts, Father went off in one direction and the ladies in the other.

"I hope Jeanette can help me," Alice murmured. "My garter twisted, and I fear I'm about to lose a stocking."

"She'll fix it," Georgiana assured her as they climbed a spiraling set of stairs. "Jeanette can work wonders." A part of the braidwork on her dress had folded in on itself, spoiling the optical effect, and the abigail had spent at least an hour last night steaming it back into shape.

"These are pretty, aren't they?" Alice said, gesturing to the portraits that graced the walls in an echoing spiral. That was new. The paintings must have been moved from elsewhere. It was the most original portrait gallery she'd ever come across. But something was off. Disorienting. She found herself counting both steps and portraits as she climbed. Calculating. Yes, the numbers were wrong. They had been hung without the proper helical proportions. How lazy.

How irritating.

"Is something amiss?" Alice asked.

"No, nothing," she said hurriedly, hoping Mama, just two steps ahead, had not heard the question. Alice didn't understand Georgiana's fascination with mathematics but didn't judge her for it the way Mama did. Of course, Alice had quirks of her own—reading newspapers in their entirety and political pamphlets from cover to cover, but not calculations of sums or observing mathematical elements in ordinary things. "It's only that one cannot stop and gaze upon the pictures as one can in a regular hall."

Alice giggled and pointed to one. "Maybe that's the point."

The elderly gentleman in a soldier's redcoat and powdered wig had a nose the shape of an anvil and was nearly the size of one. It broke the spell. Georgiana laughed too.

They found the drawing room where they straightened their garments. Georgiana thought Mama would shoo them off, but no. She followed them back down to the ballroom, where Father joined them. Mama looked about the rapidly filling room, then nodded grimly.

"I see Viscount Haslet, Alice. He's a reliable sort. But far too old for you, I think."

"He was just being kind, Your Grace. I have no expectations in that direction."

Mama's expression softened. Then she narrowed her eyes and continued searching.

Father said, "I don't see Lord Taverston yet. Ah, wait. There he is. Bothering Sir Plodgett." A strange look of amusement flitted over his face. "I'd like to have heard what he said."

"What? Why?" Sir Plodgett was not in their set.

"No reason. Just I can see Plodgett's eyes bulging from here. Oh. Lord Taverston has noticed you." He elbowed Georgiana and Alice as though they were tavern bawds. "Do you see him?

Look toward the east door. Here he comes."

Georgiana complained nervously, "Father, I certainly hope you don't intend to narrate the whole evening."

"He is striding this way. Looking side to side. Smiling—"

"Stop!" She flushed with mortification and the effort not to laugh. "Someone will hear you."

"Is that the best smile he can manage? It is more of a grimace."

"Mama! Tell him to stop!"

Alice's fit of giggles was not helping matters.

"Oh, well. He has been waylaid by Lady Drakemore. That woman. She'll be angling for him to secure a dance with that daughter of hers."

"Miss Christine is lovely!" Mama protested.

"Yes, she is. He should dance with her, of course. I'll stop teasing now. He'll be here any moment."

Lord Haslet reached them first and nodded a greeting to the Duke before exclaiming, "Ah! What a sight. The three loveliest women in the room. Your Grace. Lady Georgiana. Miss Fogbotham." He bowed to each of them in turn. Then to Alice, "What a perfect shade of blue your dress is. It makes your eyes look even greener and green eyes are, by far, the prettiest."

Alice blushed. "Thank you, my lord. You're very kind."

It was gentlemanly of him to direct his attention to Alice at her very first ball, standing in Georgiana's shadow.

Lord Taverston was not as considerate. "Hovington. Your Grace. Lord Haslet. Lady Georgiana." He nodded and mumbled something like, "milady," making it evident he'd forgotten Alice's name. Then he turned directly to Georgiana.

"How prescient of me to have secured the first dance with the most beautiful lady here. I'll be the envy of every man in the ton."

"Congratulations. I know that's important to you," Hazard drawled. "And Lady Georgiana, you will have performed your charitable deed for the day."

To his credit, Lord Taverston laughed. "Miss Fogbotham," he

redeemed himself by remembering, "Do take care of your shoulders. Hazard had been known to steer his partners into walls."

"Only once," Hazard said mildly. "And it was the lesser of two catastrophes. Shall we take a turn about the room? If we subject the Duchess to any more of our foolishness, she is likely to tuck the young ladies under her wings and bundle them home."

Lord Taverston offered his arm. "Will you?"

Georgiana nodded. She and Lord Taverston led, with Hazard and Alice walking behind. The ballroom was expansive, with a checkerboard pattern of marble flooring and high ceilings glittering with chandeliers. It opened onto a terrace. Or would when the weather warmed. Tonight the glass doors were covered with shutters. A small orchestra had set up just to the side. They had been tuning their instruments and, from the sound of it, were nearly ready to begin.

"That is a beautiful color on you."

"Hmm? Oh, thank you," she said. She hoped he would not say it complemented her eyes.

"It makes your eyes glow."

"Thank you." There must be a book men memorized. "I think the music will be starting soon. There is Lady Andini with the Earl."

He tucked her arm closer under his and watched with her. The Earl presented his sister, who welcomed them all and bade them enjoy themselves. Georgiana knew she would dance the first set with her brother but would not dance again.

The first strains of a lively country dance called to them, and they formed up their lines.

"Do you enjoy dancing?" Lord Taverston asked, putting his hands on his hips, and performing the opening steps with easy grace.

"I have heard that there are people who do not, but I have never met one of these strange creatures."

He smiled: white, straight teeth and a dimple on one side. They circled one another.

"I have. I'm related to one."

"Really?" She had to laugh. "I do beg pardon for calling your relative a strange creature."

"My brother."

"Which one?"

They separated. She faced Lord Ralston. He had taken her on two carriage rides but had not pursued her further. They exchanged smiles and breathless pleasantries until she returned to Lord Taverston.

"Reginald. The younger. Youngest, I should say."

"He doesn't dance?"

"Well, he must, mustn't he, being a gentleman?

Surely he'd told this story many times over. He timed it well with the steps. They touched hands to approach. His hands were warm even through their gloves. They backed away.

"But I fear it brings back painful memories." Taverston still smiled, but his eyes looked strained. Distracted.

"My word. How painful? Perhaps you shouldn't be telling."

"What? No. I'm sorry. I lost my…footing."

He hadn't. But they parted again. And she faced Dunstun. He stepped woodenly, stone-faced. She managed to keep her smile. Then went back to Taverston.

"Man's a pigwidgeon," he said, very low, as they circled one another. So he'd kept his eye on her.

"Perhaps he has painful memories."

"I'm certain he does. Well, Reginald's are of a different sort. You see, as eldest, I was the first to be subjected to the dancing master. At thirteen. I was still stumbling along when Crispin joined me a year later."

"Stumbling?"

They parted. She saw he was now gliding along with Alice, who was smiling at something he said.

Back to her, he continued, "Oh, I stumbled. Crispin, surprisingly, was a natural."

"Why surprisingly?"

"You'll see when you meet him."

Oh. They touched hands. He smiled, a little abashed. He had very blue eyes.

"I hope you will meet him, I should have said."

They swirled and swirled. Then slowed to begin again.

"The dancing master was a sadist. Crispin and I had to learn with brooms for partners, until Rudolfo—"

"That was not his name!" She laughed again.

"It is what we called him. He finally decided we were ready to dance with a female. We were breathless with anticipation."

She had to wait for their final steps together for the climax of the story.

"Well," he said, returning to her. "It was his great aunt. But in the end, we learned." He bowed to her as the dance concluded.

"I can say nothing about Lord Crispin, but Rudolfo taught you well. Yet Lord Reginald found it too painful?"

Lord Taverston took her arm and led her to the side of the room.

"Crispin is two years younger than I. Reginald is six. We made sure he was terrified of the dancing master. When his turn came around, he flat-out refused. Stubborn brat." Lord Taverston laughed at the memory. "He took a caning rather than a lesson. We were horrified by what we had wrought. Well, I was. So we told Father that Rudolfo was useless and that we would teach Reg ourselves. He threw up his hands and allowed it. I don't think he had been impressed with the man either, but gentlemen must learn to dance."

"But if your brother didn't suffer the dancing master, why does he hate to dance?"

"Crispin's fault. He gave the first lesson. I caught on to his game and did the same."

She narrowed her eyes at him. "Did you teach him false steps?"

"We taught him to follow." The words were delivered straight-faced, but she nevertheless caught his blue eyes twinkling.

"Oh, for Heaven's sake."

"He was—I commend him for it—excellent at the lady's parts."

"You are horrible. Your poor little brother."

"We praised him, of course. After several weeks, we beckoned my mother in to see how well we'd taught him. Crispin played a fine waltz on the piano and Mother and Reginald both just stood there, arms on waists and shoulders, each waiting for the other to lead."

"I hope your father caned you both."

"He was laughing too hard."

She giggled. It was a mean joke, but no real harm had been done.

"He did learn, of course. Eventually. The poor sod. It's much harder to learn to do something right after having learned to do it well, wrong."

"I still maintain you are horrid. My sympathies lie entirely with your brother."

He smiled. Yet there was something, something tired, in his face. "Quite rightly. Lady Georgiana, have you been engaged for the next set? Must I deliver you somewhere?"

"Back to the Duchess would be fine, thank you."

"If you have not promised the next dance, will you walk with me for a few moments in the garden?"

She should have given him the haughty look that Mama had taught her to let him know, without words, that he had crossed the line. Single ladies and gentlemen did not monopolize one another's company at balls. He knew that. People would talk. But he looked so concerned, and his voice was so earnest, that she nodded.

"A few moments."

He steered her toward the door. She did not look to see if her mother was watching. Certainly, she was, and Georgiana would receive a dressing down later.

The gardens were well-lit with paper lanterns. And many people were taking advantage of the cooling air after the warmth of the dance, so they were hardly alone. She let him escort her down a side path, but not far down it. He kicked aside a small stone, his face drooping.

"You must be thinking me ill-mannered indeed."

"I confess, I am. This is not at all the thing. You have something you wish to say to me?"

He would not propose to her now. Here. No one was as ill-mannered as that. But if he did, she could justifiably say no.

"Only that I would, naturally, have sent a tastelessly large bouquet tomorrow morning, with a variety of blooms, all in that gorgeous shade of pink you're wearing tonight." He looked rueful. "I imagine you are accustomed to men paying such dubious tributes to your charms."

She inclined her head in acknowledgment of the fact. It surprised her to hear that men recognized how ridiculous they were. But maybe not all men did. Maybe there was something a little special about this one. She should not dismiss the possibility out of hand.

"And I would, of course, request your company on a ride in the park within a day or two. My curricle should impress you. And I'm a dab hand with the ponies."

"I don't doubt it." And she expected there were seats in the Earl's box at the theater that she and Alice and Mama would be invited to share for an evening. She did not say that, did not put into words the rote nature of being courted. She did not say that she already knew the conversations they would have. They would enumerate for one another their close family members, with an amusing anecdote or two about them. He had checked that box already. He would ask her favorite flower and wear it in his buttonhole at the next ton function. He might ask her which composers she particularly enjoyed if he was musical. They would not discuss politics or social ills or, God forbid, physical ones. All this in the course of five, perhaps six invitations, after which he would have to decide whether to pursue her or retreat.

Or if he was particularly bold, he would offer for her then.

How was this enough preparation for a lifetime together? For anyone?

She saw Lord Taverston's obvious qualities. She liked that he could laugh at himself. But she did not *know* him. Nor would she know him in four weeks or eight. Not by spending twenty minutes at a time with him, chaperoned, saying all the right things. She could look at his smile, his mouth, and appreciate that it was pleasant to look at, but had no wish to kiss it.

What was it that made a person think: *yes, this is the one?*

"Lady Georgiana? This is excruciatingly difficult."

"What is, Lord Taverston?" Good Heavens. He looked harassed. Was he about to suggest they dispense with the preliminaries and settle for one another? Since they would likely end up doing so in the end?

"I'm leaving London. I should not have come here tonight, I think." He spoke all in a rush. "In fact, I'm leaving directly, which will cause talk, and I apologize in advance for any embarrassment it may cause you." How very melodramatic he was. If he had simply left, without dragging her out here, no one would have any reason to talk. Now it would look as if they had quarreled.

"My lord, I am entering this tale in the middle. Please explain. Unless it is too private to discuss, in which case, I beg to be returned to the Duchess immediately."

"We had word a few hours ago from Chaumbers. The Earl has suffered a relapse of his previous illness. My mother and Reginald have already left for the country."

She gasped. "I am so sorry!" Her thoughts had been ungenerous. The poor unfortunate family. "Naturally, you must go."

"I don't know when I might return. It will depend upon…so many things."

"Go. I'm sure that any commitments here can wait."

"Yes, but." He looked toward the garden wall. "Well, you see where this leaves me."

She frowned. He could not mean to imply that she was a commitment. That was unfair. It was too soon.

"I am not, of course, going to ask you to wait upon my return." He practically muttered the words, as if thinking aloud rather than speaking to her. "For your flowers and your curricle ride. Or my…attentions. But I would not have wanted you to think…"

"That one dance with me had sent you scampering off to the country?"

He raised his eyes to hers and his lips twitched. "Something like that."

How stupid. He should have sent word to her saying he could not make it to the ball. Did he imagine she would be heartbroken? "Go, Lord Taverston. You should have gone with—" She halted and felt herself flush at her own impertinence. "I beg your pardon. That is not my place to say."

"Of course, I should have!" He scowled. "But my father did not want us rushing to his—what we perceive to be—his deathbed. Mother believes it would frighten him if we all act as though we expect him to die. The doctors have told us not to alarm him. He is not to exert himself…" His hands had been dancing expressively until he forcibly dropped them to his side. "And I am unpardonably burdening you with my frustration."

His frustration and concern were clearly genuine. She warmed to this side of him more than to his amusing, politely flirtatious façade. But given the slightness of their acquaintance, it was true that he should not have "burdened" her with any unpleasantness at a ball. Similarly, she was well aware that it would be improper for her to respond with anything beyond polite, detached sympathy.

"Don't worry about that. It must be very distressing. I cannot imagine being in your shoes."

"You're very kind." His voice was stilted. "I do regret leaving

London just now."

"You'll regret it more if you do not go."

He sighed. "I should escort you back indoors."

Then he drew back his shoulders and the pain on his face was replaced by a more congenial mask that she expected he would wear until he was on the road to Iversley.

CHAPTER FIVE

THE COUNTESS' CARRIAGE did not arrive until the early hours of the morning. The journey, in the depths of the night over treacherous roads, had been grueling. Reginald's mother napped, but only fitfully. By the time they reached Chaumbers, he was as worried about her as he was his father. He suggested she go to her chamber and sleep first, but she gave him a shriveling look and went straight to the Earl, with Reginald following.

Olivia was seated at the bedside, pale, drawn, dressed in something wrinkled that she must have been wearing for two days at least. She stood and came to them, finger on her lips, though it was obvious Father was asleep and they'd hardly approach him yelling.

They drew off to the side of the chamber. Lamps were lit all around them and they cast an assortment of distorted shadows. Thankfully, before pointing out the superfluity of lamps, Reginald remembered that Olivia suffered from fear of the dark.

"He just collapsed," she said in a whisper. "One minute he was talking to Peters, the next he simply fell. I sent for the doctor. Peters helped me get him into bed."

"Was he conscious?" Mother asked.

"Not at first. But he was by the time the doctor arrived. He could talk but I could barely understand. You see his eye patch. That whole side of his face just droops. The eye won't close completely, so Dr. Haraldsen patched it. He can't move that side of his body at all. He told me not to send for you." She frowned at Reginald. "Only Mama. He said you boys had more important things to do." Her voice broke. "He said I should go to London. That I shouldn't miss my Season. Mama, how can he think I care about that?"

Olivia fell sobbing against their mother, who wrapped her arms around her and let her cry. It irked him that she would burden Mother, who had just ridden through the night and looked ready to topple. Then it irked him more that he hadn't appropriate sympathy for Olivia. She'd been here in Iversley for the duration, while he and his brothers had popped in and out. And she was scarcely more than a child. So he put his arms around them both. Then he wondered if he was cold and unfeeling because he wasn't crying as well.

Olivia sniffed and drew back. He handed her his handkerchief. "What did the doctor say?" he asked.

She shook her head. "He cannot say anything. We just have to see. But this is worse than last time, isn't it?"

"Perhaps not." God. He wished Jasper had come. "Olivia, Mother, go get some sleep. Both of you. I'll sit with him awhile. I'll send for you if he wakes, but you both must rest."

Mother nodded. "Come along, darling. Your brother is right." There was more color in her face. She must have feared finding they'd come too late. Then she added, "An hour or two. Then I'll come back. You haven't slept either."

"I'll be fine."

He was relieved that they left. For a minute or two, he sat holding his father's hand, but it was so cold and lifeless it made the hairs on the back of his neck stand on end. Besides, it seemed false comfort for him and none at all for his father, who looked so old. His blond hair had never really grayed but thinned to wisps. There was a coarse gray stubble on his chin, his mouth was twisted grotesquely, and that damn patch covered his eye. Reginald's own eyes ached but remained dry.

He hadn't intended to sleep, but he woke when dawn's pale light slanted through the window. He was slumped in the chair and had a painful crick in his neck. He stood and put a finger beneath his father's nose, praying he would still be breathing. He was. Reginald stretched, then went to the door of the chamber and cracked it open to spy the waiting footman.

"Will you have coffee sent up? And a few rolls."

The footman nodded and set off. He should have asked him also to send for Barclay, his valet. If Father woke and saw this black beard he'd sprouted, he'd have another apoplectic fit.

And that was not at all amusing. What was wrong with him?

He paced about the room, then thought to look at the clock. Seven in the morning. He'd drink a pot of coffee, then send for his mother, then go bathe and have himself made more presentable.

Olivia said Father could still talk.

He went to the window and pushed it open a sliver. It was to be a wet autumn, by all indications. The trees were dripping audibly, and the browning grass glistened. It was quiet enough to hear birds beginning to sing. They sounded tentative now, but in the springtime, they would be raucous at dawn. Chaumbers was not the most beautiful country house he'd ever been in, but there was something soothing about being home. Except that it would not be home, really, when he was an earl's younger brother rather than a son. He took in one more deep breath, then pulled the window shut. Some doctors insisted upon fresh air, others warned of chills. Reginald suspected it would not matter, but he would leave the window as he'd found it.

Reginald had had four months to talk with the Earl, alone without his brothers stepping on his toes, yet had managed to avoid the topic of his future. They hadn't alluded to it since Reginald had announced, at the age of seventeen, that he wished to go to Cambridge. The Taverstons, generations of them, were Oxford men. He'd been ready to put his foot down. He wanted to read with Frederick Bastion, a renowned classicist, whom neither

Father nor his brothers had ever heard of. He hadn't expected to be disowned, of course, but he had anticipated an argument. Instead, Father sighed heavily and said: *Fine, then. Cambridge will do for you fine, I think.* Whatever that was supposed to mean.

Reginald, the third son, the "clever one," was thought to be destined for the church. Because what else was he to do? From the time he was ten, Mother said, his character was evident. He was not soldier material. He would make a terrible idle man-about-town. He hated to think his ten-year-old self put people in mind of a clergyman, but there it was.

Fortunately, Father had four livings to dispose of and Reginald could expect to be given one or all of them eventually. Unless he wished to aim for a bishopric. He possessed no spiritual calling, only the right temporal connections, and, as young as he'd been, that seemed enough.

He had been at Cambridge no more than two months when he realized he could not enter the Church. He believed in God in his own way but had no desire to share his rather odd pantheistic beliefs, or force them upon people, or preach a conventional theology in which he did not believe. And he lacked the…whatever one wished to call it: the compassion for others that a minister should possess.

Unfortunately, he had neglected to tell his father any of this. He had neglected to tell anyone he had been offered a Fellowship at the University, translating from the Greek a newly discovered manuscript, one of a cache Bastion had uncovered in a monastery's crumbling library but had little time to examine. Reginald could make an entire career from studying that cache if he were to impress his mentor enough to convince him to entrust the task to him.

But a career in the murky, cold backwaters of Academia? For an earl's son? Why not a coal miner or shipwright, if he was determined to be an embarrassment to the family? Gentlemen were to be educated but not educators. That lot fell to the cleverer of their social inferiors, to those accustomed to grubbing for their guineas.

He had "put off" his ordination examination. There had been no great rush. He was young. Father was ill. That was what his parents believed, though he had not told them this with actual words.

It seemed to him the height of cowardice to hide his intentions from his father. Yet it seemed the pinnacle of selfishness to confess what would surely be seen as an absurd folly while the Earl lay there, shrunken and sallow, one half of his body already essentially dead.

The door shook, then opened. His mother entered, carrying a tray on which were coffee and cakes. She did not look rested, but she was dressed and coiffed and especially, she was poised.

"Peters brought this. I intercepted. You were supposed to call me."

"It's only seven o'clock."

"Coffee is no substitute for sleep." Nevertheless, she set down the tray and poured him a cup.

He took it and confessed. "I slept."

She snorted a laugh. It was good to hear.

"Your father did not wake at all?"

"If he did, he didn't see fit to wake me." Then he amended, "No. He's been the same." Then he lied. "I think his color is better this morning."

She poured herself coffee. She handed him a cake but did not take one herself. He was ravenous. And Cook's cakes were excellent, though he preferred her rolls. It was the fresh country butter, she'd told him once, pink with pleasure at his compliment. He devoured the cake—and found it disappointingly stale.

"Peters wishes to speak with you," Mother said.

"With me?"

She nodded. "Go see what he wants. Then take care of yourself. I'm fine here."

"All right." He drank the dregs from his cup and went out to send for Peters, but found the man waiting just beyond the door.

Peters was head butler at Chaumbers and had been for a decade. Reginald thought he was a few years younger than the Earl but as he had not changed in appearance in ten years, one could not be sure. He was competent. Haughty as the devil. Jasper liked him and would not be replacing him. Jasper liked everyone. Reginald found him stiff and self-important, but that was probably true of all competent butlers.

"What is it?" he asked.

"My lord, I regret to inform you that Mr. Bradwell has passed."

Father's steward. "Passed?" That was a gut punch. "When?"

"Three days ago."

"Has Lord Taverston been notified?"

"I just received word last night. I thought to inform him in person."

"I expect he'll be here today." Knowing Jasper, he was half-way to Chaumbers already. He would not wait to be summoned.

"Very good, sir."

"Is there anything that needs immediate attention?"

"Not that I am aware of, my lord."

"All right then. Thank you for informing me. I'll discuss this with Lord Taverston when he arrives. I'm going to my chamber now. Do you know if Barclay is there or downstairs?"

"Downstairs, I believe."

"Please let him know I require his assistance."

"Yes, my lord."

Reginald's feet felt heavy as he trudged to his chamber. Bradwell's passing was not so much a surprise as it was unwelcome news. The man had been in his eighties, practically an immortal. He'd retired six months ago when a lingering chest cold debilitated him. Truth was, he should have been pensioned off sooner, but with Father's illness, nothing had been done. As they were not to alarm Father, no one told him of Bradwell's decline. Jasper said he'd take care of hiring a new steward. Of course, it would be Jasper's responsibility soon enough. And the man he wanted, Benjamin Carroll, was the perfect choice. An Oxford mate of Jasper's. Not a gentleman by birth, but well-mannered and bright. The only problem was he had emigrated to Canada. Jasper said he would return. Reginald was not so sure. They needed him six months ago, and he had not returned yet.

He entered the bedchamber he'd left two months ago, no two and a half. Nothing had changed. Nothing but him. He felt he'd aged years. Was it only a week ago? Less? That he'd been dropped by the woman he paid to sleep with him? Ha! He sat on the bed and yanked off his shoes. Then unbuttoned his cuffs. His shirt stank and he was covered in the dust of the road.

Barclay knocked and entered. "I've ordered hot water brought up."

"Enough to bathe?"

He nodded. "It'll be easier to shave you after."

"Easier on me or on you?"

The man grinned. "Both, I suspect."

In private, he didn't stand on much ceremony with Barclay. It was too much effort. He was pleased to see that his bags had all been unpacked and his things placed where he liked to keep them. He stripped to his britches, slipped on his ratty banyan, then asked: "Did you get any sleep?"

"Enough."

"Enough to hold a razor to my throat?"

Barclay laughed. "We'll see."

That sounded too like the doctor's prognostication.

Reginald went and sat at his desk. He wrote two quick letters, one to Jasper, one to Crispin. Both said much the same thing, although Crispin's had an extra sentence or two of explanation. Essentially he said it did not look good for Father. They had best come home quickly. To Crispin, he added: *if you can.* General Wellesley might not grant him leave again so soon.

He folded the letters, sealed them, and handed them to Barclay.

"If Lord Taverston is not here by noon, post this. And send this one off to Lieutenant Taverston at once."

CHAPTER SIX

IF GEORGIANA HAD found the ton exasperating before, now she found it infuriating. Four weeks had passed since Lady Andini's ball, yet the whispers had not abated.

She sat in her favorite chair in the drawing room with her legs curled beneath her since no one was there to see. The drapes were pushed open to let in the sunshine, but there was so little of that, she lit a lamp. Her embroidery was tossed carelessly into a basket, and she held a book in her lap, smuggled from her father's library—Father wouldn't mind, but Mama frowned upon her reading "men's books." It had engaged her attention for a while, but she stalled on a set of equations that stymied her understanding. Those Hellenistic astronomers and their geometric models! She should put it down for now, but that would leave her brooding.

Oh! She *was* brooding. This would not do at all.

Mama had scolded her for disappearing with Lord Taverston but listened to her explanation and agreed it was just an unfortunate situation. Of course, she should not have gone to the garden with him. Still, under the circumstances, it had been a kindness.

A kindness. For which she was now being punished.

No, not punished. *Set aside.*

Mama said to ignore the gossip, or it would take wings. If they were to deny any understanding between her and Lord

Taverston, how would it appear if he returned shortly and began to court her in earnest? If he were detained very much longer, rumors would lose traction, and gentlemen would start to come around again.

How irritating to actually miss having suitors.

She hated that she did not know what people were saying. She could guess the gist: people were linking her name with that of Lord Taverston. It was known by now that the Earl had taken ill, explaining the son's abrupt departure. But what were the gossips reporting exactly? Mama must know but refused to dignify gossip by repeating it. Alice said she'd heard nothing, then blushed so hard Georgiana knew that she had. Wasn't fore-warned supposed to be forearmed? Yet rushing around denying everything would make it all worse. She had to rely on her mother's good sense.

And if she ended up a spinster, so be it.

She had been to the theater weekly, a recital, three teas, and five more balls. She danced. She had partners of course, but the men were reserved. She received no morning-after bouquets. She had been taken on no rides in the park. Repetitive as she had once found them, these attentions were expected. And unexpectedly missed.

She spent one afternoon with Lady Caroline Newland, a longtime friend, who asked if she might sketch Georgiana and Alice. Caroline was not without talent but had trouble finding people to sit for her after she had exhausted her store of relatives. It had been pleasant enough, catching up, until Caroline asked if she had heard any word about the Earl of Iversley.

"Why would I have?" she replied in a freezing tone.

Caroline reddened and stammered, "N-no reason. Only I thought His Grace and the Earl were friendly."

"I'm sure I don't know. The Duke does not discuss his friend-ships with me."

Which was true but disingenuous. Alice changed the subject abruptly by leaping from her stool and claiming a spider had crossed her shoe. Her cousin was a dear.

And Alice had received three bouquets this morning. Well, good for her.

Georgiana's grand pet was interrupted by the butler.

"A caller has come. Viscount Haslet."

Thank God. She sat up straight and shoved her book between the cushions. "Please bring him in." Oh, but bother. She was alone. "And inform Her Grace."

"Certainly, my lady." He stepped aside to admit Hazard, who peered into the drawing room and then paused, hand on the doorframe. His morning coat hung loosely, lending his lean torso a lazy, comfortable appearance. She felt better just seeing him.

"Shall I wait?" he asked.

"Probably." Then she threw up her hands. "No, that's unreasonable. Come sit down."

He sauntered in and took a chair a respectable distance from her, pushing aside a few pillows. He tented his fingers in front of his face.

"And how are you doing?"

"I am well. And you?"

He grimaced. "Perfect. Just perfect. What were you reading there? Something wildly inappropriate, I hope."

"Worse." She pulled it out and showed him.

"Astronomy?" His nose wrinkled. "Stars and planets and such?"

"I was hoping for pictures."

He snorted. "Stuff it back. My head hurts just from the title."

She did, just on time before Mama bustled into the room, her face wreathed with disapproval, her posture stiff. She saw Hazard and relaxed.

"Oh. It's only you."

"My dear lady," he said, in an exaggerated huff, "that is simply rude."

"Yes, it was. I apologize. I was in the midst of writing a letter and..." She glanced back at the door. "And I want to get it into the morning's post." She bit her lip. "Yes, well. I will just step out for a few minutes if you'll forgive me. I won't be long."

Georgiana stared, shocked, but Hazard simply flicked his fingers and said, "Go on."

Mama left them alone.

He looked at her and made a pained face. "How emasculating. Come, sit on my lap. It will serve her right."

"Lord Haslet!" She choked on her laughter. "You are improper."

"Too much so and not enough." He set his gaze upon the mahogany table and its burden of flowers. She noted that his cheeks had flushed slightly. Mama had embarrassed him. Oh, it made her heart hurt.

"They are all Alice's," she said, crankily enough that he would notice and be amused.

"Well, yes." He pointed to a tasteful, compact bouquet of white and pink tea roses. "Those are mine."

"Yours?" Georgiana had not read the cards. Alice wouldn't have minded, but still.

"And where is she this morning? If I may ask?" He was still looking at the flowers.

"Riding in the park with Mr. Gamby."

"Ah." He nodded and a muscle twitched in his jaw. "He's a decent sort. Dibs not in tune, unfortunately, but he has expectations from his grandfather."

"Do you know *everything*? About *everyone*?"

He looked back at her and smiled sheepishly. "I can't help it. People tell me things. However, I don't repeat everything. That is key." He lifted a questioning eyebrow.

"Don't expect any confidences," she said, tossing her head. "I'm sure you already know more about me than I do."

He chuckled. Then his thin, handsome face bunched into a knot, and he said, "I'd like to ask you something. Privately. You don't need to answer, but please don't tell anyone I asked."

She peered at him closely but could guess nothing from his

expression. "You may ask."

"What does Miss Fogbotham expect from a marriage?"

"Excuse me?" She had been traveling in the wrong direction and now drew up short. "Alice?"

"Well, girls marry for some reason. Is it wealth? Status? Children? Or something intangible."

"All those things," she answered. He looked uncomfortable and did not wear it well. So she tried to answer gently and honestly, though she could not be more confused. "I don't think Alice is overly concerned with status. Wealth is not a necessity, but comfort would be. And children, of course."

"Well, that is not very helpful. If it were wealth and status…" He turned over his hands and tried to smile.

"Are you…?" Then she rattled the thought from her head and asked instead, "Does your mother require you to pursue one young lady per Season?"

"Ha! No." He flopped back, sprawling, and rubbed his hands over his cheeks. "Not Mother. The old witch was too correct. My cousin's son just borrowed—ha! 'borrowed' as if he's ever repaid a guinea—yet another fifty pounds to keep his creditors from calling in his tickets. A little gambling at his age is nothing to carp about, but he has fallen in with the worst sort of people. He is never completely sober." He stopped, stricken. "I do beg your pardon. I really meant to address my question to your mother. And without this much sordid detail."

"Hazard, I am so sorry. And I'm discreet. I won't say anything."

"I fear it is partly my fault," he went on, as if a dam had broken. "The boy has had his hands in my pockets for so long he thinks the coat is his. And his cronies trust that I will bail him out because I always have. It isn't that I can't afford to, it's that I shouldn't. So my mother has been telling me for years."

"And you think if he were to marry Alice, it would reform him?"

"He? Bertram? Oh!" He chuckled. "No. I wash my hands of

him. I gave him the money but told him no more. Then two days later, he showed up at my home and—" He stopped. His face grew pale, and he began to blink rapidly.

"And?"

"Nothing. I forget you are a mere child and innocent. What a horrible person I am."

"You are not. What did he do? You may as well finish your sentence, or I am likely to imagine even worse."

"It isn't that terrible," he muttered. "He merely insulted a good friend of mine is all. But loosely thrown insults can be dangerous. And Bertram is not entitled to my title and fortune if he is going to abuse it. Which it seems he will." Shaking his head, he finished, "If I want a decent heir, it appears I will have to make one."

"With Alice?"

"No. Oh, bedevil it, I don't know. She laughs at my jokes. I like her. She's a sweet thing. And I don't think a title would hurt her."

Georgiana was speechless. She had thought...well, she didn't know precisely what she'd thought, but it included Hazard never marrying.

"The thing is," he mused, "I would not be a bad husband. Just not a good one. I'm not too old for children and wouldn't mind a few underfoot." He lowered his voice and said, reddening for real, "But I would not be faithful, you see." He lifted his chin and met her astonished, embarrassed gaze. "I would not demand it of her, either, once the heir was born, but I would want *him* to be mine. Silly, that, but I would. And I would give my name to any others."

"Please stop talking."

"Damn it. Yes. I will. You are absolutely right."

"Alice would not...well, she just wouldn't."

"All right. Thank you. I figured you would give an honest answer. Otherwise..."

"Yes. No. I understand. I mean, please stop talking."

They sat in miserable silence. She ached, and ached for him. But Alice deserved more. And Hazard deserved more.

"Maybe a widow?" she suggested tentatively. "One young enough for children?"

"Oh, I'm sure I can find someone," he said mournfully. Then he shrugged. "Difficult though."

She nodded. "Makes my difficulties appear minuscule."

"Hmm." He drummed his fingers on his knee. "My dear, your difficulties *are* minuscule."

"I'm sure I'd agree if I knew what they were."

It might be wrong to draw attention back to herself, but they were both too unsettled by his disclosures to continue discussing them. And switching to mindless banter seemed worse.

He snickered. "No one will tell you, eh?"

"Mama says not to pay any attention. But I can't ignore what I am ignorant of."

He glanced at the door, then back to her, before stage-whispering with mock seriousness, "Of course, you are aware there is an understanding between you and Lord Taverston."

"I should think I would know if there were."

"Well, I have heard three different versions, but they are close enough and all boil down to the same. Your fathers, or perhaps mothers, are closer friends than is commonly realized. It occurred to two of them, or all four, that a betrothal would suit everyone."

"A betrothal?"

"Oh, yes. You have been betrothed for years. Congratulations, by the way."

"This is absurd."

"Well." He leaned forward, rubbing his hands together like a good gossip should. "Last year you were *finally* of age, and quite the prize—as I'm sure you know, having startled a proposal even from the likes of me and Dunstun." She frowned at the way this story was progressing. Half-truths were being combined to form complete falsehoods. He continued, "But brick that he is, Jasper, I mean, Lord Taverston, though his heart is firmly in your grip, insisted that you should not be tied to an age-old betrothal in which you'd had no say. He did not understand, you see, the depth of your devotion, giving consideration to your youth and cloistered upbringing."

"Cloistered? Please tell me you are exaggerating for effect."

"I'm afraid I distinctly heard the word 'cloistered.' Taverston insisted you have your Season. Because, you know, of course, that a girl denied a Season is forever bereft."

"Ugh." She put her head in her hands, unsure whether she wanted to laugh or cry.

"And the pining Lord Taverston would remain secluded in Iversley so as not to encumber you. Though I'm sure every offer you received took a year off his life. You should know your steadfast devotion brings old ladies to tears."

"Surely no one believes this rot."

"The pieces all fit."

"But how does this end?"

"Happily ever after, I imagine."

How infuriating! It had taken no more than their possessing the right lineage and dancing one dance to set tongues wagging about a *betrothal.* Of course, the ton would add two to two and come up with five.

The Duchess strode noiselessly into the room, startling them both.

"What fairy story are you telling, Lord Haslet?"

"Me? Just a bit of nonsense. A play I saw at a theater that I should not be discussing in polite company."

"Honestly. We should not put up with you. I'm sorry to have been so long."

"You should be." Hazard bantered back. "I've overstayed my twenty minutes. And no one even offered me biscuits."

"How embarrassing. And you, wasting away."

He rose. Then bowed to each of them. "It's been a very pleasant visit. Please extend my regrets to Miss Fogbotham."

"You'll call again?" Georgiana asked. She needed Hazard. Not only did he seem to understand her and sympathize, but he was the only one she trusted to tell her the truth.

"You can't be rid of me. I'm like the sniffles in winter. Good day!"

After Hazard was out the door, Mama turned to Georgiana. "What nonsense was he spouting about Lord Taverston? Does he not know any better than to fill your head with peoples' foolishness?"

"I asked him."

"Even so. It was not well done of him to tell you."

"It was driving me mad, Mama."

"Are you any less maddened now?"

Georgiana drew in a breath, then blew it out. "It's hard to be patient. I want to do something. But I know there isn't anything to do."

"Well," Mama said, turning to the mantel and resting her arm upon it. Her expression was strangely discomposed. "I suppose there may be something."

Georgiana raised her head expectantly.

"The letter I received was from Lady Iversley."

She gulped. "What did she say?"

"The Earl is doing better than anyone anticipated. She did not elaborate, and I would not have expected her to, so I'm not sure what that means, precisely. At any rate, it seems Olivia will not make her debut this Season either. The girl has been stoic, but she is lonely, and Lady Iversley asks if you and Alice and I can be spared to keep her company for a few weeks. Perhaps through Christmas."

"Oh, Mama, how awful." Lady Iversley should invite an actual friend of Lady Olivia's to keep her company and provide comfort, not three strangers. They were using the poor girl as an excuse to bring her and Lord Taverston together. "That will fool no one. It will feed the fire."

"Of course it will. Or we can snuff it. I took so long because I composed a careful letter saying it might be unwise to put too much pressure on you children. But then I tore it up. You aren't children. Lord Taverston will soon be deluged with responsibilities, and it would be convenient to have *this*, at least, settled. He must have asked Lady Iversley to write."

"I am to be a *convenience* for him?" she demanded, irritated beyond measure that her mother expected her to play along with this farce, to play into the hands of the gossipy ton.

"Don't be snide, love. It's a very good match and I'm sure you can see that. Neither your father nor I will tell you whom you must marry, but frankly, you've turned down many offers that would make any other girl ecstatic. And Lord Taverston is…" She appeared to notice Georgiana's expression and stopped her scolding. She came closer and tenderly caressed Georgiana's cheek. "Dear, what *are* you looking for?"

"I don't know. Mama, if I knew, I might have some hope of finding it." She choked back her tears. Was she wrong to think falling in love required something more than summing up a man's qualities and finding them sufficient? If anyone should understand what she yearned for, it should be Mama, who *was* blessed with a love-match. *That* was what she wanted, but she hadn't the faintest idea how such matches came about. "What were you looking for when you met Father?"

Her mother sighed. "Someone kind. Someone who made me laugh."

"But surely there were other men who met those criteria. Would you have loved them the way you love Father? Does it even matter who I wed?" Her tears flowed.

"Of course it matters, sweetheart. And we would not let you marry the wrong person. We would not have let you say 'yes' to Hazard even though all we adore him. We want you to be happy and you could not be with him."

She asked, sobbing the question, not defiant but hopeful, "And you think I will be happy with Lord Taverston?"

"I think you could be. But it takes time. I don't mean a long courtship. It takes, well, years. Years of effort, and arguments, and tears, and laughter. You have to grow together. Your father and I did not find instantaneous happiness."

"You didn't?" She shuddered a breath, then rubbed her arm across her nose. She didn't know whether this was hopeful—she could grow to be happy with Lord Taverston—or terrifying—she could marry him based on that premise and then be disappointed. For the rest of her life. "I should have a handkerchief."

"I don't suppose you expected to become a watering pot. Georgiana, I tore up the letter I wrote because I realized I could not decide for you. If we don't go to Chaumbers, there may be a chance for you and Lord Taverston to court later, but there may not. It's unfair, but he may see this as a 'no' and look elsewhere. There is a chance, too, that you may yet meet someone here in London."

"But if we do go to Chaumbers, it will seal my fate."

"That is an ominous way to put it, but I think it's likely it will." She laughed a little hollowly. "The ton has already married you two off."

"Alice will miss her Season."

"Only a few weeks of it. And Lady Iversley writes that there are eligible gentlemen in the surroundings, and she will be inviting other young folks to help entertain you both and lighten the atmosphere. I don't see that it will harm Alice any. Her coming out ball is not until the end of the Season and most of the plans for it are already under way."

"I am beginning to believe the gossips are right and that you and Lady Iversley have been plotting this for years."

Mama harumphed.

Oh! She was being a child. There was nothing wrong with Lord Taverston. She breathed deeply. "I think we should go."

CHAPTER SEVEN

EVERYONE AT CHAUMBERS was on edge, from the Countess on down to the lowliest scullery maid. Reginald tried to be patient with his mother's sharpness, his sister's tears, the burnt toast, and the watery coffee. He *was* patient. But, sitting down in the empty breakfast parlor, having scooped a pile of cold eggs and limp kippers onto his plate, he found a card at his place marked with his brother's scrawled hand: *Please come to the study at your earliest convenience,* and even Reginald's patience finally snapped.

The hell.

He choked down two mouthfuls, then pushed the plate aside and rose. He stomped to the study, flung open the door, and marched to the desk where his startled brother waited.

He dropped the card on Father's desk.

"A summons, Jasper? Go to the devil. If this is how it will be—"

"What are you talking about?"

"This." He gestured to his brother, seated in his father's chair. "That!" He pointed to the card.

Jasper still looked bewildered. "I wanted to ask you something."

"Then come ask me. Don't leave me a damn card. You are not yet Iversley."

Jasper picked up the card and tore it in two. He muttered an oath.

"A bit tetchy this morning, are we, Reg?" He sounded even more irritated than Reginald felt. "Did Cook forget to bake your rolls again?" He shifted in his chair. *Father's chair.* "Sit down. Or don't. I don't give a damn."

Reginald sat. His legs felt wobbly, and his chest was tight. Moreover, his eyes burned. *The hell!* Jasper turned his attention to a pile of papers on his desk—*the desk, not his, but Father's*—and said nothing for a few moments.

Reginald steadied his breath. "I'm not prepared for any of this."

"You think I am? Damn it, Reg. I'm going to need a little help. How would you prefer for me to ask for it? I've been up since before dawn. I don't have time to lounge in the breakfast parlor until you put in an appearance. Would sending Finley or Peters for you have suited you better?"

No. Of course not. "I overreacted," he admitted stiffly. He was not used to being the one owing an apology to either of his brothers.

Jasper sniffed. "Whatever you may think, I am not chomping at the bit to take the Earl's place."

"I know you're not."

"What am I supposed to do?"

"I don't know." He flicked his hand. "Maybe buy your own chair."

Jasper stared at him a moment, then pursed his lips. "I'll put it on my list of things to do." He pulled his hand through his hair, mussing it, which brought a hitch to Reginald's throat. His brother looked exhausted.

Reginald asked, "You haven't heard from Crispin, have you?" They could really use Crispin.

"Not a word."

"Well," he sighed, "he'll just show up. That's his way."

"He'd better show up soon." His brother scowled and drummed his fingers on the arms of the chair, not absently but purposefully, as though his agitated motion could hurry Crispin along. Reginald couldn't tell if Jasper simply wanted additional brotherly support, or if he was worried Crispin…would not make it home on time. He leaned forward and reached for Jasper's fingers, laying his hand on them for a moment to stop the drumming.

"Do you think Father's worsening?"

They had thought he would die. Those first few days, he woke only to murmur and groan. Mother and Olivia spoon-fed him pap. His valet took care of his other necessities until they hired a woman to tend to them. It had been…sad. So sad. But then, he seemed to revive. They were able to prop him up in bed. His nurse and valet were even able to move him into a chair by the window for half an hour at a time. And he could make himself understood, though he didn't say much. They all took turns sitting with him. Jasper talked to him about the estate, asking a few questions, but nothing of importance. Reginald read to him— from the Bible. Reginald liked Scripture well enough; some of it was quite beautiful. But reading it like that, at his father's bedside, made him feel the worst sort of fraud.

"No," Jasper said. "He seems the same. Bad, but the same. He's a tough old coot."

Reginald nodded. "So. What did you 'summon me' for?"

When Jasper's lips twitched in half a smile, Reginald knew his apology was accepted.

"I haven't heard from Crispin, but I did get a letter from Benjamin. My letter took a long time to find him. He'd gone into the godforsaken interior somewhere. He said he would like the position if I haven't already found someone. He has a few things to take care of but then will book passage on the next available ship." He rubbed his jaw. "I don't expect him here, honestly, until summer."

"But you will hold the position for him?"

"He's the right person for it. It doesn't make sense to me to launch a search for a steward that may take until summer anyway. I don't want to hire someone just to have someone. That causes more work in the end."

"Yes. So Father has said."

"Font of all wisdom." He looked at his papers again. This time it was Jasper who appeared to be holding back tears. Reginald ignored that and kept talking so Jasper would not know that he saw.

"Well, things have been rolling in their ruts for months. I take it Father's man of business has things in hand."

"Oh, yes. I suppose. The servants are not leaving in droves. They must be getting paid. I don't know that the rents are being collected."

"I'm sure Wentworth is seeing to that." Bradwell did have an assistant; he'd been ancient, after all.

"The thing is…" Jasper leaned back in the chair. The leather squeaked. Such a familiar sound, but it seemed to startle him. He straightened. "The thing is, I don't want to present Benjamin with a slipshod set of books that haven't been cracked open in ages. I took a peek. Loose receipts are stuffed between pages. The last entry was dated eight months ago."

"God."

"I know Benjamin can straighten it all out. It isn't that I'm worried that he can't. It's simply that it's an embarrassing start. It should not have gotten to this point."

"No, of course not. But that isn't your fault."

"It isn't and it is. Either way, it's embarrassing to the family. Not that he'd carry tales. Or hold it over me."

"No. I understand." He did. Jasper was assuming his role. And Reginald was proud of him for it. It was not a role Reginald would have wanted for himself. "So what do you intend to do?"

"Ha. Well." A little of the usual lightness slipped into his voice. "I intend to dump the whole mess on you, naturally."

"*What?*" His voice rose with disbelief Of course, he wanted to help lessen Jasper's burdens, but he knew nothing about bookkeeping.

"The most recent set of ledgers is on the table behind you. Peters has a basket of receipts and bills, some of which were probably paid but he has no proof of that, and, should there be any need, there are years and years of old ledgers in the barristers on the left side of the library."

This was absurd! "I'm not an accountant!"

"You took a first in mathematics at Cambridge."

"That's entirely different. I'm not being lazy or difficult, Jasper, I—"

"Reg, you are brilliant. There is no denying it. I know it's a tedious thing to ask of you, but you'll figure it out."

Reginald swallowed his protests. It was not that much to ask. And surely, he *could* figure it out. His own interests could wait. *Should* wait. "What if I uncover all your old gambling debts?" he asked.

Jasper laughed. Reginald realized he had not heard his brother laugh since leaving London.

"Then, as always, I will rely upon your discretion, little brother."

He started to rise. "Will that be all?"

"No. One more thing."

Reginald settled back with a sigh. "I hope you didn't save the worst for last."

"Maybe. Mother has invited a few houseguests. At my request."

"Houseguests! Now? Are you mad?"

"I think it will help."

Help? He *was* mad. "Jasper, we cannot have guests. They are burning toast in the kitchen. And oh! The Earl is bedridden, in case you'd forgotten." His earlier fury returned. "Why would you do this to Mother?"

"The guests are the Duchess of Hovington, Lady Georgiana, and her cousin, Alexandra. Agnes. Something like that. Oh, God, my mind is going. I don't forget names. I *can't*." He put his head in his hands, elbows on the desk. Then he ground out, "Alice.

Miss Alice Fogbotham."

Reginald swallowed. Jasper's guests included the young lady he wished to court. His brother was no fool. He was not blind to the household circumstances. If he was nevertheless determined to pursue this course, despite the obstacles, he would need his family's support.

"And you're sure about Lady Georgiana?"

"I'm sure about her name."

"But you are not rushing into something you'll regret? Or that she'll regret?"

"I don't know, Reg," he groaned. "Do you think Cupid shot me with an arrow? But people of our station marry one another all the time. It isn't the end of the world. People speak well of her. They speak well of me. I'm sure we'll manage to rub along just fine. They'll be here in two days. Try to make yourself pleasant."

REGINALD BALANCED TWO rolls in one hand, picked up his steaming cup of coffee with the other, and set off for the library. Their guests would arrive sometime today. The funny thing was, it did help, inviting people. Cook had snapped back to form, and the kitchen staff seemed relieved to have her hounding them again. Mrs. Hardy, the head housekeeper, set the maid to dusting and sweeping and washing as if the house had been dirty, which of course it had not.

They had had two days of fine weather, so Jasper rode about Iversley, paying calls on the tenants. Reassuring them. By nature, people hated change. The Earl had been a good lord to his people, demanding but fair, generous but not gullible. Reginald would not call him kind, but he would never be cruel to those in his care. Jasper was more likable, certainly, but tenants did not necessarily want their earl to be likable. It was good for them to see that Lord Taverston was reliable and steady. And here.

Crispin had, reportedly, blown in with the wind sometime last night or early morning. Mother, who had been sitting up with Father, had seen him, but apart from the porter who opened the door, no one else had. It would be interesting to see how he took the news that the future countess was about to arrive to be courted in their presence. He hoped *Crispin* would make himself pleasant.

Reginald carried his breakfast into the library.

This should be his favorite room in the old house. Everyone probably assumed it was. But Reginald was particular about libraries and this one fell short. It was partly the architecture. It sat under the east end of the second-floor ballroom. So, back in the remote days when the Countess used to hold balls, if one happened to be a school-age boy home on holiday who wished to spend his unsupervised evening hours reading, one had to block out the sound of stomping feet and music.

Moreover, the shape of the room echoed that of the ballroom. Instead of being sensibly rectangular, with small, well-placed windows and great expanses of shelves, it was box-shaped with two…excrescences. Cubbyholes with bay windows. It made one wonder if the architect had ever seen a library before or understood how they were to be used. They were not even symmetrical excrescences, and so offended the eye. The smaller one held a tiny table with a painted-on chessboard. Two chairs were tucked beneath it. For show, he supposed. The "boys" had never been chess players.

The larger one contained a decent writing desk and a chair that could pivot back and forth. There must have been rhyme or reason for such a design, but it put Reginald in mind of a child's rocking horse. The best thing about the "cubbies" was that each could be closed off with a heavy velvet curtain, hanging from rings on a rod attached to the ceiling. The ceiling, by the by, was too low for a library. One could reach the top bookshelf with the aid of a simple step stool.

And the less said about the books, the better. It should be

enough to note that the bulk of the glass-enclosed shelves along the left wall contained old ledgers. And much of the shelving on the right contained Bibles and religious tracts.

Should one's eyes happen upon a middle shelf on the right wall, where a gap between grandfather's dusty histories had been partly filled, with no regard for order or good sense, by a few of Mother's novels, one would find the newest additions to the family book collection: Woodhouse's *The Principles of Analytical Calculation*, Maclaurin's *Fluxions*, and, of course, Newton's *Principia*. He'd thought himself clever in mathematics, taking a first, until he'd spent an evening in a Cambridge pub with a fellow named Babbage. It wasn't the ale that had befuddled him. Now he'd consigned his mathematical schoolbooks to the Chaumbers' library and recommitted himself to ancient Greek.

Reginald strode to the desk, set down his bread, and pulled shut the curtain. Two more hours, he would give it today. Then, after luncheon, he would permit himself to work on his translation until their guests arrived. Unless Crispin disturbed his plans.

He perched on the "rocking horse" and spread open the ledger. He had been approaching the task logically. Rather than diving straight in, he had first gone back to a ledger five years old, starting from the assumption that Bradwell had still been in his best form, and studied the man's system. It was not difficult to get the sense of it. There was a repetitiveness to the entries, though not all expenses were recurring ones. Five years ago: that was the year that there should have been a rather large layout for Crispin's commission, but of course, there wasn't. He wondered if Father regretted that. If Crispin did. Well, that was their business. Neither was ever going to say.

When he felt he understood it well enough, he checked himself with another ledger from two years ago. The system was unchanged, as were many of the recurring expenditures. Only Bradwell's handwriting differed. It had become shaky. That hurt to see.

He had then acquired Peters' basket. He arranged all the

scraps in chronological order and began entering them according to Bradwell's system. Some were marked paid, and he took that at face value. He had decided to make two lists of the others. One would be those he was sure would have been attended to even if they were unmarked. The others, he had no idea. He intended to send the lists to Father's man of business. If *he* didn't know, Reginald hoped the bank would.

It would upset Jasper, not to mention Mother, to have creditors banging on the door the day after Father's funeral—which wouldn't happen for some time yet, God willing—fearing they would never see their money. If necessary, he would pay something twice and leave it for Benjamin to sort out.

He had retrieved a second set of books from Wentworth, whose sole job it was to ensure rents were collected. And they had been. Reginald spent the morning transferring recent numbers to the main ledger, since that was how it had always been done. He did note that two tenants were a month in arrears. He would have to question Wentworth about that. And a third tenant was four months behind. But that man's name was circled, and the balance marked zero, with a note: *Death of babe*. He paused over that.

A policy of Father's, no doubt. Did Jasper know about it? He must. But it was important that he did, so as to continue the tradition. Reginald sighed. So he would have to tell Jasper and have his head bitten off because, of course, Jasper would already know.

He shut the ledgers and set them aside. He stood, stretched his neck, flexed his fingers, then pulled open the curtain. It was later than he'd thought. Yet no one had fetched him for luncheon. He decided to stroll to the kitchen and see when it would be served. But when he exited the library, he heard voices echoing down the hall from the billiard room. His brothers. They were not arguing, but neither were they laughing.

For a moment, his feet would not move.

Crispin had been different, harsher, when they had last seen him, just after Father's first fit. He had been granted only two months' leave, though surely his commander would have given him more if he'd requested it. And, when he saw that Father was recovering, he appeared almost peeved to have been sent for at all. Although they knew his regiment had been on the Peninsula, and that things were not going particularly well there—that much the War Secretary could not keep quiet—that was all they knew. Crispin would not talk about what he had been doing. Yet it had seemed he would have rather been there than here.

Of course, Crispin was always more or less harsh. Except for brief spurts when he wasn't. His letters to Reginald were always funny. And if one was to read a portion of his letters to Mother, it was as though a different man entirely was writing home.

Well, thank God he was back at any rate. They needed him.

Lud. He hoped Crispin had not heard about Annie and Plodgett. Reginald rubbed his jaw. He'd shaved this morning. One less thing for Crispin to poke him for. He was acceptably dressed: not as fashionably as Jasper, but not like a preacher either. He cocked an ear toward the billiard room to listen for the clink of balls bouncing off one another, but it didn't seem they were playing.

Well. Onward. Reginald was the buffer between them, and so, naturally, he would be knocked about a bit. That was his role. At least they had given him one. He just hoped Crispin would look less cadaverous than he did the last time he was home.

CHAPTER EIGHT

T HE DUCHESS' SMALL party set forth from London early in the morning in hopes of reaching Iversley before dark. The Duke had provided them with his finest carriage. It was strongly sprung, roomy with deep padded seats, and was embossed with the ducal crest. A separate carriage followed closely, filled to the hilt with their trunks and their maids. Twelve liveried outriders, armed, of course, accompanied them. Highwaymen existed, but Georgiana did not fear them.

She did not enjoy traveling. She considered it an evil necessary to conduct people where they wanted to go. It was even more unpleasant having to endure a daylong carriage ride when one dreaded arriving at the destination. She felt chilled, damp, and miserable.

This is a mistake. This is a mistake. This is a mistake.

Her thoughts rolled in a monotonous rhythm, matching the creak of the carriage wheels.

Mama and Alice spent the first hour chatting, with Mama drawing out her niece's thoughts on the various men who had paid her their attentions. Georgiana made appropriate comments but could muster no real interest in what was being said. It took several minutes, perhaps longer, before she even realized the carriage had fallen silent. Mama had dropped into a doze and Alice peered at the dead-of-winter scenery through the window where the curtains parted. She looked pensive—eyes hooded and dark curls drooping. Georgiana felt bad that she was not more supportive of her cousin. Her own discontent was already turning her selfish and ill-humored. That did not bode well for the rest of her life.

Georgiana's mind drifted back to the day she'd overheard her parents arguing. In retrospect, it seemed even more momentous than it had at the time. It was not the end of her childhood; she had already been outgrowing that. Yet it seemed the first step on the path that had led to here. Of course, those steps would have been taken regardless. There were no other paths for feet such as hers.

Father had been displaying her. It was something he did from time to time. Not often. But out of an overabundance of delight in her odd mathematical talents. When he did, she would grow a little silly with pride. What child would not bask in adults' attention? She couldn't remember who had been there that day. Perhaps Lord Billings. Or Lord Darby. It didn't matter who had been gaping and applauding. What mattered was that Mama had been looking for her. And found her. Georgiana could still see her mother's face going white. The widening of her eyes and flaring of her nostrils. The laughter in the room died. Mama bundled Georgiana off to the music room.

The little girl that she had been had not recognized her error. She took at face value her mother's scold that she was supposed to be practicing her piano, but the *extremeness* of Mama's reaction had frightened her. Naturally, she hastened to please. She plinked those piano keys for well over an hour. Yet she had done this knowing that whatever she tried would never be enough to make her mother happy. Not happy the way she had once been.

Oh, those days. She was feeling her mother's presence again after what had seemed a long absence, and she was desperate, *desperate*, for a return of the mother-daughter bond she only vaguely remembered, but whose absence she nevertheless felt deep in her heart.

When Randolph died, it was as though all the light and laughter in their family had died with him. Georgiana had been just nine years old, and time passed differently then. Slowly, slowly, she and her younger brother Charles returned to their pastimes, encouraged by Father. But there was a hole in Georgiana's life, a hole where her mother once had been. Then Mama rarely emerged from her bedchamber, which Georgiana recalled as being always dark, curtains drawn shut. When she did appear, she was so pale and hollow-eyed and listless, that it was as if a ghost had taken her place. She never took meals with them. She never spoke above a hoarse whisper.

Mama did not put off her mourning black for two years. To a girl as young as Georgiana had been, two years was an eternity. She had been left feeling, *knowing* somehow, that a mere daughter was not *enough*, could never *be* enough to compensate for the loss of a son. Yet rather than give up, poor little Georgiana tried harder.

At nineteen, Georgiana now understood what she hadn't at eleven. That Mama grieved Randolph's death differently than Father. He clutched Georgiana and Charles closer, while Mama withdrew. It had taken Mama a long, long time to return to herself—albeit a quieter, less openly affectionate version of herself.

Georgiana understood this, yet sometimes she saw herself *still* trying to win her mother's approval. To make up for her loss. No, not sometimes. Always. She was always still trying.

Perhaps it was because on that day, that long ago day, she was made to understand that the very part of herself that brought her the most joy, was the part that most distressed Mama.

When Georgiana had heard carriages pulling away outside, knowing Father's guests had left, she'd tiptoed back toward the library. While passing her mother's sitting room, she overheard them together. Her father sounded abashed. Georgiana crept closer. Mama's voice was raised.

"What could you have been thinking?"

"It was a mere amusement. Surely there is no harm—"

"She is your daughter! A young lady. She's not a substitute for—" *For Randolph. Mama would rather have Randolph.*

"Mary, stop. Georgiana is my child. I'm permitted to dote. I'm not making her a replacement. There is no replacement. But if she wants to learn—"

"She has to learn the right things! Not what you are filling her head with. The right things!"

"The right things?" Her father laughed. It was not his true laughter, more like he was trying to tease Mama from her mood. But it worried Georgiana to hear him laugh falsely. Did that mean he might sometimes speak falsely too? "Well, I think she is bright enough to learn the right things and a few of the wrong ones."

"You will make her ridiculous!"

Ridiculous.

She hadn't understood what that meant. Not then. But Mama's vehement disapproval of her daughter's—*gift*, Father had called it—seared the word into her memory, and she certainly understood what it meant now. There was scarcely any worse social sin than to make oneself *ridiculous* in the eyes of the ton.

Georgiana knew that as a duke's daughter, there was a proper way to conduct herself. So she did. Mostly. Then *and* now.

THEY STOPPED TO change horses. Then they stopped to change them again, rest, and have a small luncheon. The innkeeper's wife was solicitous, but served them a tough bit of poultry, swimming in grease, apologizing for having nothing fancier while beaming at them as if she had presented a feast. Georgiana didn't want to appear ungracious, but she couldn't eat. Mama took pity and made excuses to the innkeepers, begging a bit of plain bread for the ride as her daughter was ill from traveling. It was almost amusing how giddy it made the wife—this privilege of serving such a delicate guest.

Back on the road, they made good time. Too good for Georgiana's liking. Mama said they should arrive by dinner, which heightened her dread.

Georgiana rejoiced silently when that prediction proved premature. They reached a sodden stretch and, after creeping along at a tortoise's pace for an interminable time, they bogged altogether in the mud. While the outriders set to work trying to dig them out, Mama sent a messenger on ahead to warn their arrival would be delayed. For a short while, the carriage was jostled so roughly that Georgiana feared they would have to disembark and wait standing outside, causing her to arrive at Chaumbers with a dirty nose and messy hair. Finally, however, the coachman directed the others to lay as many branches and stones as could be gathered on the wayside beneath the wheels until the coach could be shimmied onto firmer ground.

When the same misadventure struck a second time, Mama sent another messenger. Lady Iversley absolutely must not hold dinner for them. They would not arrive until very late. She added delicately that although they were eager to spend time with the Taverstons, it might be best if they slipped in without fanfare and greeted their hosts in the morning.

"A reprieve," Georgiana made the mistake of saying, with her first smile of the day.

Her mother looked at her askance. "Georgiana, I hope your attitude will improve. A great many people have been put to a lot of bother for you. A simple 'no' would have sufficed if you didn't want to go."

There had been no such option as a "simple" no.

She wouldn't cry. She had shed enough unwarranted tears. Any other girl would be—what had Mama said? *Ecstatic.*

"I'm sorry, Mama. This journey has put me out of sorts." Her, and Mama, too. She finished stiffly, "Rest assured, I know how to behave."

CRISPIN WAS IN fine form, Reginald was relieved to see. He was out of uniform, wearing light gray pantaloons and a closely tailored waistcoat that made it evident he had put a bit of muscle back on his skinny bones. Reginald remembered when, as a schoolboy, Crispin used to wear clothing too big for him, as if to bulk out his too-lanky frame. At some point, he evidently realized the tactic made him appear even punier because now his clothes fit. Crispin was nearly as tall as Jasper, but his bouts of illness had always prevented him from accumulating weight. Even Reginald, who was a good four inches shorter, had him beat by a stone, sometimes a stone and a half. And Reginald was by no means heavily built. But Crispin must have been in health for a while. Thank God.

Moreover, his disposition was cheerier than last time. Still, he would not speak of his military experiences. Either they were too secret or too painful to discuss. Well, they did not lack for conversational material at Chaumbers.

When Reginald interrupted their bickering in the billiard room, audible from the hallway, Crispin was making it clear he had no sympathy for Jasper's fear of foundering.

"Bosh! You've been Earl of Iversley in all but name for a year and a half, Jasp. If the earldom was going to go to ruin, it would have done so by now. Just do as you've been doing."

"You have no idea how difficult—"

"Oh, bosh. They've been preparing you for this since your steed was a hobby horse. The only difficulty I foresee is telling Vanessa you're marrying a duke's chit."

That was the moment Reginald had stepped into the room. Crispin whirled around, catching the billiard balls he had been juggling, and said, "Ah, there's just the parson I wanted to see."

"How long have you been bursting to use that? You do know puns are the lowest form of humor?"

"Yes, well, I am feeling low. I saw the Earl last night."

"Oh." Reginald could not read Crispin's face. "Did I send for you too soon again?"

Crispin gave him a hard look. It might have been that Reginald *had* dragged his brother away from something more important, or it might be that the humor was inappropriate, in which case Reginald was poaching in Crispin's copse.

But then Crispin turned his face toward the wall. "No." He sighed heavily. "No. It's good that I came."

"Dr. Haraldsen told Mother that indications are favorable," Jasper said.

"Dr. Haraldsen is lying."

Jasper crossed his arms over his chest and snapped, "And now you are a physician."

"No. I am a man who has seen too many men die."

"From bullet wounds and saber cuts! That hardly makes you an expert."

"He wants to die. He's miserable."

Jasper glowered and looked as though he would say more, but Reginald tried to inject a little hopefulness.

"When he recovers a bit more, he might…"

Crispin shook his head. "He said he's made his peace with God and is ready to go."

"He said that last night? To you?" Jasper scoffed. "Why?"

"I asked."

Both Reginald and Jasper looked upon him with horror. They had been told not to alarm Father and Crispin's first words had been to ask him if he was ready to face God?

"The Earl has been stripped of the last vestiges of his authority. This is the only thing left that he can control. He doesn't want to be cosseted and lied to. He wants to prepare himself. And to let us know that he is prepared."

Jasper still looked mutinous. "Then why not tell that to Reg, who has been reading Bible passages to him for a fortnight?"

"Yes, well, Reg is a little heathen, isn't he, really? Father isn't going to meet Zeus."

He started juggling again, then challenged Jasper to a game. Reginald was not in the mood to watch one of their bouts. They generally ended up throwing the balls at each other's heads and he'd been caught one too many times in the crossfire. He left to find something to eat, then returned to his bedchamber and his manuscript until it was his turn to sit with Father. Thankfully, Father slept the whole time.

The family, except for the Earl, all came together for dinner, once Mother determined that dinner would finally have to be served without the anticipated guests. They arranged themselves back in their regular places: Mother to the right, then Crispin, Jasper to the left, then Olivia, then Reginald—with no one to his left or across from him, he felt he was hanging off the family's tail. Father's chair at the end of the table remained unoccupied. His absence had been heavily sensed the whole time, but it was ten times worse with Crispin home. Perhaps it felt more glaring to have the entire family gathered without him. Or perhaps it was the fact that they were all gathered because he was not able to be there. It made his absence seem final.

Mother asked Reginald to say grace, which he did. She always asked him, and he was generally able to say a decent prayer without giving it overmuch thought. This time he hesitated over the words. Crispin's heathen comment had stayed with him. There was too much truth in it for it not to.

Mother directed the opening conversation to Olivia, who looked a little livelier today.

"Where did you go?"

"Oh, all the old places." She beamed at Crispin. "We rode out to the lake and halfway around. Then visited the Crofts."

"She played with the puppies," Crispin said. "We may end up with another dog. Ugly things those pugs."

Olivia made a face at him.

So Crispin had taken her riding, even though he'd likely spent most of the last several days in the saddle and could have used a respite. Yet he had seen at once what needed doing. Whereas Jasper and Reginald, wrapped in their own concerns, had not bothered—had not even thought to bother.

Olivia chatted happily about the puppies and the fact that she had beaten Crispin in a race.

Crispin merely shrugged. "I was overconfident after having so convincingly trounced Jasper at billiards."

Mother said, "I'm sure that Lady Georgiana and Miss Fogbotham both ride. If the weather remains fine, you will have to arrange an outing, Jasper. And Olivia, you may take them shopping in the village. It's not London, I know, but there are a few charming shops. And I suppose the church can be visited. Mr. Brindle enjoys showing off the windows."

Crispin yawned. "Oh. I beg your pardon, Mother."

Mother slanted a suspicious look at him, then continued as if he had not interrupted. "I thought perhaps a tea. Not immediately, of course, but in a few days. We'll invite the Brindles and Sir Crawley and his wife. Do you think, Jasper, that Mr. Leighton could be persuaded to come?"

"Robert? To a tea?"

"Don't give me that look. I'm sure he drinks tea. And he may well do for Miss Fogbotham. She's a pretty girl with good breeding, but can't hope to look very high."

"Yes, well, Robert's a fine chap, but can't string three words together in a room containing females. He would show very poorly at a tea."

"A hunt then. Surely you can manage to bring a few local gentlemen to Chaumbers one morning."

"Yes, do!" Olivia said, her enthusiasm making it all too plain how neglected she had been. "And have the archery targets set up, Jasper."

"That would do very well for you," Crispin laughed. "But what about Lady Georgiana?" He pinned Jasper with his gaze. "What does she enjoy?"

Jasper returned his look. "All the usual things, I'm sure."

"We will discover her particular favorites," Mother put in smoothly. "I understand she plays the piano and sings exceedingly well. We'll have music one night. Quiet music. Reginald, perhaps you and she might give us a duet. Jasper's voice would send her running back to London."

The boys all laughed at that, mainly because Mother was not joking. The conversation shifted to other things: the villagers, unimportant news from London, if the weather would hold. The modiste Mother had requested to come to Chaumbers for Olivia had sent her regrets; the local seamstress would have to do. Reginald listened with half an ear, his mind straying to a sticky point in his translation. His eyes drifted across the table to Crispin's plate.

What now?

Crispin had not taken wine with dinner. He never drank, had not done so since his Oxford days. He had also waved off the bread. Had he eaten the soup? Reginald hadn't noticed. As their guests had not arrived, it was not an elaborate dinner. Mother dispensed with the fish course altogether and had the servants just bring the meat. But it appeared Crispin had cordoned off his beef and gravy and was eating nothing but peas and potatoes. Reginald hoped their mother would refrain from commenting, though she must have noticed. He was intrigued.

Jasper filled them all in on gossip he had collected over the past couple of days, visiting the villagers. The names were familiar, and Reginald did have fond connections with a few families, but—and this was another reason why he should not be a vicar—he was content to hear about their doings from afar.

The servants cleared their plates and brought out trays of biscuits, cheese, and sliced fruit. Crispin took only fruit. Mother's forbearance gave way.

"Crispin, eat something. For Heaven's sake. You can't afford to get any thinner."

Crispin's face darkened. When he spoke, his voice was deceptively mild. "I eat what agrees with me, Mother. And we will not discuss it further."

"If you do not care to eat what is served," she said, ignoring his warning, "at least inform Cook of your preferences. I won't have you starve."

He put an apple slice in his mouth, chewed, and swallowed, before answering, "I won't starve." Then he added grudgingly, "We simply do not eat so richly on campaign. Adam will make a list for Cook if it isn't too much trouble."

Mother's expression softened into concern. "Of course, it isn't any trouble, Crispin. I wish you would—"

"Who the devil is Adam?" Jasper interrupted.

"My batman. Or, for now, my valet."

"What happened to Richard?" Olivia asked with a giggle. Richard had been a charity case at best, and shifty at worst. But Crispin had claimed he was level-headed and fair with his pistols, which was more important than knowing which cuff buttons went with which shirt. Then her eyes widened a little. "He's all right, I hope."

"Richard is perfectly fine. He went home to his sweetheart, I believe."

"And where did you pick up this 'Adam?'" Jasper asked. "He must be half decent. Your boots are shined, and your neckcloth is sufficiently well knotted."

Crispin smiled. "Thank you, dear brother. I knotted it myself." He dropped the smile. "Adam came to me by recommendation. He suits."

"Where have you been hiding him?"

"I expect he's been with your Alfred and Reginald's Barclay, learning what he needs to know about working in this old pile. Don't look so skeptical. He has strict manners and is exceptional at making himself scarce. Your houseguests will never see him."

Jasper shrugged. "He's your valet, not mine."

Reginald decided he had nothing to add, so kept quiet. But he did wonder how Crispin's valet was going to tackle Cook. Handing her a list? He'd like to see the woman's face.

When dinner drew to a close, Mother and Olivia excused themselves to sit with Father. The boys retired to the study. Jasper poured himself a brandy, cast a look at both his brothers in turn, then stoppered the bottle as they took their seats, Reginald plunking himself onto the davenport and Crispin perching on its rolled arm.

Jasper drained his glass and set it down before focusing his scowling attention on his middle brother.

"We are trying not to upset Mother. Couldn't you have simply put a bit of gravy in your mouth?"

Crispin responded, "What exactly do you intend to do about Vanessa?"

A long silence followed. Neither bent an inch.

Finally, Jasper looked toward the wall and said, "Did you know I've put Reg in charge of the accounts?"

"Reg?" Crispin gave a mock horrified start. "The accounts? I suppose old Bradwell has been slacking?"

"He's dead."

That wiped the smirk from Crispin's face. "Damn." He considered a moment. "What about Benjamin Carroll?"

"Still in Canada. Won't be here until July. I decided Reg could take first crack at it."

"Damn." Crispin laced his fingers together and stared at the ground. After a minute had passed, he looked up. "I'm going to bed. I'm spent. Tomorrow, tell me what you need for me to do."

"You'll just do it, I'm sure, before I realize what to ask. Thank you for taking Olivia out."

Crispin's mouth tightened. "She's my sister too."

Reginald said, "Well, there will be houseguests." He echoed Jasper. "Just try to make yourself pleasant." Then he stood. "Long day. I'll look in on Father, then I'm going off too."

They left Jasper pouring himself another glass of brandy.

CHAPTER NINE

NATURALLY, THE DUCHESS' party had not been allowed to sneak in during the night like thieves. The long, twisting drive leading from the road up to Chaumbers had been lined by torches, with footmen to tend them. A bevy of grooms met the Duchess' entourage and helped everyone to get where they needed to be. Mother, Georgiana, and Alice were met on the steps outside by the Countess and Lord Taverston. Thank goodness it was dark. Georgiana shuddered to imagine how disheveled she must appear.

They were not detained any longer than necessary but were taken swiftly to their chambers. Georgiana and Alice had a room to share, which pleased them both. The Duchess was placed just down the hall. Two large, north-facing windows promised a view, though nothing could be seen yet in the night. Floral curtains and bedlinens were a soft, comforting shade of yellow. Sandwiches, a bowl of fruit, and lemonade awaited them. Georgiana nibbled a sandwich, then gave up and let Jeanette undress her. Alice couldn't even be tempted to eat or undress; she dropped onto the large featherbed and fell asleep at once. Georgiana thought she would follow. Instead, she lay staring at the ceiling, perhaps drifting to sleep but then startling back awake, time after time. Her mind was too active to let go, but too drained to think coherently.

She had not been permitted a good look at the Chaumbers' property in the dark and could remember almost nothing about it from when she had been seven years old. That didn't matter, of course. She would see it tomorrow. She had weeks to take it all in.

She had had a good look at Lord Taverston. He'd still been in his dinner clothes. He looked handsome, but...pallid. Torchlight never did one's features any favors. And, it was true they were both exhausted. She was certain she'd looked anemic as well. Everyone was excruciatingly polite. But it had been a disappointing reunion if it could even be considered such, given they were strangers.

Georgiana did not believe in omens, but overall, it had not been a promising day. And it promised to be a worse night. So when the room began to brighten, she finally gave up attempting to sleep. She slipped out of bed and tiptoed into the antechamber where Jeanette had been settled for the night rather than being shunted off to the servants' quarters at such a late hour. The maid woke at once.

"What may I do for you, my lady?"

Georgiana swallowed her apology, saying only, "It's early, I know, but I slept so poorly I couldn't lay abed any longer. I didn't wish to wake Miss Fogbotham."

"*Mon Dieu,*" Jeanette murmured, then sat up, pushing off her blankets. She wore only a shift, and her hair was down in a long braid on one side. "Would you like to dress?"

"Yes, but just something simple. I'll go down to the breakfast parlor. I believe Lady Iversley said last night that cold fare would be out from dawn until whenever we all woke, and we could partake at our leisure. It is dawn, isn't it?"

Jeanette laughed lightly. "*À peine.* You should have finished your little bites last night."

"I know. My stomach is so hollow it hurts."

"Come," the maid said, climbing from her bed, a narrow cot with a thin mattress. At least the blankets looked warm. And, to be honest, the servants' beds at Sayles and Marbury were no better. "I'm sorry I have not unpacked all your trunks—"

"No, of course not," Georgiana said.

"But I did put up a few things." She opened a wardrobe and removed a pretty sprigged muslin. She frowned, considering, then said, "Yes, this should do. With your wrap. It is cold in the air."

Georgiana agreed. It was attractive, fairly simple, and comfortable. A little dressier than what she would wear in the morning at home, but not outrageously so. Jeanette helped her into her things and buttoned the long row of buttons down her back. Then she brushed Georgiana's hair until it shone and twisted it into a chignon.

"Simple now," Jeanette said. "The better to stun him at dinner. I think the green gown tonight."

Georgiana smiled weakly. "Thank you."

Did she wish to "stun" him? If he acted besotted, would that be better or worse? Probably worse. She was not quivering with excitement; why should he be?

"Will there be anything else?"

"Oh, no. Just let Miss Fogbotham know where I am when she wakes."

"In the library?" Jeanette asked, a twinkle in her eye.

"Maybe," Georgiana admitted. "After I've eaten something. Unless the family is all up and I have to allow myself to be entertained." She left Jeanette but suspected the poor girl would not return to bed. Rather she would finish unpacking and seeing to their clothes.

Georgiana crept downstairs and found her way to the breakfast parlor, relieved she remembered the directions she had been given last night. The ground floor was very quiet, but it was not as early as she feared. Fires had been started and there were servants moving about. The door to the breakfast parlor was ajar. She hoped there would be no one in it. Especially not the Countess or Lord Taverston. She took a deep breath and stepped inside.

At first glance, the morning room appeared very formal. The walls were papered with a dark blue design and the wood floor was nearly black. Food was laid out on a substantial Italianate sideboard. But a wall of windows, drapery tied back, brightened the space. Georgiana smiled to see the formality was softened by plump, somewhat worn, mismatched seat cushions on the chairs. Left on the bare-of-linen table, which could easily seat twelve, was an empty coffee cup and a plate containing crumbs. Her fellow early bird was already gone. Good.

After surveying the offerings on the sideboard, Georgiana scooped a few dried berries into a bowl and drenched them with cream. This was lovely. She was tired of jams. She also took a thick slice of bread and slathered it with butter. How delightful to be alone since she intended to gorge herself. She felt as though she hadn't eaten for days.

She was thirsty too, but not for coffee. Her stomach was not yet settled enough for that. Instead, she took a half cup of tea and drowned that, too, with cream. She sat at the table, two seats from the detritus of the previous breakfaster. A folded newspaper lay on one of the chairs, but she didn't bother to pick it up. She was tired, tired, tired.

When she finished her meal, she crumpled her napkin and laid it beside her bowl and cup. A maid came in and started. "Oh! Milady." She curtsied. "I beg your pardon. May I bring you something?"

"No, thank you. Everything is lovely. I'm just finishing."

"I'll come back to clear."

"You needn't. I'm going now." She stood. "Perhaps you might direct me to the library if the Earl permits visitors."

"Oh, he never minded, milady. And I'm certain Lord Taverston won't. I'll show you."

The maid led her away from the breakfast parlor, down a long corridor. She could hear a faint whistling of the wind outside, and it grew chillier the farther they walked. She pulled her shawl tighter. This might not have been such a good idea.

Near the end of the corridor, the maid stopped abruptly, curtsied again, and said, "That's the door there. It won't be locked." She giggled. "Mr. Taverston says there's nothing there to steal." Then she gasped, looking mortified. "Beg pardon, milady. I didn't mean…"

Georgiana smiled. She rather liked that the poor girl was a little gauche but trained well enough to recognize when she'd said something amiss. A lax household would be terrible, and she didn't expect Lady Iversley would be lax. But Georgiana disliked households where the servants were all impeccable and all terrified.

"I'm just going to keep myself out of the way until the others wake."

"Yes, miss," she murmured, curtsying again and then hurrying away.

Georgiana opened the door. It swung soundlessly on its hinges. For all it was tucked away as an afterthought, the room seemed well maintained. It was even a little warmer than the hall had been. She glanced about and noticed a small brazier set near the wall, in front of a curtain that must be keeping out drafts, and a second curtain, parted only enough to let in a little light. Surely the brazier was not lit. That would be foolish, an unattended fire in a library.

Unless, she thought, nose crinkling with distaste as she looked around, they hoped to burn the room down. What a sorry excuse for a library!

The carpet was nice at least, thick underfoot and woven with the Earl's coat of arms. There were two leather chairs with end tables in corners and an overstuffed kissing chair near the right wall. The left wall's shelves held rows and rows of what appeared to be account books. Lord help her. She moved to the right wall and scanned. Hardly better.

Oh! For a moment, she didn't dare breathe.

The Principles of Analytical Calculation.

She was dreaming. None of this was real. She was still in bed next to Alice.

She ran her fingertip down the spine. It felt real.

Timidly, she pulled it from the shelf and opened it. Then put it to her nose and breathed in the scent. It was real. Heavens, her fingers were trembling. She had never seen a copy before; it was not the sort of book her subscription library lent out. She hadn't dared ask Father to purchase it. Oh! Her knees felt weak.

She stole a peek at the page she had turned to at random. But the words and notations swam before her eyes. She shut it quickly. She had weeks to pore over it. Perhaps a lifetime. She was not going to sully the experience by attempting to read a page when she hadn't slept in two days.

When she replaced it, gently, onto the shelf, she saw Newton's *Principia*. An old friend. Smiling to herself, she picked it up and took it to the kissing chair. Settling in, tucking her feet up beneath her, plumping up the pillows, wrapping her shawl tighter—though, in truth, it was warmer than she had first thought it would be—she opened the book. She would read the preface—again. That would require no great effort and, oh! She could think of nothing more soothing to her unsettled heart.

REGINALD RUBBED HIS eyes and realized he'd been staring at the same column for several minutes without actually seeing the figures. They would not add up. His scratch paper was covered with numbers, tallied, and crossed out. This was a waste of time.

In anticipation of the day's festivities, he'd come early to his cubbyhole to work for an hour or two on the manuscript. It had been months since he'd sent any pages back to Bastion. The man had likely given up expecting more. But he couldn't concentrate on the Greek when the ledgers lay there before him accusingly. If he pushed on through, he should shortly have the books finished and ready to present to Benjamin. Then he could get back to his Greek. But his brain was not working properly. He kept skipping numbers and adding wrong.

He needed a bit of fresh air. Unfortunately, the morning fog had not burned off and it was now starting to drizzle. Which meant—God only knew what—card games or poetry readings or, Lord help him, charades. The puzzles were always so obvious. He had to pretend to be stumped or else he would annoy his fellow players.

Hopefully, the bulk of the entertaining would be Jasper's responsibility, aided by Olivia and Mother. It would be wearisome having to witness his brother courting. Wearisome and embarrassing.

Well. He could go have another cup of coffee, and take it out to the small terrace where it was roofed. He stood and rattled back the curtain.

A body sprang, with a startled shriek, from the kissing chair, and something thudded to the floor.

"Good Lord!" he exclaimed, his heart banging in his chest.

A lady stood before him. A houseguest. Lady Georgiana or Miss Fogbotham? Good God. He drew in a steadying breath.

Whoever it was, she moved her leg, her foot he supposed, with two quick jerks as if to nudge under the chair the book that she had dropped. They all read those silly novels. He didn't know why they imagined it was a secret.

"I beg your pardon," she said, pulling her shawl up over her shoulders like a surrogate dignity. "I didn't know anyone was here."

"Neither did I."

She'd been exceptionally quiet. Asleep, obviously. Her hair was mashed to one side and her eyes were a bit puffy. Surely this was the cousin. He tried to set her at ease. She was, after all, a guest in their home.

"We have not been introduced, but at this point, the formality would appear to be moot. I am Mr. Taverston." He bowed a little. "The youngest son. And you are Miss Fogbotham?"

"No, unfortunately. I am Lady Georgiana."

He bit his lip. *How awkward.* "How long have you been here? In the library, I mean."

She looked to the wall clock, then groaned, "Nearly two hours."

Both their heads turned, as if connected by a string, to check the library door. It was firmly closed. A shiver ran down his spine. This was the fabled situation where a young man must go, hat in hand, to speak with a girl's father and pray not to be shot.

Lady Georgiana turned back to face him, her eyes a bit wide. "This is not going well, is it? What should we do?" Her calm impressed him.

He considered for a moment, then said, "Jasp—that is, Lord Taverston is not generally an early riser. And Lieutenant Taverston, unless his habits have changed, will go for a long morning walk before breakfasting. Olivia sleeps late. So we really need worry only about my mother."

"And mine."

He nodded, feeling rather sick.

"I don't suppose that window behind you opens?" she asked.

He turned and looked at the bay window. "Why?"

"Well, you could climb out, couldn't you? Walk around the house. Approach from the front. Say you have been out walking? Like Lieutenant Taverston does?"

"In the rain? Without my coat?"

She frowned at him, and he realized he sounded rather missish.

"I *could*," he amended quickly. "But I usually work in the mornings and walk later in the day. My habits are well known. My brothers would be on me like terriers on a rat. And I'm not a good liar."

"Generally, that recommends a man, but it doesn't help now."

"Can *you* li—um… prevaricate?"

She flushed. "Perhaps if we simply confessed? It is rather funny, don't you think?"

Funny? They would not actually be forced to the altar. But Jasper would be annoyed that Reginald had put Georgiana in such an embarrassing position, even unwittingly. And Jasper wouldn't blame her either, but he'd be peeved at the error.

"God," he groaned. "You don't know Crispin." Only Crispin would find it amusing—he would never let them live it down.

"I could slip out. Return to my guestroom."

"Would anyone ask where you've been? You can't say the library. Wait! I know. The music room is three doors down the hall. You play the piano, don't you?"

"Am I to go bang on the keys?" She sounded faintly amused.

"No, but there is sheet music on the piano and more in a basket on the shelf. Collect a few pieces and take them to the breakfast parlor. Someone is bound to be there. Say you've been poring over them for over an hour and hope for some advice on which ones Lord Taverston would prefer to hear."

He thought it a clever suggestion, but her flush deepened and she frowned. "For someone who claims he does not lie, you have apparently mastered deceit." She adjusted the shawl which had slipped down her shoulders. "You are not the only one with established habits, Mr. Taverston. My family will also notice something amiss if I behave out of character. And I am not a coquette."

"I beg your pardon." He made a short, apologetic bow, and felt himself flush at his own gaucheness. This was why he did not like to meet new people. Jasper charmed multitudes, while *he* could not…well, he could not.

The lady tilted her head then, her eyes peering upward as she tapped her finger on her chin. "Although…" she mused. "It would appease Mama to see that I have chosen to make an effort."

An effort? To do what, exactly? "Excuse me?"

"Nothing," she said. "Is the music room to the right or the

left?"

"Left."

"You do know that when we're introduced later today, you'll have to pretend it's the first time. Can you prevaricate that much?" She looked at him with one of her eyebrows raised, as if she was skeptical of his ability to lie.

Prevaricate, rather. He drew himself up. "I believe I can muddle through a pretend introduction," he replied, amused to think he and his sister-in-law would always have this little deception to smile about.

She smiled at him. "Thank you. I do apologize for upsetting your morning."

"Not at all."

It occurred to him that she was an exceptionally pretty woman. Though not at all in the way that Annie had been. Even disheveled as she was, Lady Georgiana was proper. She would be perfect for Jasper's countess. Proper yet just addle-pated enough for him to mollycoddle. Reginald made a polite bow and let her go.

Then he went to the kissing chair to retrieve the novel she'd hidden. He knelt on the floor and reached for it. Bulky thing. He pulled it out.

Principia.

He looked at the closed library door and then back at his book.

Good Lord.

CHAPTER TEN

THEY GATHERED IN the drawing room for introductions before luncheon. Reginald thought his acting was acceptable. It required only his being courteous, quiet, and uncomfortable in new company—his natural state. A little added uncomfortableness drew no attention.

To be charming was Jasper's natural state. He focused upon the Duchess first and foremost, while complimenting both the young ladies equally. He did not make it obvious that he had brought Lady Georgiana here for the purpose of wooing her, which seemed to set her at ease. It must have been an awkward business for her as well. Miss Fogbotham was reserved but had a laugh that suggested she would be delightful once she settled. Their mothers appeared sincerely pleased to find themselves in one another's company.

It was only Crispin who didn't play his part well. His responses were brusque, and he remained standing while everyone else was seated. When they rose to move to the dining room, Crispin excused himself. "I'm afraid I've developed a headache. I'll take luncheon in my room."

Crispin did not get headaches.

Mother frowned and excused him. Jasper, too, looked annoyed but hid it before their guests might notice. Jasper offered the Duchess his arm to lead her in first.

In the general bustle from room to room, Reginald found Lady Georgiana at his elbow, so he offered it to her.

She whispered, "Lord Taverston *does* rise early. He was in the breakfast parlor. He'd been in his study all morning."

Father's study.

He whispered back, "What did you do?"

"Fudged. Smiled prettily, showed him the sheets, and asked him what music he most particularly enjoyed."

Smiled prettily. She would make a fine coquette. Except…

"Were you reading *Principia?*" He kept to a whisper.

Her brow clouded. "Reading *what?*" She cleared her throat softly. "Do you mean that fat book in the library? It put me right to sleep." Then she squeezed his arm. "Stop whispering." And said aloud, "Why, yes, Mr. Taverston. This is the perfect time of year for a visit to the country."

"You'll enjoy Chaumbers, I am sure."

She had told the truth earlier. She was no better a liar than he was.

Mother had arranged the seating, placing Lady Georgiana beside Jasper. The numbers were horribly uneven, so she moved Reginald between the Duchess and Miss Fogbotham. They were both accomplished conversationalists. His only complaint was that he had very little chance to listen in on what Jasper and Lady Georgiana were saying. Her expression was politely pleased, though not animated.

After luncheon, it was still raining, so they returned to the drawing room and played a few hands of whist. Reginald suggested speculation next, but Jasper shot him down.

"You never let anyone else win."

Crispin entered the room. "Billiards?"

Lady Georgiana nudged Miss Fogbotham, murmuring something that made her laugh and then shake her head.

Jasper said, "Not billiards. Something the ladies will enjoy."

They fell into a discussion. He heard Lady Georgiana echo speculation, but the company seemed weary of cards. Reginald rose and sidled up alongside Crispin, who had remained close to the door. Although he had learned it was unwise to question his brother as to the state of his health, nevertheless, he asked, "Headache gone?"

Crispin did not look at him, but said, "I didn't have a headache."

"I didn't think so."

"I didn't want Mother glaring at my plate in company."

That was quite an admission for Crispin. Reginald said, "You can't take all your meals in your room."

Then Crispin did spare him a look. "If you must know, I had a boil on my arse. Adam lanced it. I should be quite comfortable by dinnertime. Satisfied?"

"All except for the part where your valet lances your boil."

Crispin's eyes glinted for a second, then he shrugged. "His talents are legion. Would you like to exchange Barclay for him?"

"No, thank you." He would take his boils, or any similar such, to a surgeon.

Crispin smirked at him, took a step forward, and said, "A drizzling day calls for a game of charades."

GEORGIANA ENJOYED CHARADES well enough although she had a tendency to evaluate clues too literally. Alice, who was much slyer, had a true gift for the game.

Mr. Taverston had excused himself and departed the room without fuss. Lord Taverston sat down beside her.

"Don't mind Reg. He doesn't believe in fun."

"Doesn't he?"

"Perhaps that is overstating. He merely defines it strangely."

"While Jasper's definition of fun is any game he can win," Lieutenant Taverston said.

"Pot accusing the kettle," Lord Taverston gave back.

"Well, it is true I won't race Olivia again. That's no fun."

Olivia laughed. "I'll give you a handicap. Have you noticed Jasper has not yet had the shooting targets set out?"

"It's raining!" Lord Taverston protested, his bright blue eyes wide with theatrical defensiveness.

"Are you playing or bickering?" Lady Iversley asked, but she sounded teasing as well.

The drawing room was spacious yet intimate. The overall sense was of a pleasant warmth, with furnishings of burgundy brocade, walls the color of butterscotch, and a toasty fire in the hearth. It had a good sense of home. And truly, Georgiana liked this family. There was a lot of love here. One could hear it in their laughter. But she hadn't sorted them all out yet. Olivia was clearly the pet. Mr. Taverston, "Reg," played the role of the family killjoy. And Lord Taverston took their teasing well, as though he had already decided to be a jovial patriarch—but perhaps the easiness of his disposition was a display for her sake. As for Lieutenant Taverston, she could like him, too, but there was a darkness there. Not a meanness. More something secretive. He was so very thin, she wondered if he had been wounded on campaign. Perhaps he was in pain. It was none of her business, of course, but it would be difficult to be asked to become part of the family and still be left wondering. She was a little fearful of offending him.

The game was soon underway, with Mama joining Georgiana and Alice to even the teams. Lady Iversley read from a new book of riddles called, *The Frolics of the Sphynx.*

"An easy one first," Lady Iversley said. Her tone of voice changed, singsong, as she read the riddle, "'An insect industrious and the fruits of another, form a hero in history, famed as a lover.'"

Easy? Georgiana puzzled over it anxiously. Busy bees were industrious. Fruits? What did insects make?

Alice cried out, "Ant-honey." Her eyes flashed with humor and triumph.

The Lieutenant let out a long whistle. "To arms, Taverstons." He leaned over, patting his knees eagerly. "We have competition."

Olivia gave Lord Taverston's arm a shove. "Pay attention."

Lord Taverston protested, "I am!"

The Countess thumbed through the book. "Here's one. 'My first is a meat, most savory to eat, my next does derision infer; my whole is a bed, which when I shall wed, twill not serve for me and for her.'"

The room fell silent as all brows furrowed. Georgiana chewed her lip.

After a few minutes, Lord Taverston chuckled and said, "Ham-mock."

So he was clever as well as handsome.

Naturally, they all clapped and cheered. Georgiana eyed him sidelong, searching for evidence of smugness, but saw none. His smile was gently amused, his posture was relaxed, and his hands were folded loosely in his lap. He looked amiable.

"Another!" Lady Olivia demanded.

Rather than chastising her forward daughter as Mama might have, the Countess nodded and continued.

"Try this: 'My first is provided with fruit or with meat, and when it is seen it is greedily eat. If you are my second, I pity your head. And my whole can't be found of one color, 'tis said.'"

Alice *hmm*'ed and stared off into the distance, thinking. Georgiana watched the Taverstons, who were exchanging looks back and forth as if reading one another's thoughts. Lord Taverston started to say something, then stopped, shaking his head. If he were to guess wrong, his teammates would have to silently wait for their opponents to come up with an answer unpressured.

Georgiana struggled a little desperately: *Eaten with fruit or meat—bread? Pity your head-ache? No.*

Lady Olivia snapped her fingers. "Pie-bald!"

"Good show!" Lieutenant Taverston cried.

The next was a lengthy one that no one could decipher.

Eventually, Mama provided the answer, but admitted she'd heard the riddle before, so they should not win the point. The Taverstons took the next three, noisily, with much commentary, before Alice answered one. Then Lord Taverston again. The contest was becoming a rout. Or a competition amongst the Taverstons—leaving their guests behind. Lady Iversley took notice.

"I think I've exhausted the riddles for this evening," she said, closing the book. "Let's play something else."

"Oh, one more. Please, Mama?" Lady Olivia begged.

"One more?" Lord Taverston made a similar, though gentler, plea after giving his sister a soft look.

Georgiana did not mind watching the siblings entertain one another. She found it sweet.

She added her voice to the choir. "Just one more?"

Lady Iversley reopened the book. "'My first is ready to fulfill, each new intention of the will; my second's neither more nor less, than a redundant part of dress; my whole resembles wedding bands, in coupling two unwilling hands.'"

Georgiana looked to Alice who gave a small shrug, then frowned with determination.

Olivia said, "Han—"

"Bootlace!" Lieutenant Taverston foiled her guess.

"Bootlace?" Lord Taverston repeated with exaggerated scorn. "How do boots—"

"When I use *my* boot, my will is fulfilled. Sometimes the infantrymen need a swift kick."

"But lace is a critical part of a dress, not redundant," Lady Olivia corrected him, laughing.

"Coupling two unwilling hands?" Lord Taverston shook his head.

"I have done so with my bootlaces," the Lieutenant said, with mock affront. "With prisoners, sometimes, one must make do."

"Oh, bosh," Lady Olivia said.

Alice interrupted. "I believe the answer should be handcuff."

"Miss Fogbotham is correct," Lady Iversley said.

Lady Olivia slapped Lieutenant Taverston's shoulder. "I was about to say 'handcuff.'"

He pouted. "All right. Mother, give us another chance. Livvy's in a pet."

Lady Iversley sighed a long-suffering maternal sigh. "Last one. 'My first is a counterfeit greatly in vogue, with the loit'ring truant, or sluggard at school, though I hope from my heart the sophistical rogue may be flogged for so craftily playing the fool.'" She raised two fingers. "'When the tempest is up and the busy wind sighs, o'er the high-swelling waves which are dark with the storm, my next all the hurricane's fury defies, and proudly presents its unchangeable form.'" She held up three. "'Of my whole I shall not give you more than a hint, it derives, like Antaeus, its strength from the earth, and on Irishmen's bosoms will always imprint, a token of love from the place of their birth.'"

Irishmen? Shamrock. Sham. Rock. It fit, didn't it?

Lieutenant Taverston called out, grinning, "Clod-dock."

"Crispin!" Lady Olivia's scowl was contradicted by the giggle that followed. "That isn't even a word."

"It is. Those rings they wear. Love and loyalty and whatnot."

Lord Taverston burst into laughter. "Claddagh. Claddagh."

It was impossible not to laugh along. Lieutenant Taverston could not maintain his frown of indignation and his infectious hooting started them all up again.

When the laughter subsided, Lady Iversley turned to Georgiana. "Have you guessed it?"

"Shamrock," Georgiana said, feeling relieved to have contributed something.

"Yes," Lord Taverston said. "Now let us close and call it a draw before Crispin humiliates us further."

Lieutenant Taverston merely grinned, but Georgiana noted that Lady Iversley seemed well-pleased with him, which was good to see after the tension at lunchtime.

Yes, Georgiana liked the Taverstons very much. They were *comfortable.*

But then, Lord Taverston had not yet begun to court her in earnest.

GEORGIANA WORE HER sage green gown to dinner. It was very simple, other than that the sleeves were puffed, and the neckline showed more than just a hint of bosom. It was closely fitted, which lent it an elegance and made her feel more mature. Jeanette fussed with her hair for over an hour, braiding it and twisting it, then teasing out a few small wisps to curl.

Alice murmured, "You are so beautiful. They will all fall in love with you."

Startled, Georgiana turned to look at her cousin, who had sounded wistful.

"That is not my goal," she tried to joke.

Alice laughed, and the impression of her unhappiness was dispelled.

"No, of course not. What a mess that would be. But I can certainly see you as a countess."

When they gathered again in the drawing room, they didn't have much time to sit before dinner was announced.

This time Lady Iversley placed Georgiana between Lieutenant and Mr. Taverston and across the table from Lord Taverston. He was polite to Alice on his right, and teased Lady Olivia on his left, but mostly, he kept his eyes upon Georgiana, even while she was attempting conversation with his brothers. His expression was one of approval rather than admiration. It was silly of her to be so persnickety, but it did seem he had skipped a step.

In fact, the whole evening was a half-step off. Mr. Taverston's conversation, benign on its surface—asking about her childhood, her governess, what languages she spoke—was standard fare. (He spoke German, French, and Greek, and read Ancient Greek and Latin besides. He wasn't boasting; she'd asked the reciprocal question of him.) Yet she could not help thinking that he was trying to discover if she knew what she had been reading in the library or had merely grabbed from the meager offerings at random.

She should have alternated her attention more between Mr. Taverston and Lieutenant Taverston. But that usual polite convention, too, was one step off. Perhaps Mr. Taverston was monopolizing her as a kindness because one could not easily converse with the other man, not at the table. He was too odd.

He did not partake of the common meal but rather was served a single plate of food from which he ate at a glacial pace, the whole evening, and touched nothing else. Not even wine. His dinner comprised a tiny piece of hake and a large pile of asparagus, both without sauce, and a mix of lettuce and cobnuts. He spoke across the table when he had something to say and addressed himself occasionally to her when she did attempt to draw him in, without ever alluding to his eccentricity. Of course, she kept her eyes off his plate, but it was an effort.

She was quite exhausted by the close of the meal. The ladies then removed to the drawing room and the men to smoke and drink brandy, or so she assumed. For all she knew the strange creatures were doing headstands on the terrace.

JASPER BECKONED HIS brothers to follow him to the study after dinner, saying they would rejoin the ladies shortly. This bit of manly performance seemed rather unnecessary in Reginald's opinion. But in truth, his sulk stemmed from the fact that he was out of sorts with himself.

He was not given to gawping at women. He supposed he appreciated a fine figure as well as any man, but staring had always seemed rather pointless. He had gawped at Annie, of course, when she was lying naked beneath him. But there was rather more to that than feasting his eyes.

Yet he had had a hard time keeping his eyes off Lady Georgiana. A wisp of hair seemed to be tickling her neck and he'd wanted all evening to brush it, gently, to the side. And, well, yes, her cleavage. He had as much trouble keeping his eyes off *that* as she had had ignoring Crispin's heaped pile of asparagus. What a farce! And when he did focus on her face, he kept seeing in his mind's eye how she had looked rising from sleep that morning.

So he'd grilled her on her education as if focusing on her brain. And when she responded in kind he sounded like an egg-headed braggart. She must think him the worst sort of bore.

He followed Crispin into the study, *Jasper's* study. Jasper the soon-to-be earl with his soon-to-be countess.

Jasper poured himself a brandy and didn't even bother to offer one to Reginald.

"Sit down," he said, gesturing almost grandly as he sank into the leather chair. The creak it made did not startle him anymore.

"I'll stand," Crispin said.

"Suit yourself. Reg?"

Reginald sat.

"Well, what do you think of her?" He looked rather proud.

Reginald made himself shrug. "She's pretty."

Crispin caught back a snort.

"You don't think she's pretty?" Jasper said, incredulous.

"I laughed at Reg's usual understatement. I will understate as well. Her manners are acceptable."

Jasper looked blank, but Reginald laughed. Crispin had noticed how well she ignored his plate.

"What is this about, Jasper?" Crispin asked. "You don't need our approval. You have Mother's."

Jasper was quiet for a moment. Then he said brusquely, "You're right. I don't. It looks to be less dreary tomorrow. I think I should give her a tour of the property. Save the house tour for the next time it rains. And I've invited the Willowsetts and Robert Leighton to come hunt with us the day after tomorrow, so long as it's clear."

Crispin nodded. Reginald did too, though it annoyed him that he would be left so little time for any of his work.

Jasper continued, "I think it's best if everyone goes on the tour. I don't mean Her Grace or Mother, of course. That's a little too much chaperoning."

Crispin shook his head. "I'm not riding tomorrow."

"Six is a more comfortable party than five. There will be pairs. It will be easier for me to talk with Lady Georgiana one-on-one."

"I understand, but I said I'm not riding tomorrow."

Jasper's voice hardened. "And I said I would like you to come."

Crispin raised an eyebrow. Then he said in a low tone. "And I said I will not be riding."

Reginald said, "Crispin has a boil on his arse."

Crispin closed his eyes and let out a slow breath, almost as though he were counting.

Jasper flushed. "We will make do with a party of five. I hope you can join us for hunting the following day."

Crispin turned, flung open the door, and stomped out, slamming it.

They were quiet for a moment. Then Jasper said, "Is he angry at you or at me?"

"Me, I suspect. *I* am angry at you."

Jasper's eyes went wide. "What did I do?"

Reginald stood. "Nothing."

Nothing at all, except discover Lady Georgiana and claim her as a matter of course.

He left the study to see Crispin had not gone far. He was leaning against the opposite wall. Resigned to being scolded for peacekeeping—as well as the sin of alluding to *any* blotch on Crispin's health—Reginald approached him.

"Are you waiting to plant me a facer?"

Crispin's lip curled. "Let's make a deal, shall we?" He waited for Reginald to nod, then said, "You keep my confidences and I'll keep your secrets."

Had his gawping been obvious? The trick with Crispin was never to acknowledge that he had the upper hand. Crispin often bluffed.

"I don't have secrets. I'm not that interesting."

"Then why are you wearing that guilty face? And sulking like you want to wish Jasper to the devil?"

Reginald tucked his thumbs into his waistband. And prevaricated. "Do you know that chair in the library? In the bay window?"

Crispin's eyes lit. He might not know where Reginald was leading but was ready to follow. "The one that bucks you off if you forget and lean back?

"I would like to swap that chair for Father's chair in the study." He emphasized the word *Father* with a petulance that was only partly feigned.

"Ah." He nodded, satisfied. "Jasper is sitting a little too comfortably?"

Reginald lowered his eyes and let himself look more guilt-ridden. Crispin snickered.

"Sentimental idiot. It's just a chair. But I'll meet you in the library at midnight, eh?"

CHAPTER ELEVEN

T HE DAY WAS lovely, the sky bright blue, the clouds no more than threads, and sparse fall flowers were still in bloom. It was a good time to get outside and take the fresh air. So said everyone at breakfast. Everyone except Lieutenant Taverston, who had not been there. His absence should not have disappointed Georgiana, but it did: what would the man have eaten? Then she was ashamed of her own curiosity.

Five of them marched down to the stables. Georgiana's riding habit was black with white frills, and Lord Taverston complimented it twice before they reached the gate. She thanked him without pointing that out.

Georgiana did enjoy riding so long as there was no galloping involved. She was a bit taken aback when she saw the spirited mount being led out for Lady Olivia, but thankfully her own horse and Alice's were more docile.

Lord Taverston held her stirrup. He looked so handsome in his buckskin riding breeches and brown jacket, smiling his one-dimpled smile, that she could not help lightly frosting him. Wooing should be an effort, not a given.

They rode off across a grass-and-mud meadow: she and Lord Taverston to the front, the others behind. They followed a track to the lakeside. The surface of the water was still as glass and reflected the blue of the sky. She noted the boathouse, and that several large flat stones had been laid near the water.

"Do you swim from there?" she asked.

"We do, but only in the summer months. Crispin might still, but the rest of us are more sensible. We can take a boat out another day if you wish."

She nodded. "I like rowboats." Then, to move things along, she said, "My brother Charles does too. He's a strong rower."

"Charles is at school?"

"Yes. His first year at Oxford."

"Does he like his studies?"

"I believe so, though he complains horribly."

She made herself smile. It was an unfairness she had long made her peace with; if she had been permitted to go to Oxford, she would not have complained. She made do with the books her father allowed her to sneak from his library, books her mother would disapprove of. Charles used to discuss them with her, but their interests did not coincide, and now that he considered himself grown, his interests were more "important" than hers, in his opinion anyway.

She did love her younger brother dearly, even if she was envious. He had his faults, as all brothers must, but he was a good young man and smart. If he was getting into trouble at school, she suspected it was of the temporary variety. But she didn't tell Lord Taverston any of this. Nor did she mention Randolph. He'd died while away at school. An accident was all she was ever told, though she had heard whispers he had fallen into a fire. But this was not a topic for today's conversation. Besides, they had finished with siblings, and he was already beginning a brief history of Chaumbers and the village of Iversley.

"We should have brought a picnic!" Lady Olivia exclaimed, drawing up alongside them near the water's edge. She managed her horse so keenly that Georgiana felt perfectly green.

"We just finished breakfast!" Lord Taverston laughed. "But yes, we can come again with a picnic." He turned to her. "If you like."

"I do enjoy picnics."

"Well, if the weather remains mild, we'll return another day." He pointed away. "If we follow this path, it will take us to a fork. One path will lead to the village, and another continues around the lake."

"Mama thought an excursion to the village on Saturday would be clever," Lady Olivia said. "We can go to the shops—"

"Why don't we let Lady Georgiana choose?" he interrupted, firmly but not unkindly. Even so, his sister looked chastened.

Georgiana said, "I am curious about the lake. Why don't we continue along it?"

"All right," he said, smiling. Evidently, she'd made the correct choice.

Georgiana glanced at Lady Olivia, who looked as though she felt out of place. She would have said something warm to draw her in, but Alice called, "Olivia, please come tell me if this is true. I think Mr. Taverston is telling me a Banbury tale."

Olivia made a soft noise to her mount and returned to her group.

"Shall we?" Lord Taverston asked.

They continued. Behind them, merriment erupted. The two girls, who were already using one another's Christian names, were giggling ferociously at something. Then Mr. Taverston's deeper laugh rang out. Georgiana felt a surge of…resentment. Who said Mr. Taverston was not fun?

Lord Taverston continued to point out features of the landscape. It was all quite nice, nothing as grand as Sayles or as charming as Marbury, but she was not so spoiled that she could not recognize that other people's homes could also be nice. A good thing, she supposed, if she was going to be Iversley's countess.

The path narrowed. Their chaperones fell farther behind. Lord Taverston returned to the subject of Oxford. "I was merely a fair student. Obtained my gentlemen's degree and was out in two years. Reg was the family scholar."

"You skipped over Lieutenant Taverston."

"Oh, yes, well, Crispin. He didn't finish." He cleared his throat. "He caught the soldiering fever, you see. A terrible row, but off he went." He chuckled. "We expected a bigger row when Reg announced he was going to Cambridge. He does things like that. Well, I guess they both do."

"Things like what?"

"Make up their minds that they want something, then just pursue it." He gave her a meaningful look. "I suppose we all do that, come to think of it."

"Cambridge though," she said, shifting the focus. "That must have come as a surprise."

"Yes, quite. How about you? Did you like your governess? Were you a mischievous child?"

The conversation rolled along its predetermined course. She answered many of the same questions she had answered earlier for Mr. Taverston, but she was quite sure Mr. Taverston had been fishing for other information. *How much of a bluestocking was Lady Georgiana and should he warn his brother?* And she had been careful with her responses. It had made that conversation more of a challenge than this one. More interesting. She wondered if Lord Taverston was paying as little attention to her casual replies as she was to his.

He asked about Sayles next. She described the grandeur of the cliffs. The pretty wilderness walk.

She might never have been so bored.

And behind them, for the duration of the outing, she heard the girls' chatter she could not make out, laughter she could not join in, and, often enough to believe he was involved in their discussions and not merely putting in a comment now and then for politeness, she heard the rumbling of Mr. Taverston's voice and his clap of laughter.

On the return, during a lull in their own conversation, a thought struck her. Had Mama and Lady Iversley plotted more than one match? Did they think Alice and Mr. Taverston...

Why not? And how happy, of course, Georgiana would be if it were true. They would be sisters as well as cousins. She didn't know where Mr. Taverston intended to make his home, but surely it would not be far from Chaumbers. Unless he settled in London.

Alice and Mr. Taverston. They would make a wonderful match, wouldn't they? Or maybe not. At any rate, the thought did not make her as happy as it should. She didn't dare investigate *that* any further. She didn't like that the term "sour grapes" came most quickly to mind.

AFTER RETURNING THE horses to the stables, they climbed the hill to the house and separated. Georgiana and Alice went to their room to bathe away the scent of horse, then rest, then dress for tea. Mama informed them they had decided to take tea on the terrace, as the weather was so gentle. Still, she suggested, it might be wise to wear something warm.

Georgiana decided on a simple cotton floral and wrapped herself in her shawl. Alice wore a pretty, pink-and-gray-striped dress that was perfect for autumn and made her look gay. They went down the stairs arm in arm.

"You and Lady Olivia were having a grand time this morning."

"Yes, we were. She's so funny. Even Mr. Taverston was in stitches."

Georgiana supposed none of it would be as humorous repeated. She sighed and said, "I hope I will have opportunity to spend time with her."

"I suspect you will have a good deal of opportunity." Alice looked at her sidelong. "Did you enjoy the ride? The estate is beautiful."

"Yes, it is." It was too soon to burden Alice with her misgivings. Surely she was just nervous and would soon adapt. She should ask Alice how she found Mr. Taverston's company.

Lieutenant Taverston met them at the bottom of the stairs.

"Ladies, they are setting up the tables outside, but tea service will still be another half hour. I hope you are not too peckish?"

"Why, no," Georgiana said. She was afraid to ask if he was.

He grinned. "Good. Jasper is detained for a bit." He wrinkled his nose. "Correspondence to see to. And Reg has disappeared as he is wont to do, so I am afraid you are left with me to entertain you until teatime."

"Only if we aren't pulling you from something you should rather be doing." They didn't need constant entertaining. In fact, she had been hoping for a spare moment to return to the library and be sure *Analytical Calculation* was still there. It must belong to Mr. Taverston, as he was the reputed scholar. She worried that he might not want her handling his books, especially after she'd mistreated his *Principia*. But surely he would not pack them away.

"I was hoping you might be interested in a game of billiards." Lieutenant Taverston focused on Alice. "I thought Jasper might have spoken out of turn last night when he dismissed it as nothing ladies would enjoy."

Alice flushed but answered truthfully. "I do play with my father sometimes."

"Ha! Come along then. Olivia is awaiting us. We'll play teams."

Teams. So Georgiana would be needed as a fourth, even though she could not play well and would have preferred a little time alone. She trailed along behind, thinking Alice was having more success at this country gathering than she was. If only they could trade places! Alice would make a much better countess. Not only could she adorn an earl's properties and run his household, but she would be rapt if he should come home prattling about Parliament and bills and such.

They reached the room, which was shouting distance from the library—but, of course, she was not supposed to have discovered yet where the library was.

Lady Olivia was waiting for them, wearing a lively look of expectation. The younger sister possessed the golden good looks of her elder two brothers. The square jaw might have lent her a slightly masculine appearance if not for the long lashes framing her wide blue eyes. Mr. Taverston had gotten his mother's dark hair and more angular features. The Earl, she recalled, had been fair.

"They do play," Lieutenant Taverston announced, with a hint of I-told-you-so.

"Alice does," Georgiana said quickly. "I am not at all skilled."

"Then you should be on Olivia's team. She's the best of us."

"Pooh!" Lady Olivia cried. "I've only ever beaten you twice."

"Fine. You take Miss Fogbotham and I'll take Lady Georgiana. You may lead off, Miss Fogbotham."

Lady Olivia asked, "Cue or mace?"

"Cue," Alice said.

"Leather tipped?"

"Of course."

Lieutenant Taverston laughed. "And for you, Lady Georgiana?"

"The same, I suppose."

Lady Olivia placed three balls on the table. "House rules."

Alice nodded. Then she bent over the table and used her cue to tap one ball into the others.

"Cannon!" The Lieutenant said. "Good for you!" He turned to Georgiana and swept his hand to the table. "Lady?"

She grimaced and tried to mimic Alice. Her ball rolled slowly to one side and stopped. She gave her partner an apologetic shrug.

"Well," he said, forcing a frown to cover his laugh. "A game try. Olivia?"

Lady Olivia smirked and lined up for her shot. The game was interrupted by Mr. Taverston bursting into the room, carrying a large bucket. He looked angry. No, he didn't. He looked as if he were trying to look angry but was more likely to laugh.

The Lieutenant said, "Oh, good idea. The pockets are likely a bit too small for Lady Georgiana."

Lady Olivia slapped her cue against his arm. "Crispin!"

Mr. Taverston said, "This was in the library. In place of the chair."

The words made no sense, but the Lieutenant gleaned something from them because he crossed his arms and said, "An outrage! Did you fall in?"

"No, it was upside down."

"Small favors."

"Do you have any ideas?"

"We'll think of something."

Lady Olivia put in, "You're being very rude. What are you talking about?"

The Lieutenant laid his cue across the table. "I think it's teatime. Olivia, dear, take our guests up to the south terrace. We'll be right behind you."

Lady Olivia tossed her head. "I hate when you get like this." But she looked rather gleeful, so presumably her brothers were pranksters, not madmen. "Come along, Alice. Lady Georgiana."

"Please just call me Georgiana," she said, as Lady Olivia linked her arm through Alice's.

"And I am Olivia. Phew, that's much better, isn't it?" She put her other arm through Georgiana's and led them both out the door.

CHAPTER TWELVE

GEORGIANA ALWAYS ENJOYED the excitement of a hunt, even though she tended to bring up the rear. She had a good seat but not a *very* good one and, frankly, did not show to best advantage on a horse. Particularly not compared to Olivia.

Their party was supposed to have been increased by the addition of three local men but at breakfast, a message arrived from Mr. Leighton, the curate, with his regrets. Lord Taverston said the Willowsetts would meet them at the stable. The twin sons of a well-to-do squire in the neighboring village, they were frequent visitors to Chaumbers.

Lord Taverston was his usual well-mannered self at breakfast, but Georgiana thought he looked tired.

He had joined them late for tea the previous afternoon and had been out of sorts. She wondered if his correspondence had been troubling, but it was not a question she could ask. Besides, how troubling could correspondence be compared to what he faced here? After tea, he had gone to spend time with his father. His brothers also took their leave. Mr. Taverston had to do some "work," whatever that meant, and Lieutenant Taverston went to the stables to be sure his hunter—which had taken a stone in his hoof and was being seen to by the grooms—would be sound for the chase. So they said. But the two had set off with an eagerness that didn't seem appropriate to the tasks. Olivia grumbled that they were up to something, and the ladies retired to Lady Iversley's sitting room where the girls recounted the doings of the day.

Later, at dinner, Lord Taverston had been polite but distracted. That was reasonable as he had come directly from his father's sick room. Georgiana was once again seated beside him; however, this time her mother was on her left, so Georgiana found herself making more effort to be engaging. Even so, he seemed less engaged. It was quite dispiriting. If this was courtship, what would marriage be like?

She was glad to find him in better spirits this morning.

They all went down to the stables. Georgiana wore her prettiest riding habit, a dark blue velvet with a very smart matching hat. Lord Taverston paid her the requisite compliments.

The horses led out by the grooms were fresh ones, gorgeous creatures. Lord Taverston helped Georgiana to mount, then signaled to the groom to bring his own hunter. She happened to be nearby Lieutenant Taverston who chuckled and muttered, "Bloody hell."

She soon saw what he was laughing at. Lord Taverston's horse was a magnificent chestnut, but upon its back was a dirty, battered saddle that should long ago have been tossed into a bin. To her shock, he swung his leg over as if it were the most natural thing in the world.

"Lud!" Olivia shrieked. "What is that?"

Lord Taverston smiled. "This? I stumbled upon it where it shouldn't have been and thought it would suit much better on Skylark than where it was." He raised his chin. "Are we done now, boys?"

Lieutenant Taverston laughed out loud. Mr. Taverston coughed and said, "Here are Jeffrey and Jeremy." He doffed his hat and waved it.

Hardly a satisfactory explanation; nevertheless, all attention turned to the newcomers, two pleasant-looking young men, identical in appearance except for the color of their jackets. Jeffrey wore red, Jeremy blue. They were sandy-haired, apple-cheeked, and dressed like dandies. They rode sturdy horses, thankfully not matched. Georgiana had met identical twins before, but none quite so identical.

And they were young. Sixteen? Seventeen? They greeted the Taverston brothers, were introduced to the Taverstons' guests, and then attached themselves to Olivia with jostling devotion. Olivia treated them as the chums they had likely been, without encouraging any hopes it would be ridiculous of them to have. Their infatuation would have been embarrassing if there had only been one of them. With two, it was comical.

The houndsman brought out the dogs and then they were off.

Lieutenant Taverston and Olivia shot out in front, the Willowsetts in frantic pursuit. Mr. Taverston rode alongside Alice, urging her on. Lord Taverston, bringing up the rear with Georgiana, had a strained look on his face that she could only interpret as frustration with her pace. "Go on," she laughed. "I am accustomed to straggling. I don't mind."

"I daren't with this saddle," he grumbled, then quickly amended, "I much prefer riding with you to racing my siblings."

"What a fudge!" she teased.

His rueful smile was one of his better ones. "We can overtake them. They are going the long route in order to jump the hedge. Olivia feels it doesn't count as a hunt unless she can jump at least once. The hedge doesn't extend this far so if we keep straight, then bear right, we should meet up with them on the opposite side. Does Miss Fogbotham jump?"

"How high is the hedge?"

"Two or three feet, but no matter. Reg will ascertain which way to bring her. Or, if she wishes, he'll lift her over and then jump the horse."

"You've thought of everything."

"If we don't, Mother does." Then he grinned at her. "I can go a *little* faster."

"Oh, well, yes, so can I."

So they picked up their pace and rode to the rendezvous at a loping run that provided less chance for talk. That was fine with Georgiana. They soon came to the hedge and went a short distance alongside it before Lord Taverston drew rein.

"Can you hear them? They'll come up over that ridge, then take the hedge. The ground is fairly level on either side, but the approach is quick."

She *did* hear a cacophony of loud happy shouting and hounds baying.

He said, "We can await them all here. Who do you think will be over the hedge first? Olivia or Crispin?"

Georgiana answered, "Jeremy. Or maybe Jeffrey?"

He laughed. "Don't lay wager on it."

The shouting grew louder, and she heard the horses. Twenty yards ahead, the first rider appeared, flying over the ridge: Lieutenant Taverston, going hell-for-leather. Olivia appeared moments after, bonnet fallen to one side, dangling by strings. Lieutenant Taverston soared over the hedge and continued a short distance while he slowed. Olivia followed, chasing her brother, shouting and laughing.

Then came the Willowsetts, their horses neck-and-neck, crowding one another as they approached the hedge. Georgiana cringed.

Lord Taverston muttered, "Idiots! Spread out."

Just before the jump, Jeremy's horse shied. Georgiana gasped and Olivia cried out. Jeremy was thrown against Jeffrey's horse as they both went over the hedge. The horse landed badly. He stumbled a few steps then his forelegs crumpled. Jeffrey, thankfully, slid clear.

Everything next happened at once. Mr. Taverston and Alice stopped on the far side of the hedge. Mr. Taverston dismounted, dropped his reins, and caught Jeremy's horse. He handed both the reins to Alice and then hurdled the hedge. Lord Taverston and the Lieutenant also dismounted.

All three converged upon the catastrophe.

Jeffrey stumbled toward his brother, aghast, making incoherent apologies, but the Lieutenant had beaten him there and was already kneeling in the grass, tending to the injured boy. Lord Taverston blocked Jeffrey's approach.

"Take Jeremy's horse back." Projecting calm and authority, he seemed every inch an earl. "Tell Mundy to come with the cart."

Pale and shaking, Jeffrey quieted, staring at him helplessly. He tried to nod.

Lieutenant Taverston called, "Have them bring Adam also. And send for Dr. Haraldsen."

Georgiana's attention shifted. The Lieutenant had removed his neckcloth and was pressing it to Jeremy's head.

"My God!" Jeffrey moaned. "I didn't mean to crash into him."

The men were all speaking loudly over the restless whinnying of the horses and one's frantic squeals of pain. Nevertheless, Lord Taverston sounded calm.

"Of course not. You were both riding like gudgeons. Now go fetch the cart if you want to help."

Olivia rode closer, calling, "I'll come with you, Jeffrey."

Georgiana felt useless. Sickened. It frightened her how still Jeremy was.

Lieutenant Taverston glanced up, looked around, and shouted over the noise, "Georgiana, go to the bag behind my saddle. There are spirits and bandages. Will you bring them?"

A shot rang out. Abruptly, the world became silent. Everyone turned to the downed horse. And Mr. Taverston. Whose pistol now pointed at the ground.

"Right," Lord Taverston said finally. "Jeffrey, Olivia, go."

Jeffrey clambered over the hedge to retrieve his brother's horse from Alice. Olivia jumped hers over neatly. Georgiana slipped from her own saddle to fetch the spirits and bandages. She had to pass close by Mr. Taverston, whose head was lowered and whose expression was wooden. Unthinkingly, she put her hand on his arm for a moment in passing. He did not look up.

What an impressive trio the lords of Iversley were, Georgianna thought. In a crisis, without conferring, without argument, each had leaped to a separate, necessary task as if their assignments had been preordained. And Mr. Taverston undertook the most thankless.

⇻⟫⟪⇷

ALICE PEELED OFF her gloves and dropped them on the bed. Jeanette stood ready to help them change for tea.

"It was horrible. That poor boy. And Georgiana! You were so brave. I don't know how you did it." Alice sank onto the bed.

Georgiana did not have gloves to remove. Lieutenant Taverston had demanded them of her before allowing her to remount. They were bloodstained. Very. She hadn't noticed. He apologized and said he would see to replacing them. She said she had other pairs. It had been a rather inane exchange.

"There is, I think, a bit of blood on my sleeve, Jeanette. And mud on my skirt. If it won't come out—"

"I will see to it, my lady."

Jeanette helped her to remove her garments, then produced a bowl of hot water so that she could thoroughly clean her hands and arms and knees.

"Will he be all right?" Alice asked. "He looked horrible. And his brother was so contrite. And Olivia was so upset. They were trying to impress her."

Georgiana sniffed. A sorry way to go about it.

Alice was not finished. "Whatever made you kneel in the dirt? It was wonderful of you, of course, but I couldn't have brought myself to do it. I mean, I couldn't have helped with the bandages. How did you know what to do?"

"I did what Lieutenant Taverston indicated." She shuddered, picturing the profusely bleeding gash on Jeremy's head, and his leg, bent at that unnatural angle, also cut and bleeding. "I couldn't merely fetch for him. He only has two hands and needed at least four."

"And that strange man who returned with the grooms? Adam? Who is he?"

"Lieutenant Taverston's valet, apparently."

Alice's expression turned incredulous. "Do you believe that? He doesn't act like a valet."

He did not. A short, doughy man, he had a Greek complexion and wore military clothes that fit so poorly they appeared borrowed. The moment he'd appeared, leaping from the cart, Lieutenant Taverston had yielded to him, gesturing for Georgiana to back away. "Let my valet have a look." They'd spoken in low tones over the boy, who was no longer in a faint. His bleeding had been staunched. He'd ground his teeth and manfully tried to hold back his moans as Adam lifted the bandages, touched his bent leg, and then murmured questions at him.

Georgiana heard only the end of the discussion when Adam said, "Clean break. The doctor can set it. Brain is bruised. He should be moved as little as possible for a sennight."

When they finally made it back to the house, they discovered Dr. Haraldsen had been sent for but had not yet arrived. Poor Jeremy was carted off to a guest chamber in a different wing. Jeffrey was sent home to explain things to the Squire.

"I think Adam must have worked with the army surgeons. He appeared to have some knowledge," Georgiana said. How he'd ended up a valet, she could not guess.

Jeanette held up two dresses. *"Rose? Ou jaune?"*

Both were reworked from last year. The colors were pale, the fabrics medium-weight, the styles demure, though the ruffled trims had been replaced with braiding and the cut was a bit more daring. They were too similar to choose between.

She sighed. "I don't care."

"Oui. La jaune." Jeanette placed the pink back into the wardrobe. "And for you, Miss Fogbotham? Would you like your blue

muslin? With the green trim?"

"Yes, fine." Alice sprawled on the bed. "Are you going down straightaway, Georgiana? I can't face them just yet. Tea won't be for another hour. I need to lie down. Is that weak of me? I don't think I'll ever go on another hunt."

"I don't want to see anyone either. But I'm too agitated to lie down." She bit her lip. "I think I'll slip off to the library and see what is there." She hadn't mentioned finding the *Principia* earlier. If the books were still there, she would tell Alice about them. She wanted to share her excitement. But if they were gone, it wasn't worth mentioning.

Jeanette dressed Georgiana first, fixed her hair pins, then let her go and turned her attention to Alice, whose hair always took longer to tame because of the tangle of curls.

Georgiana went downstairs. Passing the open parlor, she saw Lieutenant Taverston inside, pacing. He looked up at the sound of her footsteps and called out, "Lady Georgiana, may I speak with you a moment?"

"Certainly." She stepped to the door.

"I must apologize."

"No, please! I was happy to do what little—"

"Not for that. I appreciate your help and thank you for it. I apologize for the liberty I took in addressing you." His cheeks held a faint flush. She would have thought nothing could embarrass him.

Confused, she asked, "Liberty?"

The pink faded and his lips curled on one side. "I called you 'Georgiana.'"

"Oh, for Heaven's sake. Well, I didn't notice."

"Neither did I. Jasper told me I did."

"And ordered you to apologize?" *How beastly.*

"No, that was my own initiative."

"Well, your apology is accepted of course, but is entirely unnecessary. In fact, I hope you will continue to call me Georgiana. After the day we've been through…"

"And you must call me Crispin. Please do. And Miss Fogbotham must as well."

"Very well." She smiled at him, thinking she'd been silly to have thought him intimidating. Then she frowned. "Oh, but how awkward."

Crispin laughed. "Yes, that's the fun of it. If you are amenable, I'll let Reg know."

"Oh!" She bit her lip to keep from laughing as she caught on. "Are you trying to plague Lord Taverston?"

"It's what we do." His eyes gleamed. "Or if you prefer, I'll warn Jasper and then we can plague Reg."

"No, not him. Not after he had to put down that horse."

The spark in Crispin's eyes faded. He scowled. "I'd have sooner shot Jeremy. That horse was innocent."

"Lieutenant Taverston!" she gasped.

"Crispin." He reminded her. Then said, "But yes, I'm sure Reg was devastated. Yet you know, there could have been no choice, and acting promptly was merciful." She nodded. He said, "Our mothers are in the ladies' parlor, if you're looking to join them. Olivia has taken to bed. She feels worse than Reg."

"I…" She hesitated, then plunged ahead. "I was hoping you would have a library I might sit in. Libraries are calming to me."

He gave her a curious look, then said, "Ours is not. It's jarring. But it's at the end of the same hall as the billiard room. You're welcome to use it, though you might want to bring your own reading material. And you may find Reg there. You have that in common."

"Oh." *Rot.* She would never get another look at his books. "But I shouldn't disturb him."

"He won't mind. I suspect he's having trouble concentrating on his tasks. You can tell him we have all adopted each other's Christian names except for Lord Taverston. And ask him what he is sitting on."

"I beg your pardon?"

"Go on. Take his mind off the horse. It's a game we're playing."

She shrugged. "All right. If you say so." She left the parlor.

Forewarned, she could leave the library door wide open. And they were not meeting in secret if Crispin knew. She wouldn't stay long, just long enough to peek at the shelf. And involve herself in Crispin's games. She shook her head, thinking of Mama's reaction. This was a terrible idea. But at least it was no longer dull.

CHAPTER THIRTEEN

REGINALD TRUDGED INTO his bedchamber and shut the door firmly before stripping off his gloves and jacket. A bowl of water had been set on the dresser, so he dunked his hands, then pulled them out and plunged his head in. The cold was bracing.

Behind him, the door opened and shut. Barclay exclaimed, "My lord! There is warm water on the way, if you would be patient."

Reginald lifted his head. Water ran off his hair and down his shirt. Barclay dropped Reginald's best boots, freshly blackened and oiled, to fetch him a towel. "Was it a successful hunt?" Barclay ventured.

"No," he said, rubbing himself dry. "One of the Willowsetts took a tumble. Broke his leg and rattled his brains."

"Ah. That explains the hullabaloo downstairs." He nodded at Reginald's riding boots. "May I help you with those?"

Reginald glanced down. They were caked with dirt and there were bits of hedge stuck on. He hoped he hadn't tracked all that up the stairs.

"Yes." He sat down and let his valet pry off his boots, then set them outside the door to tend to later. He was still motionless, staring vacantly at the wall, when Barclay offered him his banyan.

"No. Tea clothes, I'm afraid." He scowled. "I don't think I'll survive two weeks of this. God forbid three."

"I don't suppose Lord Taverston will require three," Barclay said wryly.

Reginald lifted his chin and stared. It was not the farthest step over the line he had permitted his valet, but it rankled. Barclay turned hastily to the clothes trunk to find suitable tea wear.

"Trousers rather than pantaloons," Reginald suggested, injecting enough warmth into his voice to counter the stare. He said nothing further while Barclay tended to him—undressing, shaving after the warm water arrived, dressing. He was oppressed by his thoughts.

That horse! What a waste of a noble animal. Inviting the Willowsetts was a mistake. The two brothers had been making cakes of themselves over Olivia for months. And now farce had turned to tragedy.

Jeremy would recover, so long as his head had not been thumped more severely than Adam suspected it had. They would have to see what Dr. Haraldsen thought. But it might have been a worse tragedy. Indeed, for the first few minutes, Reginald had worried the boy had broken his neck.

He shuddered. Too much illness and death. He didn't know how Crispin stood it.

Of course, the looming storm of grief hanging over them all kept death at the forefront of Reginald's thoughts. He kept pushing it back and pushing it back, but it hovered, nevertheless.

And Lady Georgiana. He had determined to avoid her as much as possible. *He* would not make a cake of *himself.* Not over Jasper's intended.

But God. The way she had gone straight to Jeremy's side, heedless of her dress, unfazed by all that blood. Unbothered by Crispin, who must be cool as ice in battle. And she had, with tender mercy, attempted to comfort *him* as well, yet he had not dared even acknowledge her kind-heartedness.

He hoped he hadn't looked like a fatwit.

Barclay put the last twist in his neckcloth and knotted it.

"There you are, sir." He still sounded contrite. "Is there anything else? More cologne?"

"The devil! There is more than enough in the neckcloth. My eyes are watering."

Alarmed, Barclay leaned toward him and sniffed. Then he chuckled, sounding relieved. "Very funny. I didn't use even a drop. Hardly a dab."

Reginald stepped away. "I'm going to go sit with the Earl for a bit. I'm not ready to return to the crush that our drawing room has become."

⤐⤐⤐✕⤐⤐⤐

FATHER WAS AWAKE, sitting in his chair by the window. He wore a nightshirt and bed jacket and had a blanket over his knees. His eyepatch had slipped down his cheek. His nurse puttered around the room but didn't appear to be doing anything of note.

Reginald said, "If the Earl is set for now, you may go have your tea. I'll be here for a while."

"Very good, sir." She wiped her hands on her apron and shuffled out.

"How are you today, Father?" he asked, dragging a chair over beside him.

"Bored." He sighed. "Hell of a thing."

A hell of a thing? Reginald wasn't certain he'd heard right. He hated asking Father to repeat himself when it was so difficult for him to speak. "What is?"

"Dying."

Reginald blinked. His eyes watered threateningly.

Father went on, "Crispin said," he cleared his throat, "better than dead." He laughed, short and chesty, then coughed. "Not so sure."

Reginald hoped his father wasn't looking to him for some sort of homily on the soothing delights of Heaven. Especially as the sun was casting a disturbingly brilliant sliver of light on the carpet like some sort of omen. Or like Jacob's ladder.

"Well," he told his father, "I've learned not to argue with Crispin."

"Ha!" He patted the arm of his chair, a gesture meaning Reginald should sit. He lowered himself into the chair he'd brought near. "What…a hunt?"

"Yes. Today we attempted to hunt. Jasper invited the Willowsetts. Jeremy suffered a fall at the hedge."

"Better seat," he sputtered.

"I thought so too. But…" he stopped and turned up his hands. He didn't want to upset the Earl with tales that the Squire's boys were bothering Olivia. Probably today had been the last of that. "Accidents happen."

Father nodded, the movement emphasizing the sagging of his face. Noticing that a trail of drool had trickled from the down-turned corner of his father's lip, Reginald picked up a handkerchief from the blanket and dabbed the side of his father's mouth, then lifted the eyepatch back into place.

"Would you like me to read to you? I thought, perhaps, from Psalms?"

"No." He breathed noisily. "Talk."

"All right." Reginald tensed. "About anything in particular?"

"Lady Georgiana."

He tried to ignore the heat creeping up his neck. "That topic is best directed to Jasper, don't you think?"

"Crispin says." He paused to breathe. "Too good for him."

Reginald snorted. "Well, Crispin would say that."

His father half smiled. "Pretty child. Good parents. But."

"But?"

"Hasty."

"Well." He thought a moment, then said, "Jasper is not one to dawdle once he's made up his mind."

"Heh." After a moment's silence, he said, "Tell me."

"All right. Lady Georgiana is a beauty. A rare beauty. Fair with just a little red in her hair."

"Fiery?"

"No. She's very proper," he assured him. Then amended, "Without being prim."

"Clever?"

Reginald stopped himself from saying he believed she was intelligent rather than clever. He didn't know for sure that she had been reading Newton. "I expect so. I haven't spent much time with her, but she speaks well."

The Earl grunted.

Reginald said, "I'm sure she'll make him a splendid wife. Mother thinks so."

"Tell him…" His good hand balled into a fist on his lap.

"Tell him what?"

"Give up Vanessa." He scowled, wheezing. "Give her up."

Reginald flushed. Father knew about Jasper's mistress? Obviously, he did. But that was something sons did not discuss with fathers. At least, not this son. *Good Lord.* He hoped Father didn't know about Annie.

"I'm not telling Jasper what to do. For one thing, he doesn't listen to me, and for another—"

"He listens." Father's chest rose and fell. "To you. Tell him."

"I'm sure Crispin already has." Reginald could not imagine why their father was making an issue of this. "And Jasper will say it's none of my concern." Nor was it any of Father's. But the man looked so sorrowful, Reginald said, "Vanessa never struck me as a woman who would remain a married man's lover. If Jasper doesn't set her aside, I suspect she'll drop him."

He braced for the name "Plodgett" to come from his father's lips, but the words that did emerge were even more of a shock.

"Should've married her."

"Vanessa?"

When his father nodded, Reginald did also, but warily. He wouldn't expect the Earl to champion the cause of a girl who'd followed the drum. Besides, it was too little too late. She was a fallen woman in the eyes of the ton.

His father rubbed his good eye, then dropped his chin to his chest.

"I've good boys," he mumbled. "All of them. Good boys."

"Thank you?"

His father did not respond to the jest. "Where's Nurse?" He coughed. "I want…lay down." He shifted restlessly. Contorting his face, he coughed again.

Feeling panicked, Reginald stood and put his hand on his father's shoulder. "I'll send for her. Try to be still. She'll be back in a moment." He straightened his father's blanket awkwardly and repeated, "Be still."

Then he walked quickly out of the chamber, told Father's valet to go in, and sent the footman for the nurse. Alone, he leaned against the wall and wiped his smarting eyes.

What kind of clergyman ran from a sickroom? He'd been about as useful as a cow in there. He pulled away from the wall, giving it a backhanded punch with his fist. *Oh, Father! Damn it all.*

He should have gone to the library. Buried himself there with inanimate things. Things that would never die. Things he could not disappoint.

GEORGIANA REPLACED THE *Analytical Calculation* carefully back in the exact spot where she had found it. She'd read three pages and was confident of her understanding of only one paragraph at most. Still, she refused to be discouraged. Naturally, it would take multiple readings. And a lot of careful thought. It would likely take years for her to grasp the whole of it. Perhaps the rest of her life. That thrilled her a little. She felt awake for the first time in a long while.

If Mr. Taverston dared pack up his books, she would have to find a way to steal that one.

Thank goodness he was not there. Georgiana had called out

to be sure when she first entered the room and had received no answer. Now she glanced at the curtain, remembering again her shock when he had appeared there before.

What had he been doing so silently? Was this where he worked? What on earth did he do?

She looked back at the door, which she had left ajar. Then hesitantly, guiltily, she crept toward the curtain and pulled it back a few inches. That was his desk. A ledger rested on it with a few scattered papers nearby. There were numbers and notes on them, written in a bold hand, but most of the figures had slashes through them. Nothing was there that made any sense. And she had no business looking at it anyway. There was also a leather case closed with a clasp which looked as though it might contain something more substantial. She wouldn't touch it, of course. She couldn't explain why she wanted to. Her curiosity about it was a mystery. She was not generally a nosy-body, especially not enough to go rifling through a man's papers.

What had Crispin said to ask him? What was he sitting upon? She pulled the curtain back a little farther. A stool was set partially under the desk. But what an odd stool. The legs looked to be of uneven lengths and the bottoms were roughly sawed. The seat had been painted to resemble a chessboard.

"Lady Georgiana?"

Heavens! She whirled around. "Oh! Mr. Taverston, you frightened me."

"Again? Then I apologize once more." He appeared more concerned than angry as he waved a hand toward his desk. "May I ask?"

Heat rose to her cheeks. "It is I who should apologize to you." This was not something she could explain. Not readily. She stalled. "Lieutenant Taverston said I might find you here."

"You were looking for me?" His expression darkened.

"Oh! No. I mean, not at first. I was looking...well, for the library. I asked him where I might find it and he said you might already be here."

"Ah." His posture seemed to lose some of its tension.

"But I came anyway. Because I was agitated. And libraries calm me."

"Yes. I remember. They put you to sleep."

She dropped her chin, mortified.

He said, "And you worried I might be behind the curtain again, waiting to jump out and startle you?"

"Oh, do stop teasing!" she begged. She hated that he was so peeved. But what should she expect when he caught her practically rummaging through his things? Things he had taken care to hide behind a curtain. "Let me explain. Crispin said—"

"Crispin?"

"Lieutenant Taverston."

Laughing roughly, he said, "Yes, I know who Crispin is. What has he done now?"

"He says, well, first, he accidentally called me 'Georgiana.' Then he apologized for it and, to tell it quickly, we agreed to use Christian names. Except…" She blushed again. "Except not to tell Lord Taverston. But to tell you. Am I making sense?"

"Yes." He rubbed his nose. He looked embarrassed. "It is the sort of thing we do. Annoy each other. It must seem rather childish."

"No," she protested. Silly, yes, but not childish. "I think it's lovely how you rally one another."

"Well." He reddened, as though touched by her words. "Then my name is Reginald. Or Reg."

"I think Reginald. Good Heavens. My poor mother."

A smile flickered across his face. "And is Miss Fogbotham in on the game, *Georgiana*?"

"She will be." Now she relaxed. She knew how to explain her odd behavior. "There is something else."

"Is there?"

"Crispin told me to ask you what you were sitting upon. He wouldn't say why." She bit her cheek and pointed to the stool. "I'm afraid curiosity got the better of me. Why are you sitting on that?"

"On what?" he stepped forward and looked around her. Then he snickered. "Well, I always hated that table."

She looked at him questioningly, but he merely shook his head.

"It's too involved to explain." His fingers flexed. "More childishness."

"More rallying," she said gently. "This must be so difficult for you all. And then to have to entertain us as well." She bit her tongue. How was he supposed to respond to that except with bland reassurances?

He sighed. "Yes, you are a pestilence."

She started. Then laughed. He would not have said it if he meant it.

"Is it teatime yet, Reginald? I'm famished."

He offered his arm. As he led her out, skirting the kissing chair, he glanced at the bookshelf, then away. He cleared his throat. "You're welcome, naturally, to borrow anything you like."

How nonchalant. *Ha!* And what would he make of it if his *Analytical Calculation* went missing? He wouldn't catch her out that way. But he was onto her. To misdirect him, she was going to have to take one of those awful novels back to her room.

She smiled and said, "Thank you. I may."

CHAPTER FOURTEEN

I F ANYONE NEEDED rallying, it must be poor Lord Taverston, Georgiana mused, as Jeanette brushed out her hair. Not only had the hunt he planned been a disaster, but the whole evening had fallen apart.

No sooner had they gathered in the ladies' parlor for tea than the butler had announced the arrival of the Squire and his wife, as well as poor Jeffrey. They bustled in, full of concern and apologies, insisting they would remove Jeremy to home at once. It fell to Lord Taverston to take them to see their son and to explain to them the doctor's orders. Jeremy was not to be moved: he must remain in bed for a week. Lord Taverston assured them it would be no trouble at all to keep him. The upshot was that the parents had left Jeffrey behind to keep his brother company and to fetch and carry for him so that the Taverstons and their guests would not be disturbed.

Of course, that meant having another chamber opened for the boy. And then, to prove Jeremy was welcome and no trouble, the men all took their dinner in his room. Lady Iversley and Mother used the opportunity to sup with the Earl. That left the girls to their own devices. Olivia suggested they eat in the garden.

Georgiana found it exceedingly pleasant. Olivia was friendly and chatty and very interested in hearing about "all the eligible men in London." She insisted she did not regret missing another

Season, saying there would be plenty of men left for her to flirt with next year. And if she didn't "take," she said, with a waggle of her eyebrows, there was always Jeffrey. Or Jeremy.

Georgiana told them both about Crispin's suggestion. Olivia thought teasing Jasper was fine sport and wished she could address him as "Lord Taverston" also, but that would give away the game too quickly. As for Reginald's odd choice of chair, Olivia confessed to complete ignorance but then wondered if it might be related to Jasper's odd choice of saddle. She promised to ferret out what was going on. She hated—she said with a laugh—being left out.

They had had a grand time. Until the rain started, and they had to abandon their desserts and run inside.

Now, Jeanette put the last few pins in Georgiana's hair. *"Très belle,"* she pronounced. "What do you have in store for today?"

Georgiana sighed. "Likely a tour of the house." It was still raining. She stood. "I suppose I'll wander downstairs and see who's stirring." She had spent part of the night pondering what she had read. She might have figured something out—she needed to reread that page. How she wanted that book! It almost made her wish Lord Taverston would get it over with and propose to her. The sooner they were wed, the sooner she could reveal her true self.

She was being melodramatic, of course. Save for one small quirk, this was her true self; it had to be.

There were two men in the breakfast parlor this morning: Mr. Taverston—Reginald—and Jeffrey. Reginald had his head bent over a book, with a plate of eggs and sausages next to his elbow and coffee beside the plate. Jeffrey was at the sideboard, piling two plates and trying to balance them.

Without looking up, Reginald said, with a hint of impatience, "Just ask a maid for help, for God's sake."

"No, no. I won't be a bother. I said I would see to anything we need."

"You're going to need a broom and a mop."

Georgiana said, "You might simply ask for a tray."

Reginald's head whirled. He saw her and quickly stood, while Jeffrey cried: "Oh! Splendid idea. Yes. A tray. Will they have one in the kitchen? I'll go see." He hurried out, leaving his plates on the sideboard.

Georgiana eyed the plates. "I gather Jeremy's appetite was not harmed."

"What? No. I suppose not. Good morning. Thank you. For someone who swears he won't be a bother—"

"He's a pestilence?"

He laughed. Georgiana picked up a plate and some toast and approached the table. There was a piece of paper next to the book. She saw now that the book was a ledger, spread open. She stepped closer. Her eyes ran down the right page to the tally at the bottom.

"Eighty-seven pounds twelve shillings three pence," she said, "Not eighty-three, six, and three."

What had she done? She spun around, dizzied, swaying on her feet. The plate fell from her hands and shattered on the floor. She needed to flee, but Mr. Taverston caught her wrist.

"Georgiana? Georgiana, are you all right?"

She felt his hands on her arms. He scraped his chair back with his foot.

"Sit down. Please." He guided her into the seat.

She had no choice but to sit. Mama would—*oh!*—she would weep. How could she have been so unguarded? So stupid?

"Georgiana?"

"I'm fine. It's nothing." She tried to smile. "A little faint. I didn't sleep well last night."

He was regarding her much too carefully. Then he said, "I knew a fellow at Cambridge with that talent. Remarkable. Put all his classmates to shame."

"Please." She winced. "I'm sorry. It doesn't...I don't..." She dropped her head into her hands. Mama would be so disappointed in her.

"I want you to know, I did come up with the correct answer on my first try." His voice was softly jocular. "But arithmetic is not my strength, so when I add long lists, I always tally up at least twice." He slid a piece of paper out of the ledger and along the table in front of her. "See?"

She shut her eyes. Then realized how idiotic she must look, so she opened them. He added in groups. Next added the sums. *Amateur*.

Oh, God help her. She couldn't bear it. "There." She pointed to one of the groups. "There is your mistake."

He stared at it a moment. She could practically see gears grinding in his brain. Then he smiled. It dazzled her.

"Yes, I see! How embarrassing. God." He pushed that page aside and the ledger forward. "What about this?"

He pointed to the sum at the bottom of the left page. Tempting her. No, *encouraging* her. Then he glanced away, picking up his coffee to sip, as if aware that an audience could fluster someone working a puzzle. *Ha!* As if sums so simple could possibly daunt her. She could not have turned away from the numbers if she tried.

Well, then. She scanned the column eagerly, her dizziness gone. The numbers fell into place like old friends. "That's correct," she told him.

"It should be. I got the same answer three times. And this one?" He turned back several pages.

She shook her head. "Close. You're off by three pounds. Because there." She put her index finger on the offending row then jerked her hand back, resisting the strange urge to caress the page. How she missed this! "That five should be an eight."

He squinted. "Yes. That isn't my handwriting. That was Bradwell. But how did you know?"

"Because…" She hesitated. But it was too late now. She'd gone too far and the devil of it all was, *this* was more interesting than anything she had done since her debut last year. Perhaps even before that. "Because it was an eight on that previous page."

He flipped the page then flipped it back again. "Recurring expense. But you can't tell me you memorized the whole column."

"No. It's not memory. More like recognizing a pattern. From those groups you added before."

He looked at his scratch sheet, then back at his ledger, then sat heavily beside her.

"That's extraordinary. I've never seen—"

"Oh, please!" she groaned. She was making herself ridiculous. "Please don't tell anyone. It's horribly pushing of me to have corrected you. And then to display this…these…" She echoed her mother's long-ago disparagement. *Parlor tricks.*

"Parlor tricks?" His mouth twisted. "Whoever used those words is sadly ignorant."

"The Duchess."

He reddened. Then he said, "If she stands by her words, I stand by mine."

"Ladies do not show such an interest in *numbers*." She said it as though it was something despicable; it's what her mother would have said had she been in the room.

"Ladies help keep household accounts."

"Not in their heads." She stared at the tabletop. *How mortifying.*

His mouth shut. Then he smiled again as if to reassure her. "I should think you would have guessed by now that Taverstons are not sticklers."

"On the contrary," she retorted, annoyed that he did not see what an embarrassment this was. "Lord Taverston seems to me to be quite a stickler."

Reginald's face shuttered down. "I see. Yes. Well, he isn't, really. Not when you get to know him better."

Jeffrey blundered back into the room with a maid, who was carrying an empty tray. "These. And coffee. Thank you. I can take it up myself."

"It's no bother, sir."

Reginald said, "Gertie, I knocked that plate on the floor. Would you take care of it?"

"Yes, milord. I'll bring a broom."

"You can take the tray up to the lad first. The mess can wait."

"Yes, sir."

Jeffrey waved his thanks to Reginald and followed the maid from the room.

Reginald stuffed the loose paper into the ledger and closed it. He took a drink of coffee and stood.

"I shouldn't work here. I'll take this back to the library."

"I didn't mean to drive you away. You haven't finished your breakfast."

"It doesn't matter. I've had four rolls." He tucked the book under his arm. "I believe Jasper is giving a house tour later. If you'll excuse me until then." He bowed slightly and went to the door, where he paused and turned. "I meant it when I said you could borrow any of the books that you might fancy to read. And if..." he hesitated. "If there is anything you'd like to discuss, from the books, I mean, if you should tire of charades and cards..."

"Thank you. But..." She shook her head. She had already gone beyond the bounds of what was proper. Reginald might have been entertained by her odd little talent in the moment, but upon reflection, he would surely find her ridiculous—as Mother had warned. After all, what use was there in a lady who did sums in her head? Ladies were supposed to have ornamental skills before marriage: painting or playing the pianoforte or arranging flowers. After marriage, they needed only to know how to run a household—and, of course, give their husbands sons. Georgiana sighed.

"No, you're right," Reginald said, reddening as though he had as much cause to be as embarrassed by his offer as she had for inspiring it. And then he turned and walked away.

REGINALD HAD NEVER been jealous of Jasper. People might have found that hard to believe, but it was true. He had been annoyed by him, sometimes resentful, but never jealous. They were too different. Jasper had never had anything that Reginald truly wanted.

But Crispin was right, even if he had been joking. Georgiana was too good for Jasper. He saw her as a perfect potential countess, one who was beautiful to boot, and he'd looked no further. The truth was, if Jasper had witnessed Georgiana's *parlor trick*, he wouldn't have been pleased. It wasn't that he would see it as a fault *per se*, but Jasper would not want a wife smarter than he was. After all, Jasper could barely put up with a younger brother who was smarter. Hence the constant ribbing.

And Georgiana…*Lud*. In ten seconds, she'd caught mistakes it had taken him ten minutes to make.

He strode into the library, into his niche, and set the ledger on his desk. Crispin had been busy: Father's chair was tucked back behind it. He wondered absently what Crispin had put in its place.

The devil. Georgiana was not only better at arithmetic; she had better sense. Pushing him away. What had he been thinking, asking her to discuss Newton with him? That he had something of more value to offer her than Jasper did? The better course was to avoid her. He had *nothing* to offer. *He could offer nothing.*

Besides, Jasper had seen her first.

CHAPTER FIFTEEN

"AND HERE," LORD Taverston said, pushing open a door on the second floor, "is the ballroom. Not as grand as the Atherton's, but it serves the purpose."

"Oh, it's beautiful!" Alice exclaimed.

Georgiana agreed. The delicate appearance of the floor's mosaic tilework made her want to tiptoe across. She said, "The chandeliers are exquisite. And the color of the walls? Like daffodils."

"Those glass doors on the far side lead to our large terrace," Lord Taverston said. "We can go out and look if you'd like."

"It's the same view, Georgiana," Crispin said, "that you can see from the library. We're just above the music room now."

"And where would the billiard room be, Crispin?" Alice asked. "Relative to this."

"We'll see that next, Alice. There are retiring rooms just down the hall."

Lord Taverston frowned but didn't seem annoyed. Maybe puzzled. "One room at a time, please. The ladies have already seen most of the house. I'm trying to stretch out the rest of this tour."

Georgiana said, "Let's do go out onto the terrace, Lord Taverston. Just for a moment. I don't believe the rain is coming down too strongly."

He linked his arm through hers and led her to the glass doors, opened one, and ushered her through, beckoning the others to follow.

"If you look that way…ha! And imagine it without the fog, you'll see where we were riding. The lake is over there. And just at the south end of the lake, there is a folly. We'll go out that way the next time there is sunshine."

"It's quite pretty, even with the fog," Georgiana said. It *was* pretty; she was not simply being agreeable. The fog sat lightly upon gently rolling grounds that retained a hint of what would be lush summer verdancy despite the winter's brown. The lake in the distance was just discernible as a splash of gray-blue rimmed by a blur of trees. She turned to Reginald, who had been trailing along behind, not saying a word.

"Why do you keep the curtains closed all the time in the library? They block the view!"

He chuckled. "Not my view. And no one uses the library except me."

"She has a point though," Lord Taverston said. "You go in there and block out the world."

"I look out at the world. I block out my brothers."

His brothers both laughed. Georgiana fidgeted. She should not have mentioned seeing Reginald in the library. What if Lord Taverston wondered when that had been?

Alice said, "Lord Taverston, have you held many balls here?"

"My parents used to. Twice a year. Once in the summer when they would have house parties, and once at Christmastime for the locals. It was a nice tradition. I'd like to reinstate it someday. Mother stopped holding the ball about five years ago when Crispin marched off with his regiment."

Neither Georgiana nor Alice knew what to say to that. It seemed there might be something painful, or accusatory, in the statement. But Olivia laughed.

"Crispin was the piano player."

"You could have hired someone!" Crispin protested.

Lord Taverston smiled and said quietly, "There were professional musicians. Not Crispin. I think Mother was looking for an excuse. It was a lot of work. Come, let's go back inside. It's a bit drizzly." They all stepped back inside. "Where should we go next? The portrait gallery?"

"Show Georgiana the retiring rooms while we are up here," Crispin suggested.

"They are not much to look at. And we still have the Conservatory. That's Olivia's domain."

"Which is closer, Lord Taverston?" Alice asked.

Georgiana could not help smirking. Alice was having too much fun with the game.

"The portrait gallery. It's on this floor, but the west wing."

"Crispin," Georgiana said, joining in, turning her head to see the Lieutenant. "If the Conservatory is Olivia's domain and the library is Reginald's, what is yours?"

"The stable," he said. "And Lord Taverston's is the study."

"All right! Enough!" Lord Taverston burst out laughing. "You've painted me flying above my consequence and I object. Who is behind this? Crispin or Reg?"

"Olivia started it," Reginald said.

"Bosh!" Olivia cried. "Only with Alice and Georgiana!"

"Well, who else is there?" Crispin asked. "The Duchess?"

"No!" Olivia shrieked. "Crispin, even you wouldn't dare!"

"Lady Georgiana, Georgiana if I may," Lord Taverston said, drawing his elbow in toward his body, pulling her closer, showing her his white teeth and dimple, "do, please, call me Jasper. And allow me to show you the portrait gallery."

"Yes, of course." She smiled, but a shiver ran down the back of her neck. She should have anticipated where the game would lead. Georgiana and Jasper. The courtship was progressing apace, despite yesterday's interruptions. She would rather go backward than forward, but how was she to stop something with so much momentum?

⇶⇷

REGINALD FELT DRAINED. Everything worth seeing had been shown. Even his "domain." Crispin had nudged him when Jasper caught sight of Father's chair, but Jasper said nothing. In fact, he gave no indication he'd noticed. But, of course, he had.

The party returned to the drawing room for tea. Jasper was still holding forth, replying to a question Alice had asked. It still chafed, though it shouldn't, the way that Jasper was acting "the Earl."

"The reason it has such a modern feel is that a fire destroyed about three-quarters of the original house, back in my grandfather's time."

"How awful," Alice said.

Jasper escorted Georgiana to a seat and finally released her. He went to stand by the mantel.

"It was terrible, of course, but grandfather was a young man with young ideas. He hired a friend as his architect and told him he wanted something modern and grand. The architect was no one with a name, just an artist with a good deal of ambition. He may have had a vision, but we'll never know."

"Didn't he design Chaumbers?" Georgiana asked.

"In part. You see, he saw the commission as his chance to do something extraordinary. To make his reputation. He presented grandfather with design after design, each more whimsical than the last. The story has it that Grandfather finally flipped over one of the drawings and sketched out what he wanted. Something resembling this pile of stones, and demanded the architect give him that."

"So your grandfather designed this?"

"It would have fallen down by now if he had," Crispin muttered.

"I think," Reginald put in, "Grandfather can take credit for the bay windows in the library."

His brothers both laughed. Even Mother, who had joined them mid-explanation, seemed amused.

"Suffice it to say," Jasper continued, "the house got built as some sort of agglomeration of the two men's plans. After which, neither would take credit, *and* they were no longer friends."

Georgiana protested politely, "But it's a beautiful home."

"It grows on you," Jasper said. "At least, I hope it does."

The room quieted. Georgiana appeared embarrassed. Reginald felt annoyed. Jasper was doing it far too brown.

"If you will sit down, Jasper, I will pour," Mother said. "Lady Georgiana, your mother is writing a letter to the Duke and says she will not be down for tea." She poured and Gertie distributed the cups, then biscuits.

"Has there been any word from our young invalid?" Mother asked.

"I peeked in on him earlier," Reginald said. "He and Jeffrey were playing cards. I declined to join them."

Crispin added, "Adam said his eyes are clearer and he is answering questions more appropriately."

Mother gave Crispin a chilly look. "I'm not sure we need the opinion of your valet."

He pursed his lips, then nodded. At that point, Reginald could not help noting he'd taken no biscuits. Had he put anything in his tea? Was he living on air?

In part, Reginald understood their mother's concern. Throughout Crispin's youth, the many physicians they had brought in had told her she must make her son eat. Yet now, he seemed to be taking this Adam's advice as gospel, and Mother clearly thought he was starving himself. But though he appeared thinner, he looked better. Mother must see that. Crispin was seeing to his own health in his own way.

Well, whatever she was thinking, Mother had learned not to argue with Crispin in public over his physical state. "We hoped we might have music tonight," she said, shifting her focus to Georgiana.

"That would be delightful," Georgiana replied. Then, a little mischievously, she added, "I hear Lieutenant Taverston plays the piano."

"In fact, he is a very nice accompanist. If you—"

They were interrupted by Peters.

"My lady, my lord," he announced, "there is a Mr. Tibury calling."

Mother held up her hand and he brought forth a card. She scanned it. It seemed to Reginald that she grew pale.

"I don't know a Mr. Tibury. Do you, Jasper?"

He shook his head.

"My lady," Peters said, "he says he was summoned by the Earl."

Jasper frowned. "The Earl is not receiving. If he wishes, I will see him in my…in the study."

"Very well, my lord." The butler retreated.

Mother said, "I don't think you should receive him. You have guests. And we don't know his intentions."

"Well, we won't know if we send him away."

Crispin said, "Maybe just see him in the small parlor."

"What would that help?"

Crispin shrugged. Jasper closed his eyes a moment, then opened them and said coldly, "What will I be sitting on?"

"A stack of Bibles."

Jasper glared at him. "Put the chair back. And stop."

It had, perhaps, gone on too long. Reginald stood and said, "I'll move it all back." He felt Georgiana's eyes upon him, and the childishness of the prank seemed all the more pronounced.

Peters returned. "My lady, he has a letter. From the Earl. Who wishes to see him."

Mother stood. Flustered, she said, "Yes, well then. Take him up. I'll come as well."

Jasper said, "Mother, you needn't."

A man, a stranger, stepped into the room. The butler's eyes flew wide.

"Sir! You have not been admitted!"

"No. I have not." Mr. Tibury stood before them, all affronted dignity. He was soberly attired. Rather cheaply. But his gloves were immaculate, and he had removed his hat. He was heavy set, square-jawed, with nondescript brown hair but striking blue eyes. About Reginald's own age, he guessed. And he looked familiar, though Reginald was certain he'd never seen him before.

Jasper rose. "You understand, Mr. Tibury, that you are intruding upon a family gathering, and that my father is quite ill."

"I do understand that." The man's lip curled. "And if he hadn't sent for me, believe me, I would not be here."

"Come then." Jasper went toward the door. "Mother, you needn't trouble yourself."

But Mother stood also. She looked very pale. "I think I should."

All three left the room. Peters pulled the door shut.

"Who was that?" Olivia demanded.

Crispin chewed his lip. Reginald said, "God only knows. Jasper will straighten it out."

Crispin said, "Or vice versa. Are we still having tea, or should we adjourn? Reginald and I have a chair and Bibles to transport. We can reconvene at dinner."

REGINALD DIDN'T KNOW to where the ladies had retired, but he and Crispin went to the library to retrieve the chair. It was a heavy thing. Crispin left him to heave it back up the stairs, saying he had hauled it down. Then they each brought back half the pile of old Bibles and religious tracts.

"A shame," Crispin said. "I thought this was the capper."

"I thought sawing the legs off the table was cleverer."

"Hmph."

They put the books back on the shelves. Then Reginald shifted a few. Crispin looked askance.

"Can it matter?"

"No. The whole thing offends my sense of order."

"As in Newton next to Radcliffe?"

Reginald threw up his hands. After a moment, he asked, "Had you ever heard of Tibury?"

Crispin shook his head. "But I think Mother has."

He was thinking the same. "Any guesses?"

"Nothing I would posit out loud. You?"

"No. If you're positing anything at all, you're ahead of me."

He hoped Jasper *would* sort it out.

CHAPTER SIXTEEN

"The violet," Jeanette said decisively. "If you are to be singing, you will want the violet."

Dresses were laid out all over the bed. Georgiana looked them over with a jaundiced eye. The modiste had prepared her a wardrobe for a London Season, not for whatever this was.

"Isn't that style a bit much for a house party?" It showed too much neck.

"It is perfect for standing up to sing. Very dramatic."

Georgiana grumbled, "I don't think we need any more drama."

Alice giggled. "Wasn't that just awful? Who do you suppose he is? He looks like he could be a cousin, didn't you think?"

"A cousin!"

"He has that chin. Or maybe it was the blue eyes."

"A cousin, yet no one had any idea who he was?" Georgiana laughed at Alice's fancy.

Alice shrugged but a smile played on her lips. "Maybe the Earl and his brother had a falling out. They haven't seen one another for years. And now the nephew has appeared with demands upon the inheritance."

"Good Heavens. You have it all figured out?" Georgiana entered into the spirit. Tapping her cheek, she speculated, "But why then, would the Earl have summoned him? And why would he have looked so annoyed to be here?"

"Oh, I don't know." Alice pouted. "And I don't suppose we'll find out. It's abominably nosy of me to want to hear what happened."

"I suspect if Olivia finds out who he is, she'll tell you. No matter how lurid the secret is."

Alice giggled again. "The only person in this house I suspect of having lurid secrets is Crispin. Adam is no more a valet than I am. And aren't you curious to see if he eats anything tonight?"

Georgiana huffed. "We are awful."

Jeanette's little smile showed she was having difficulty pretending not to listen. She approached with Georgiana's violet gown in hand.

"And, with this, the silver chain and pendant," Jeanette said. "And pearls in your hair."

"You don't think that's excessive?"

"*Non.* If anything, it is too tame."

"*Hmm.*" She frowned skeptically. "All right."

Then she recalled her maid's secretive smile. Servants knew everything.

"Jeanette, are they talking about Adam downstairs?"

"*Bien sur,*" she murmured, "but what do they know? Nothing."

"What do you know? Have you spoken with him?"

"In passing. His French is very good."

"His French? I thought he looked Greek. Or Italian."

"He is Greek. It is where he…" She searched for the English translation. "Picked up his little knowledge of medicine. But he learned French in France before he went to the Peninsula."

Alice gawped. "To do what? That sounds like a resumé for a spy!"

"Alice!" Georgiana laughed. "Estranged cousins? French spies? You read too many novels." But she couldn't help asking Jeanette, "Did he say how he met Lieutenant Taverston?"

Jeanette shrugged. "*Non.* But for certain Lieutenant Taverston would not bring a spy to his home."

"If he knows," Alice said, pressing her point despite its absurdity.

"I do not believe Lieutenant Taverston is anyone's fool," Jeanette said. "Now let me prepare you, or you will be unacceptably late for dinner."

Jeanette dressed them both. For Alice, she chose a beautiful lavender gown, light in shade, suitable for a girl who had only recently come out. It was a much better choice than Georgiana's violet-colored gown for a house party that was essentially a vigil.

"Are we ready?" Georgiana asked, peering at the figure in the mirror as she pulled on her dinner gloves. The silver pendant dipped down between her breasts. In the candlelight, the luster of the pearls would draw attention to her red-gold hair. But her shoulders were bare, and she had gooseflesh. At least no one would ever suspect that figure of pondering mathematics.

"Ready and eager."

"Then let's go down."

REGINALD WAS THE first to arrive in the drawing room. When Crispin showed up a few minutes later, Reginald sniffed a laugh. They were both dressed as if they were expecting a momentous event: Crispin in uniform, starched and polished, and Reginald in his best cutaway jacket and fawn pantaloons. Barclay had even given him a second shave and put an intricate knot in his neckcloth.

Crispin sat down on the davenport beside him and clenched his hands on his knees.

"No Jasper?"

Reginald shook his head. "Mr. Tibury is gone, however. I do know that much."

"Well, yes. I didn't expect Mother to invite him to dinner."

"I hope he didn't upset Father."

"If he did, it's Father's fault for summoning him. The poor fellow clearly wished he were elsewhere."

"Hmm."

Jasper strode into the room, dressed like a pink and wearing a scowl.

"That," he said, "was intolerable."

"Enlighten us," Crispin replied.

Jasper went over to the sideboard and poured himself a sherry. "Reg?"

"Will I need it?" he joked.

"Yes."

Reginald swallowed hard and stood. He went to take the drink from his brother. Jasper said nothing more, so Reginald took a gulp, then gave him a look that said: *Now?*

"Mr. Tibury is a curate in Ipswich."

"A curate!" Crispin let out an exaggerated whistle as if awed. When no one laughed, he said, "I wasn't expecting that, but he looks it. And what, pray, does the Earl want with an Ipswich curate?"

"To give him the livings in Fremont and Bellwether."

Neither Reginald nor Crispin had any immediate response, not a spoken one at any rate. A thousand jumbled contradictory thoughts crashed through Reginald's brain so that he could not have spoken if he tried.

Jasper went on. "Mr. Tibury was flabbergasted as well."

"Start from the beginning, please," Crispin said.

"That is the beginning. Close to it. The interview was short. Father doesn't have words to waste." Jasper drummed his fingers on the mantel. "Taking him up there, Tibury was as indignant as he seemed when he invaded us at tea. He didn't say much, just exuded indignation. He did say he had never intended to intrude upon—" Jasper's lip curled. "—*the lords of Iversley.* He sneered it, just like that."

"Ha!" Crispin seemed almost amused. "People don't sneer at

us." He turned to Reginald. "Do they?"

Reginald could not joke. He felt too sick. And too relieved. There should be a wider range of human emotion. It should not be that being scorned by his father in favor of a stranger would feel exactly the same as being dropped by his mistress for Plodgett.

"Well, this man sneered." Jasper downed his glass and poured another. "Though, to be fair, seeing the Earl affected him. I doubt he expected to find him so ill."

"He knew Father?" Crispin asked.

"Seemed to."

"And Father knew him?"

"If he did, he pretended not to. Not by sight. The thing is, I don't think he was overjoyed that Mother and I accompanied Tibury. But honestly, he needed one of us to translate. He's getting harder to understand." He breathed out sharply. "In a nutshell, someone wrote to Father on Tibury's behalf. He's an excellent curate and so they put forward his name for Mr. Codworthy's eventual replacement. Father read his references and, well, there it is. He told this Tibury fellow that he would add a codicil to his will that the livings would go to him." Jasper's voice rose, then fell. "I'm sorry, Reg. I'm not going to ignore his wishes…that is, unless you…"

Reginald shook his head.

"Damn it, Reg. Say something!"

"There are—" Reginald had to clear a rasp from his throat. "There are four livings. And there are many, many, worthy, educated men who would be grateful for even one. I had no expectation of hoarding all four."

"But Tibury didn't even appear grateful! He said, stiffly as you please, that he was not in any position to refuse!"

"Framingham is the best of the four," Crispin said, so gently it embarrassed Reginald. It embarrassed him even more because he didn't want Framingham or any of them, but to say so would only make him sound petulant. And hurt. And damn it all, he *was* hurt.

"I don't understand why Father didn't say something to me first," Jasper grumbled. "He just—I've been beating my head against the wall, sorting out the mess everything has fallen into the past eighteen months, and he just goes and does this. Reg, if I had known—"

"It isn't a tragedy."

"Nor a mystery," Crispin said. "Father hasn't any muscles left to flex. Handing out a living..." He shrugged. "It was something he could still do. Don't begrudge him that."

"I don't," Reginald said.

"I wasn't talking to you."

"I don't either!" Jasper's voice rose again. "You think I begrudge him his last few breaths? The hell—the both of you! The hell with you! That damn chair! Do you think I want this? Any of this? *Any* of it? Do you think I enjoyed tossing Vanessa aside like...like... Tearing each other apart by *correspondence?*"

"Shut up!" Crispin said, springing to his feet, catlike, over the back of the davenport and putting his hand to the door. He closed it softly. Then turned and said low-voiced, "They're coming. Jasper, get hold of yourself."

Jasper drew a long, shaky breath. Then he tossed down the rest of his sherry and poured yet another but set it down. He ran a hand through his hair. Then he nodded.

Crispin opened the door. He swooped an elaborate bow. "Ladies, welcome."

If Reginald envied his brothers anything it was this. How easily they could project ease. They might have been sparring over billiards. Meanwhile, he still felt jellied inside.

And the ladies entered, Georgiana, vibrant as a thunderclap, striking Reginald like a blow to the chest. No, he didn't envy Jasper anything but her. She was so, so beautiful. And she was the same woman who had almost tearfully begged him not to let anyone know she was intelligent. No, not intelligent. Brilliant. Was she supposed to hide that? For the rest of her life, was she supposed to hide herself?

He shuddered. Just as he was going to end up with the Framingham living, with a few dusty Greek texts on his shelf that he never looked at anymore, pretending to be a man of God. Avoiding his brother and his brother's countess. Hiding from this. From *her*. He looked up.

Jasper had gone to the door to draw in the ladies.

And Crispin, Crispin had already welcomed them. Now, to Reginald's dismay, Crispin was looking closely at *him*.

AT DINNER, NO one discussed the strange visitor. Georgiana found it maddening. Of course, it was none of her business, but at least Lady Iversley or Jasper might have laughed and said: *What an odd little man.* Ignoring him and his visit gave it more consequence rather than less.

Like Crispin's plate.

The soup course was pea with a good deal of salt but no meat. Crispin consumed a large bowlful. Then came the fish. Bream. It was very good with a heavy, peppery cream sauce. Crispin's was served plain. And then there was boiled beef and carrots. For everyone except Crispin. Who had a bowl of thick gruel comprising, it appeared, oats and dried fruit, as though he were a horse.

No one commented. Georgiana wanted to scream. She felt she was in some bizarre bit of theater. As if the Taverstons were testing her to see when she would break.

Alice looked so bottled up, Georgiana worried she would break first. The Duchess, of course, coolly appeared to notice nothing amiss. But that wasn't fair, since she had not witnessed the entrance of Mr. Tibury.

Table conversation was insipid. They would be going into the village tomorrow, so every shop had to be described in detail.

Dinner finally ended, but there was to be no reprieve. The men were not even to be permitted their brandies as Lady Iversley marched them all to the music room.

It was—as she had discovered earlier, when searching for sheet music to help her prevaricate—poorly designed for a music room. Which made more sense now that she'd heard Chaumbers' history. The piano was too close to the wall and the marble floor was half-covered with a thin carpet. The acoustics would be terrible. With the piano taking up space where it was, chairs could not be arranged except in front of the windows, which were drafty.

If she were in charge, she would move the billiard table to the library, the library shelving here, and put the piano in the billiard room. She put the thought from her head.

Alice was importuned first. She played a sonata. Then Olivia played something more lively.

"Shall we have a song next?" Lady Iversley asked. "Will you sing for us, Lady Georgiana?"

"Yes, I will." *Why else would I be wearing this dramatic dress?* She moved to the piano and shuffled through the music.

"Crispin will play for you."

Crispin rose, wordlessly, and came forward. He sat at the piano and waited for her to hand him a sheet. It was an aria, but not a particularly difficult piece. He looked at the music, then nodded and handed it back to her. He began the introduction from memory, which gave her courage. It was terrible stumbling through a piece when talents were mismatched.

She joined him at the appropriate moment, and then the music carried her along. She had a strong voice and she'd had an extraordinary teacher, but she'd been to enough operas to know how real singers should sound. There was no danger she would abandon society for life on the stage.

She finished her part and Crispin drew the piece to a close with a lovely, improvised tail—an effortless talent. The room was still. She opened her eyes, blinking, to find her mother's eyes glistening, Lady Iversley smiling approval, and Reginald rubbing his nose.

"Where have I heard that before?" Jasper snickered. His attention appeared to have turned to his youngest brother rather than the performers, but even so, Georgiana started at his taunting tone. She could not consider mockery an appropriate response to *anyone's* singing. "It was at a party, I think. Reg, do you remember? Who was the girl?"

Crispin pulled something from his pocket and lobbed it at his brother's head. It thonked him right between the eyes. Georgiana jumped.

"Crispin!" Lady Iversley cried. "Good Heavens! Why on earth—was that an *apple?*"

The ladies all appeared similarly wide-eyed with the same confusion Georgiana felt, but Jasper merely picked the apple up from the floor and took a bite. "My mistake. Reg doesn't go to parties." He sounded smug.

Reginald said nothing. He simply looked embarrassed for no discernible reason.

Oh! It was maddening. Nothing the lords of Iversley did made any sense.

CHAPTER SEVENTEEN

GEORGIANA WAS NOT, by habit, an early riser, but one would never guess this by her behavior at Chaumbers. She could not sleep. She intended to wait for Alice to wake too, but peckishness overcame her nerves.

She had hoped she would not stumble upon Reginald in the breakfast parlor again. Even so, she was disappointed to find that he wasn't there. Rather, it was Crispin she found lounging at the table with a newspaper. He didn't even rise when she came into the room. *Odd man.* She put a bread roll and a spoonful of berries on her plate, then sat down.

"Good morning," Crispin said, without looking up.

She noted he was drinking weak tea. His plate held an apple core, which was somehow appropriate.

"Good morning," she replied, wincing inwardly to hear her voice's false brightness. She was still unsettled by the Taverston brothers' own strange performance the night before. Although she did not believe Jasper had been mocking her singing *per se*— he couldn't have been *that* ill-mannered—he had certainly been making fun of *something.* Crispin obviously knew what it was, and if it was what Georgiana thought…

He folded the newspaper and laid it on the table. "You sing beautifully. I meant to say so last night, but everyone else was telling you that, so I thought it would make more of an impression to wait."

She blinked at him. It had seemed strange that her accompanist had been mute, even when she'd thanked him and told him he played well. "You are an odd man."

He laughed. "I suppose I am."

"I thought it was your habit to go walking in the mornings." She put a berry in her mouth and looked up at him.

"I'm not odd enough to go out walking in this downpour." He sipped his tea. "I'm afraid there will be no excursion today to the village shops."

"We can go another day."

"How very rational of you."

It was hard to tell if he was in a good humor or a grumpy one. She decided to assume it was good. If she could have only one of her questions answered—the one that had kept her up last night—she would consider herself satisfied. And Crispin was the only one she dared approach.

"May I ask you something?" It was important that she know.

He set down his teacup and ground his jaws. Then he said, "I have a delicate digestion. I am on a program to see what agrees with me and what doesn't."

She stared at him, agape.

He put his thumb under her chin and pushed her mouth shut.

"I answered the wrong question."

A huff of laughter popped out before she stifled it. "Good Heavens. You can't possibly think me so rude."

His face reddened. "Well, I'll thank you not to refer to it again."

She nodded.

"*Ever* again."

"I won't!"

"Then what was the question you were going to ask?"

She took a breath and dove in. "Why did you throw an apple at Jasper?"

"Because he was being an arse. Excuse my language."

"Was he…was he making fun of me?"

Startled, Crispin looked her full in the face. "Of you! How could he possibly make fun of you?"

She had given the evening a good deal of thought and it was the only answer she had. She'd seen Jasper's expression after she'd finished singing. It was not only mocking but a little bit mean.

"Because," she said, almost whispering now in her embarrassment, "I wore that frightful dress, and sang an aria, and he said," her voice got even quieter, "there was a girl."

Fury whisked across his face. "Georgiana, no. No one would ever compare you to an opera singer." Then his laugh rang out but even that sounded angry. "Well, that came out wrong. You have a superb voice. And your dress was stunning but perfectly proper. Jasper was not making fun of you. He was making fun of—" He halted abruptly, blinked a few times, and finished—"of me."

"Of you?"

"Well." He rose from the table and poured himself more tea from the pot on the buffet. Behind her back, he continued in a calmer tone, "There was a party and there was a girl who sang, and I found her very pretty. And that is all I will say on the matter."

"Oh." She let out a long sigh of relief. So Crispin had once been enamored of an opera singer. And he was embarrassed to be teased about it. "Well." She pulled off a piece of her roll. "I should imagine you won't be joining *me* for breakfast again any time soon."

He sat back down beside her, grinning broadly.

"No, next time I'll take my chances with the weather."

He drank his tea while she ate her roll.

"These are so good!" she exclaimed. Their own cook's rolls were not half so delicious.

"Oh, God." He groaned. "Yes, I know."

Her eyes widened. "I'm so sorry," she said, mouth full.

"Georgiana, do me a favor. Reginald is almost certainly in the library. Go pester him."

She swallowed. "I shouldn't."

"Yes, well, you shouldn't be eating Cook's rolls under my nose, either, but you're doing that."

She scrambled to her feet. "But I can't bother him if he's working."

"Go. Go." He shooed her. "Take all the rolls with you."

"There are half a dozen!"

"That will make him very happy."

She hurriedly piled six rolls on a large plate and scurried away. As she left, she heard Crispin snap his paper back open behind her and she felt fortunate he had not smacked her with it.

THE LIBRARY DOOR was wide open. And so were the curtains. Reginald was seated on a spindly chair that matched the one in the second little nook. Georgiana knocked lightly on the doorframe, then went in. Reginald's head came up from his ledger. He didn't look particularly happy to see her, but neither did he look displeased.

She held up the plate. "Crispin was in the breakfast parlor, trying to read a newspaper. He sent me here with these for you. I must have been annoying him."

"Crispin is shockingly easy to annoy. Come in. Come." He stood up. "Whereas *I* am pleasant to anyone bearing Cook's rolls."

She crossed the carpet and joined him in the nook. Then she realized at once that she shouldn't have. Especially because he wasn't wearing a neckcloth, and the top button of his shirt was undone. She set the plate down, intending to leave directly. But the ledger over which he had been hunched was surrounded by scratch paper and scribbled calculations, and she couldn't tear herself away.

Reginald noticed her lingering, though she imagined it was hard for him not to—leaving a plate of rolls should only have taken a moment. He picked up a bread roll and gestured to the papers. "Does this mess make your head hurt?"

She knew he was not referring to the splash of papers but rather the inefficient figures upon them; but she refused to be so thin-skinned as to now imagine *he* was mocking her.

"I confess it does. Why are you spending so much time on accounts? Surely you have a steward."

Good Heavens. Intrusive questions were now rolling easily from her tongue.

He rubbed his stubbled cheek. This sleepy, somewhat rumpled look was oddly attractive on him. Of course, she'd never seen a gentleman, or any man, so...*mussed.* Yet somehow, she didn't believe she'd find dishevelment attractive in any other man. *Faith!* This train of thought was terribly inappropriate. She forced herself to focus on his words. "We did. The man passed recently and hadn't been keeping up for several months. I don't think it was topmost in Jasper's mind until he saw how muddled it had become."

"But surely he doesn't expect you to be his steward!"

"Oh, no. Jasper's expectations are more in line with my father's. Fairly medieval ones. First son heir. Second son soldier."

She finished the triad. "Third son to the church?"

He nodded. Then yawned before sitting wearily back down. "Jasper has a man in mind to take over, but he wanted the books a bit cleaner before handing them off."

"And then?"

"Then?"

"What will you do with yourself?" She couldn't really see him as a clergyman. "What would you be doing if you weren't poring over these ledgers?"

He hesitated, then gestured to a leather case on the floor. It was the clasped one she had noted before. "In there, I have a manuscript, in ancient Greek, that was presumably meticulously copied by monks a few hundred years ago. If Bastion is correct—"

"Frederick Bastion?"

His eyes glowed a moment and he said, "Yes. By God, how do you—"

"My brother Charles has mentioned him. I've only heard the name. Sorry, go on."

He gazed at her a moment as if he were going to say something different, but then continued, "If he's correct, there is no one alive today who knows what these manuscripts say."

"Plural manuscripts?"

"He has twelve of them."

"And *you* are going to learn what they say." Oh! Now *this*! Gooseflesh rose on her arms.

"Well, a few pages of one." He rubbed his hands down his thighs and smiled ruefully. "After that, I suppose I will settle into a living at Framingham. But!" He tapped the ledger. "I have forbidden myself to work on the Greek until I get these accounts sorted."

It occurred to her she could sort them out for him. But putting her nose into the Taverstons' finances would be—it would be heinous.

It would also be fun. "Are you even almost finished?"

"I thought I was." He shook his head. "I was rattled yesterday, by that mistake of eight versus five. What if I've been sloppy, reading others' handwriting? So I've been double-checking some of the receipts and they look correct, but what if they're not? I really don't want to go through them all again. Then I remembered what you said about patterns."

"What I said?"

"Yes. Most of the expenses are for the same things over and over. If the cost was the same each time, I wouldn't have to sum it all up each time."

Well, obviously. "But?"

"But the cost is not always the same. Sometimes it's more, sometimes less. I'd have to look deeper into the invoices to see why. And, well, the devil. It's too boring to contemplate."

She laughed lightly. "I can imagine."

"So I went back to assuming the entries I'd made were correct and just tallying them to get the whole thing finished." He pointed to his scratch paper. "And I shouldn't have been working on it so late because none of my sums came out the same twice."

"You should have gone to bed."

"Yes, but then here is the worst of it. When I started this whole project, I thought I'd be clever and start by looking at the account book from five years ago. Bradwell was taking care of things then. So I decided I would simply do as he did."

"That makes sense."

"But because I have become so hopelessly muddled that I can't even add and subtract anymore, I thought—last night I thought I'd go back to that first book and just…tally the columns." He frowned. "Like a schoolboy exercise."

"I'd call that a drastic measure." She picked up one of the rolls and broke off a piece, but she was fidgety, not hungry, so she set the bread down. "I hope you aren't redoing all the books for the past five years."

"It wasn't my intention but now—" He pulled his hand through his hair. "I was up all night."

She tried not to think of him sitting here through the night. There was something more intimate about that than picturing him in bed. *Which she would never do!*

Reginald opened a worn book with a frayed cover and pushed it in front of her on the desk. He pointed to a column.

"Please tell me I'm wrong."

Georgiana drew a breath, debating whether to look. But she knew she was going to. It was either look at the page or at the hollow at the base of Reginald's throat, right there in front of her. She turned to calculating the costs and revenues and then compared her result to the total that had been recorded at the bottom.

"That is incorrect." The significance of that fact gave her a cold, heavy feeling in the pit of her stomach. "Have you another ledger? Another year?"

He pulled out another from a short stack on his desk and opened it to a page he had dog-eared.

"Six years ago. Randomly selected quarter. This page."

She ran her finger down the column. Then looked into Reginald's pallid face.

"Oh," she said, full of sympathy, but unsure what else to say. They were each off by thirty pounds. If that was true of every quarter, the books were off by one hundred and twenty pounds a year. For who knew how many years.

"Damn it!" he swore. "I'm sorry. I should not have burdened you. God! If I wasn't so tired I never—I'm sorry, it's inexcusable. I just hoped I was wrong, and you would—"

She waved his protest away. Now was not the time to be polite. Or ladylike, for that matter. No matter what Mama thought. "How many have you checked?"

"Three quarters. From randomly pulled years."

"And they are all off?"

He nodded. "Not always by the same amounts. But usually close. Maybe I'm wrong." He heaved a sigh. "But if I am, it's not by much. I was concentrating on the numbers without paying much attention to what they were for, so after I talked to you I realized I should be looking for patterns, but..." He waved a hand toward the bookshelf where she had seen rows and rows of old ledgers. "It will take years."

"If your steward was dipping—"

"But he wasn't! Not Bradwell. I would stake my life on his honesty. And his competence. I can't make sense of it."

She said nothing. His father's steward had been stealing from the family. And now the man was dead, and nothing could be done. And his father was dying. Reginald wanted to do this one simple thing for his family, and it had devolved into a nightmare.

He murmured, "And I feel as if I could decipher the books..."

Oh, Reginald. Her heart broke for the man because she knew he wanted to do what he loved, what he lived for, and was instead trying to reconcile himself to doing what was expected.

Gently, she said, "It's not ancient Greek. You can't translate it."

"No. No, it's not Greek, unfortunately. It's numbers."

Numbers.

"I—"

"Oh, God, Georgiana. No. I'm not asking you, of course, I'm not. I'm just bemoaning my own inadequacy. I know Bradwell is not an embezzler. But something is not right. And I'm concerned this is something that will come back to haunt Jasper. He should at least know there is something hidden. And the answer is in those books somewhere. The money came in. It went out. It *has* to add up."

He could not have seduced her more effectively than that.

"I'll help you."

"I can't ask that."

"Reginald, you can't put something like this in front of me and then snatch it away. It would be as if Bastion took away that manuscript and said, 'Never mind.'"

He looked at her hard, then shook his head.

"Bradwell was the family's accountant for forty-seven years. *Forty-seven.* Do you know how many ledgers that spans? Jasper is not going to let me lock you away in the library—"

"Reginald—"

"—for hours at a time, days on end. He has a million things planned."

"Reginald, I don't think he'll notice." She looked down at her hands and willed them not to tremble with excitement. "It won't take me all that long."

CHAPTER EIGHTEEN

L ADY GEORGIANA STEWART had just made an unimaginably arrogant statement about her own mathematical abilities. Yet the scholarly gentleman sitting before her did not shy away, grimacing with distaste. He smiled.

It was not only the turn of his lips, but the way his sky-at-dusk-blue eyes suddenly appeared to be lit from behind, crinkling at the corners—it took her breath away.

He said, "I won't get in your way. Just tell me what you'll need."

"Oh." At best, she'd expected him to hand her a stack of ledgers and fire off a plodding set of instructions, then breathe down her neck. Because what else could she have expected him to do? But this man, this unbearably marvelous, sensible man, ceded control over a problem. With a smile. To a woman.

It came to her all at once. A revelation: *This is the one.*

Her mind began reeling back to every interaction, every moment they had shared since he'd frightened her awake and they contrived to lie to their loved ones. She had known then. And later, when he took it upon himself to put that horse out of its misery, and when he had watched her do sums in her head and been impressed rather than appalled. Rather than intimidated.

Well, no. It was easy to look back and believe she had known all along, but she knew she hadn't. And she couldn't be in love with him. She had known him for less than a week. But she could love him, given time.

At once came the horrified realization that she *would* love him, given time.

She could not marry Lord Taverston.

Georgiana stepped away from the bay window, praying her face had not betrayed every thought in her head, every emotion coursing through her body.

Think, Georgiana. Think.

He had asked her what she needed to proceed. She needed two things: a course to follow and a course to appear to be following. *An alibi.*

She pulled a Radcliffe novel from the shelf, opened it, and stared blankly while she gathered herself, then returned to the desk.

"I will sit here." She pointed to his chair, and he quickly stood. "I'll sit in the light, with the curtain mostly closed, and pretend I'm reading if anyone approaches."

"Have you read it?"

"Of course not."

"*The Italian* is Olivia's favorite. I'll jot down a quick summary. Just in case."

"You've read it?"

"As I said, it's Olivia's favorite. Regrettably, she needed someone to gush to about it."

Georgiana sighed, feeling for him. "Why are you assigned all the worst jobs?"

He looked amused, so clearly he didn't realize she was referring to shooting the horse. The two were not exactly comparable.

"When we are finished," she said, trying to sound casual, "will you let me borrow your Woodhouse?"

"Yes." He shifted his gaze aside. "Or if you'd like, I'll read it with you."

He was offering to tutor her. Not in a condescending way. Merely carefully. It would mean continuing to meet in secret.

She slid into his chair. "Have you a clean sheet of paper?"

He produced one. Then he pushed the inkwell closer and handed her an odd metal-pointed pen.

"I've never used one of these."

"They're very clever. A schoolfellow gave it to me. He's working on a patent."

"Hmm." She set it down. "I think we would be very fortunate to discover any patterns if we just pluck out ledgers at random. I'd like to approach this somewhat differently. I have some questions, but they may seem intrusive."

"Ha! Well, I think we've moved past that. I have faith in your discretion."

As well he might, given he knew the worst about her.

"Bradwell has been the family's steward for forty-seven years? Was this all under the Earl?"

"No, my grandfather brought him on."

"How long did he serve your grandfather?"

He squinted. "Well, that would be arithmetic, wouldn't it?" He rumpled his already-mussed hair. She felt a tightening in her chest, along with an absurd desire to fix his hair with her fingers. "Father is sixty-two. He rose to Earl at age thirty."

"So," she cleared her throat and focused. "I expect we will not need to look at the first fifteen years. But I'll check one of the early volumes just to be sure. My reasoning is that I want to use major family events as touchpoints. If these…discrepancies started at some distinct time, for some distinct purpose, it seems likely we can identify the trigger by correlation."

"Give me an example," Reginald said.

She frowned with concentration. "Don't take offense."

"I won't. It's a hypothetical."

Ah, she adored him. How he spoke. How logically his mind worked. How he was not reluctant to admit to having questions.

She decided not to start with the obvious: embezzlement. Instead, she said, "Let us say the Earl wants a particular bill passed, very badly, and stoops to bribery."

He smirked. "Ha! Good Lord, you're offensive."

She refused to be distracted by his teasing. "If we were to check the books around the times of debates of bills you know he supported, we might find a time where money unexpectedly and unexplainably starts to flow out."

"Bradwell would have had to be in league with the Earl."

"That will be true no matter what we find. Unless Bradwell was acting on his own."

He scowled at her and was about to protest again, but she kept talking.

"In which case, I expect that instead of finding approximately one hundred and twenty pounds disappearing every year that a particular type of bill comes up, we will find there will be quite small, randomly occurring discrepancies to start, gradually becoming larger and more regular as he grows more confident that he won't be caught."

He sulked. "Wouldn't it be quicker to start from the beginning and look for your gradually increasing thievery?"

"Yes, but I am giving your man the benefit of the doubt."

The crease of annoyance disappeared from his brow. "All right. But obviously, we are not looking for Parliamentary bribes. What are we looking for?"

"I don't know. It isn't as though I've done this before." She dipped the pen in the well and stared down at the empty page. "But I want to try to narrow down the number of books we must examine. If something obvious jumps out, that would be wonderful. If not, once we know the timeframe during which all of this is occurring, we can narrow our focus to try to determine what it is."

He moved out of her peripheral vision, and she heard him dragging the second little chair closer. Her breath quickened in an odd way. She held up her hand, motioning him to stop.

"I have just a few questions. Then I think you had better go get some sleep." She added quietly, "And change your clothes."

His eyes grew wide, and he grasped the top of his shirt. "I beg your pardon. You should have said—I should have—oh, my God! You must think—"

"I think you need some sleep."

"Yes, yes. I'll go. Immediately." He stood immobile, his face as red as a brick.

"Reginald?"

"What?"

"Before you go, tell me when your parents married, how old you all were when you went off to school, and when Crispin went into the army. That should be enough to get me started."

REGINALD WAS CERTAIN he would never be able to sleep. He was mortified. He might never sleep again. How could he have—how could she have allowed him to—*God!* Talking about embezzlement and bribery while standing around half-dressed.

He was disgusting.

He didn't see how he would get through the next few weeks without Jasper calling him out. *Damn it.* For honor's sake, he would have to allow Jasper the first shot. He snorted. And probably the second shot also. Jasper couldn't hit a cow at ten paces.

He took off his jacket and boots and sat down on his bed. Shivering, though he was not cold, he pulled a blanket around his shoulders and then lay back to stare at the ceiling.

He could, he was fairly certain, manage to slog through account books without making an arse of himself. Not even he was green enough to imagine this was the sort of activity that would turn a woman's head. Or a man's—even if men's heads were notoriously easy to turn. He could surely work in close quarters with Georgiana for a week or two without putting a knife in Jasper's back. *Huh.* As if he could even succeed if he tried. How hubristic to think he—a third son!—could compete with an earl for a duke's daughter. How ludicrous to imagine competing with Jasper at all.

But. After the next few weeks, after sorting this, after Father…passed, after Jasper ascended to the title and wed, what was *he* going to do?

He closed his eyes and tried not to picture Jasper and Georgiana together. Setting up their nursery. Throwing Christmas balls at Chaumbers for the good folks in Iversley.

Framingham was not far enough. Nor Bath. Not even Cambridge, not even with twelve untranslated Greek manuscripts awaiting him, nothing, without her, would be enough.

⋙✕⋘

THE BED SHOOK, and Reginald woke to see that Crispin had flopped down on its edge.

"Are you awake?" Crispin asked.

"I am now." He sat up and swung his feet, like blocks of lead, to the floor. "What time is it?

"Nearly teatime. What the devil happened to you? Reg! Those are last night's pantaloons! Were you out on a drunk?"

"Yes, obviously. Because that's what I do."

"Did you ride over to the Boar's Head in Grosling to give Maggie a bang? I know it isn't your usual practice, but after Annie threw you over—"

If only Jasper, for once, could keep his mouth shut. Crispin was probably wondering what was wrong with Reg that he hadn't sought out a lightskirt for some convenient solace. Crispin did not see the point in mistresses, preferring, so he said, variety, and the method "pay-as-you-go."

He muttered, "Maggie is yours."

With a wicked smirk, Crispin said, "Maggie is everyone's. That's rather the point."

"Everyone's except mine. And Jasper's."

"Oh, right." He looked at Reginald sideways. "I'd forgotten. Our unwritten, unstated rule."

Reginald felt his blood run down to his toes. Crispin was surely not saying what it sounded like. He had not let his attraction to Georgiana become obvious.

"If you must know, I spent the night in the library, working on the damned accounts."

"If they are in that much of a state, leave them for Benjamin. That's what Jasper will be paying him for."

"Believe me, at this point, I would like nothing better than to dump the whole mess into Benjamin's lap."

Crispin pulled a small cloth bag from his pocket, pulled open the drawstring, and plucked out a couple of nuts. "Why don't you?" He tossed them into his mouth.

Reginald hesitated. He couldn't involve Crispin. He shrugged. "I will. But there are a few stray bits missing and I don't want Benjamin thinking I did a half-arsed job."

Crispin snickered and munched a few more nuts. "You've never been half-arsed in your life." He looked up. "You're more of a whole arse."

Reginald stood and went to his dresser. The water in his washbowl looked filmy. Yesterday's wash water. Barclay needed a talking to.

"Did you come to wake me up for a reason?"

"No reason."

"May I ask you then, to get the hell out?"

Crispin grinned at him. Then asked, "What's missing?"

"What?'

"From the receipts? What's missing?"

"I don't know. If I did, it wouldn't be missing." He downplayed it more. "I warned Jasper I was likely to stumble onto his gambling debts."

Crispin laughed. Then said, "But that would have come out of his allowance. Bradwell wouldn't have bothered itemizing the trifling bits that we spent. Can you imagine?"

"Hmm." The devil. The allowances. By now, Georgiana would have discovered how much he was worth. How much smaller could he possibly be made to feel? His allowance was not insubstantial, but to a duke's daughter, it would appear paltry.

"Well," Crispin said, "I suppose it wouldn't be so bad for you. Item one: books. Item two: coffee. Item three: books."

Reginald pushed back. "You forget. Item four: opera singer."

"Yes, but Bradwell would have said, 'Good show, lad. About time.'"

"Ha, ha. As you leave, can you find a footman to send Barclay up?"

Crispin put the bag of nuts back into his pocket. "I suppose I need to be direct. Though it goes against the grain. Are you all right, Reg?"

"All right? Why wouldn't I be?"

"For one thing, look at you. For another, you slept away the entire day."

"Was it charades or whist?"

Crispin blinked. Then he said, "All right. I'll give you a pass on the hiding and pretending to sleep. But the third thing is Mr. Tibury."

"Oh, for God's sake." He had forgotten about Mr. Tibury. "That bothers me about as much as Plodgett does."

"It bothered me. And it bothered Jasper. And not only because Father didn't consult him. It was unfair of Father not to have mentioned something to you."

"If anything, I give Father credit for knowing that I wouldn't care. And stop looking at me like I am a dissection specimen. I'm telling the truth."

Crispin stopped inspecting him and turned to studying his own hands. "If we're being truthful, I give him credit too. I was a little concerned that he may not be in his right senses. That happens with apoplexy, you know. I worried that he'd been bamboozled. But he was sound asleep when I went to sit with him last night, so I went through his correspondence."

"How contemptible of you."

"I found Tibury's references, and they are not only legitimate but strong. Very strong. I suppose you could say that it gave me some satisfaction to be proud of the old dog. I suspect, sick as he is, he considered the matter very carefully and concluded Tibury was the best man."

"Thank you?"

"Well, face it, Reg. You've never expressed any actual interest in the church. Maybe theology as a concept, but not service to the church. I'm not saying you would not be a fine clergyman if you put your mind to it. You could do anything you set your mind to." He smiled. "Except soldiering, of course."

Reginald felt moved by his brother's concern. "I don't want to be a clergyman. That's the truth of it. But I've never had the courage to tell the Earl I don't."

"An awkward and largely unnecessary conversation. But he's still of sound mind. You could still talk to him."

Reginald shrugged. Crispin had always been tighter with Father than he was, except for that one horrific row, which had blown over quickly enough. Crispin didn't avoid awkward conversations—he barreled right in.

"Maybe. Though it will sound pettish to tell him I don't care what he gave to Tibury because I didn't want it anyway." He picked up his wrinkled jacket from the floor and winced. "Barclay will also believe I was out on a drunk." He threw it onto a chair and turned back to his brother. "Crispin, I am going to piss now. So unless—"

"I'm an officer in the King's Army. Pissing men don't faze me. Unless you plan to aim for my boots."

"I won't miss."

Crispin hopped up. "Don't be late for tea. Jasper is convinced you're sulking and if he scolds you publicly, I'll have to find another apple."

CHAPTER NINETEEN

GEORGIANA MADE DESULTORY conversation in the ladies' parlor where they all, even Jeffrey, awaited Reginald before tea was served. When he entered the room, apologizing to Lady Iversley for his tardiness, Georgiana's spirits lifted. Then they plummeted because her heart should not be beating faster at the mere sight of him.

He looked better. Not *better* exactly, but rested. His nascent beard was gone. His hair had been tamed. And he wore a neckcloth with a particularly high knot as if to make up for his earlier dishevelment.

She imagined she might distinguish among the lords of Iversley just by their clothes.

Jasper dressed to perfection. He had a bit of the Beau Brummel about him. His attire was of the most recent fashion but without any of its flamboyance. His tailoring was exquisite but not fussy. His collar was bleached and starched, but the points were not so high as to pierce his earlobes. His boots were kept shined to a gloss, but he did not embellish them with tassels or extra buckles. He wore one ring, not more. There was nothing ostentatious about him, yet he would gather all eyes in a ballroom.

Crispin was a military man. Whether in uniform or civilian clothes, his appearance was that of an officer, though she could not say what it was exactly about him. But the man carried bandages and spirits along on a hunting frolic, one safe enough to include ladies, on family property. That was Crispin.

And Reginald? He effaced himself. He dressed carefully, not to stand out but to blend in. Georgiana would wager he didn't even realize that that was what he did.

Teatime conversation centered on arrangements to attend church the following day. If it rained, they would take the carriage. If the weather was fair, they would walk. How far was the walk? Oh, not so very. Three-quarters of an hour. A little laugh—the boys could do it in half that.

Georgiana could scarcely bear it. She and Reginald avoided looking at one another so assiduously that she was certain everyone must notice their efforts. But no. They droned on.

Then the decision was made to walk in the garden. The rain had ceased. The evening was pleasant. The late-fall blossoms, so ephemeral, must be enjoyed. Lady Iversley shooed the young folks outside. She was going to sit with the Earl. Mama was going to her chamber to write home.

On the way out the door, they collected their wraps. Reginald happened to pick up hers, and he draped it over her shoulders.

"Anything?" he murmured.

"Not yet." She had discovered quite a bit, but nothing pertaining to the matter, except that it did appear nothing had been amiss in his grandfather's time. She knew that Reginald's allowance was one-fifth of Jasper's. Crispin's had been too, but ceased temporarily when he went into the army, then, after a few months, he was allotted just fifty pounds per year. That was typical enough for young men whose fathers had means to supplement their soldiers' pay, though it seemed a miserly sum in this case. Moreover, as far as she could see, no commission had been purchased. Which made no sense. Earls' sons did not enlist. And enlisted men rarely ever rose to an officer's rank. But none of this was any of her business. "I need that plot summary."

His lips twitched. "Olivia?"

"Found me after only two hours." She'd had to put her hands over her ears and command Olivia not to say anything until she had finished reading the novel. It was too, too engrossing and she didn't want even one twist of the plot to be spoiled.

Reginald moved away from her. She stepped closer to Olivia and Alice, but Jasper swooped down and claimed her arm.

The garden was remarkable. The fragrance alone would have made the walk worthwhile. The paths swirled and crossed one another. Little fountains appeared in niches. Although there were few blossoms, the pruned bushes were flourishing. But, as the others moved along one of the wider paths, Jasper stalled, then took her down another.

Please, no. Not yet.

He pointed out a supposedly rare flower from Belgium and said there was a cherubic statue with Olivia's face that she would enjoy seeing. The voices of the others grew more distant.

She would simply tell him no. She didn't owe him a reason. Not even after she'd agreed to come here. She had not committed to anything. And as for ton talk—surely out of sight was out of mind. For Heaven's sake. Refusing a man was not difficult. She had done it sixteen times her first Season! All she need do was give him a gentle but brook-no-argument "No."

"I suppose," he said, speaking low, "you have been wondering who Mr. Tibury is."

"Who?" She laughed with nervous relief. "Oh, no. Well, no. It isn't any of my concern."

"It's no scandalous family secret." He smiled his ingratiating smile. "He is the curate in one of the towns a few miles away. The Earl has the disposal of a few livings and two of them are likely to become available within the next couple of years. Perhaps sooner if Mr. Codworthy wishes to step aside. Anyway, some of Mr. Tibury's friends wrote to the Earl advocating for him. And the Earl summoned him to offer him the livings and his congratulations."

"Oh." That was an anticlimax. "Odd that he seemed so

peeved to be here."

Jasper chuckled. "In the poor fellow's defense, he *was* summoned, he came all that distance, and Peters nearly turned him away at the door." He shook his head. "If Father had only warned us of Mr. Tibury's coming, he'd have received a better reception, I assure you."

"Oh, but you can't fault the Earl."

"Of course not." Jasper paused and nudged her arm so that she would face him. "You are looking especially lovely today. But then, you look especially lovely every day."

"I think that is definitionally impossible."

He moved closer. She stepped back. But there was a rose bush right behind her. With thorns. She flinched from it. He put his hand on her back as if to rescue her from the roses. And kissed her.

Her response was immediate. She slapped him furiously and shoved him away. It was the most horrible, the most humiliating, the most ruinous thing ever to happen to her. If she were not so angry, she would burst into tears.

With his hand on his cheek, which bore a reddened mark from her palm, he looked as mortified as she felt.

"I beg your pardon," he said stiffly. He rubbed his cheek once, then dropped his hand. "I didn't mean to take advantage. I thought a kiss would not be unwelcome."

Well, obviously, he'd thought wrong! She didn't need to reprimand him further. The slap had taken care of that. "We should rejoin the others."

"All right." He gestured for her to proceed. He followed. As they neared the main path, he offered her his arm and said, "Please?"

They could not storm back from a private meander crab-faced and at odds. It would make what had happened obvious to everyone. At least her slap mark had faded. Not gone, but it was not an obvious handprint. She hadn't meant to hit him that hard. She took his arm.

"I am sorry," he murmured.

"Yes," she said, because she could not think of a suitable reply, but wanted him to know that she had heard.

Maybe that would be the end of it. Surely he would not ask for her now. Mama would be disappointed, but Georgiana would be relieved.

REGINALD GRITTED HIS teeth and took his place at the table. Because tea had been substantial, dinner would be light and informal. Mother said she was remaining upstairs with Father. However, there were still eight at the table because Jeffrey had joined them. Adam would be supping with Jeremy. No one pointed out that that was odd.

Reginald would rather be anywhere but here. It seemed a preview of the rest of his life, sitting "below the salt," with Jasper as head of the household and Georgiana at his side.

The garden walk had been bad enough. Reginald would have given his right arm to be the one leading Georgiana off alone to stroll along quiet paths. Jasper had acquired that right, somehow, over the course of a week, while the best Reginald could hope for was an hour or two squirreled away in the library with a pile of dusty ledgers forming a wall between them, door wide open. And even *that* was not strictly permissible.

No! It was not permissible at all! Involving Georgiana in the task Jasper had assigned to *him*, displaying the family's crooked books—good God. What had he been thinking?

Thankfully, he had no opportunity to sulk and stare. He was seated beside Olivia, who had him on one side and Jeffrey on the other. The misadventure must have knocked sense into the boy, because he now was shy and embarrassed around her, rather than slavish and show-offy. Reginald thought it a sad state of affairs when the flow of light dinner conversation depended upon him.

Even tasking himself with this, he could not rein in his too-frequent glances at Georgiana. She spoke more to Crispin than to Jasper, but that could be because Crispin, eating so little, talked so much. If Reginald didn't know better, he would say Jasper was brooding, but Jasper didn't brood.

After the last course was served and tasted, Jasper sent the ladies off, suggested Jeffrey go relieve Adam, and asked his brothers to join him in the study. When Reginald waved off a glass of brandy, Jasper did not pour himself one either. He sat glumly in his chair.

Crispin sat. Reginald followed suit.

"What's wrong?" Crispin asked.

"What's right?" Jasper replied.

"That bad? Has this sulk anything to do with the imprint your cheek acquired during your little detour?"

"Imprint?" Reginald asked. He hadn't a clue what his brothers were saying.

"She slapped him."

"Slapped him?"

"Stop echoing me!" Crispin laughed. "Yes, you dolt. Why do you think Jasper has been acting like a whipped dog since we left the garden?"

"What did you do?" Reginald demanded, whirling to face Jasper. He started to rise from his seat, but Crispin pressed a hand on his leg.

Jasper said, "It was stupid. I rushed things. She's a lady, and painfully innocent, and I tried stealing a kiss." He huffed. "You'd think I'd torn a button off her bodice."

It took every ounce of reserve not to draw Jasper's cork. Reginald didn't trust himself to speak. He didn't dare move, he was so furious.

Jasper said, "This is farcical. I'm not terrifying. She didn't have to hit me."

"Never been slapped before?" Crispin teased.

"Of course not." He put his elbows on the desk, scowling,

then said, "I wasn't anticipating a slap this time."

"Why did you rush?" Crispin asked. "It's only been a week. Or were you overcome with longing?"

"Ballocks." He shook his head. "The devil of it is, I think I've set this courtship back weeks. I'm going to have to walk on eggshells."

"Again, Jasper, why the rush?" Crispin pressed. "You never—"

"And that's the problem. I never. I acted as though I had all the time in the world. And now Father is dying."

"Father is. But you are young and hale."

"Did you not see Jeremy take that fall? My God. I thought he'd snapped his neck. That could be me."

"You don't ride like a bacon-brain."

"My horse could step in a hole. I could fall down the stairs."

"You could, but the odds are slim."

"Crispin," Jasper sounded impatient. "Who is my heir?"

Crispin's face went slack. When he spoke again, his voice was weak. "I see." Then he wrung out a wry smile and managed to inject a bit of his usual irony. "Well, then, it would be best if you were to acquire at least two sons before the year's end. Because, in the event, I would immediately take a bullet and leave poor Reginald in charge."

"You are both being absurd," Reginald managed.

"Quite so," Crispin agreed. "Jasper, you did not maul Georgiana in an effort to secure the succession."

"I did not maul Georgiana full stop. I don't believe I even kissed her. Her reflexes are faster than Gentleman Jack's."

Crispin laughed. "Good for her. Now, Jasper, be honest. Why are you going about this so ham-handedly? Could you not have waited...a month to court her back in London?"

"No, I could not. I didn't want to risk her accepting someone else. I want her for my countess. She's perfect."

Reginald pressed his fists against his thighs. He couldn't listen to this.

"Perfect as a countess?" Crispin pressed. "Or perfect as your wife?"

"Perfect full stop."

"I can't argue with you." Crispin turned. "Reginald? Anything to say?"

God! He ground out, "You've made her your captive. She can't accept anyone else."

"Except she is not my captive. There is no set date for their departure. They might leave any day. And as yet, we have no firm understanding."

"You have *no* understanding," Crispin said. "I thought she was here as Olivia's guest."

Jasper stood and began to pace. "That was a flimsy pretext, and you know it. You and everyone else." Then he returned to the desk, opened the top drawer, and pulled out a folder. He flipped it open to reveal a stack of letters. He picked up the first and closed the folder.

"From Hazard." He handed it to Crispin. "Skip the hellos. It's the second paragraph."

Crispin glanced down, frowned, then read aloud:

'You know, my dear friend, that I am not known to gamble excessively, but I am not morally opposed to the practice. If I can beat the odds in a wager, I'm sure you agree it would be foolish not to seek advantage where I can.'

"What is he going on about?" Reginald grumbled.

Crispin continued, "Here is the crux:

'It is being said that the banns will be read before Christmas. Wagers at White's are now running sixteen to one. If you would be so good to announce AFTER the holy day, I would be ever so grateful. Please respond quickly. If the odds go any higher, I will likely lay down a pony whether you reply or not. Keep that in mind. Give my love to Lady Georgiana.'"

"What a blackguard!"

"Not at all," Jasper said. "It is simply his way of letting me know where things stand. Georgiana and I are the talk of the ton.

It isn't so much a matter of why am I rushing, it's what are we waiting for? We are going to be betrothed. We are going to marry. Taking baby steps is…" He sniffed. "Well, but if that is what Georgiana wants, of course, I'll step slowly."

And, of course, Reginald would step away.

CHAPTER TWENTY

THE FOLLOWING MORNING, it rained. They rode to church in two carriages—the Taverston siblings in one, Lady Iversley and their guests in another. Georgiana sat facing the Countess, a froth of skirts, reticules, umbrellas, and lap blankets surrounding them.

"Is everything all right, Lady Iversley?" she asked, deciding it was impossible and a little unkind to ignore the lady's red nose and swollen eyes.

"Oh, dear child, I'm afraid no. It is not."

Mama, beside her, patted her hand.

Lady Iversley said, "The Earl took a turn last night. He has been coughing quite a bit and last night he became feverish. We had Dr. Haraldsen come in the middle of the night."

"I'm so sorry."

"I didn't want to leave him this morning, but Reginald said prayer would be best for the Earl and that going to church would be best for me. I suppose he's right. Crispin asked Adam to sit with him. I don't know why but the Earl likes that man."

Mama said, "You're very fortunate in your children."

"Yes, I am." She added with an attempted smile, "I just hope the boys don't fall asleep in church. They were up all night."

There was nothing else to be said. But it reminded Georgiana that the reason she had been asked to come to Chaumbers in the first place was because the Earl was ill. Dying. How could the Taverstons bear it? If Father were dying… No. She couldn't even think of it. And how would Mama survive the heartbreak? Lady Iversley was so brave.

They all were. Oh, maybe she should excuse Lord Taverston his false step. He'd assumed they were practically betrothed. How could he have known she had fallen in love with his brother?

They completed the journey in silence.

The carriages were brought up to the front of the church and they hurried inside, trying to avoid the rain. Although small, it was a well-proportioned building, clearly not designed in the style of Chaumbers. No visible depredations had been visited upon it over the centuries. It even retained its stained-glass windows.

The Taverstons took their seats in the family pew. For a moment, it seemed that Georgiana was going to be ushered in beside Jasper, but that would crowd them all and likely displace either Olivia or Reginald, so she pretended not to see the way they were shuffling about. Instead, she followed her mother and Alice into the pew behind—where she could readily study the Taverstons. She hoped the rest of the congregation was not studying her.

The Taverstons did not fall asleep, despite the best efforts of Mr. Brindle, the rector, to lull them. He spoke in a quiet monotone, with a message so uninspiring she wondered if he had composed it over his breakfast that morning. Much more interesting was the fact that Reginald had pulled a pair of spectacles from his waistcoat and wore them during the sermon, then deposited them back into his pocket when Mr. Brindle was done. She hadn't realized he was nearsighted. And how like him to suffer the indignity of wearing spectacles rather than squinting and pretending he could see just fine.

When the service ended, the Countess was obliged to accept the good wishes and concern of her fellow parishioners, but no one attempted to keep her for long. The ladies returned quickly to their carriage. On the other hand, Lord Taverston *was* being detained.

Lady Iversley sighed. "I'll have luncheon delayed. Poor Jasper. Everyone is in such a hurry to curry his favor." She grimaced. "No, that's unkind of me. I should not have said that."

But it was the truth.

Lady Iversley smoothed her dress and shifted in her seat. "Lady Georgiana, I think that while we are waiting for the boys and Olivia to return, I will take you and Miss Fogbotham to see the Earl. If you are amenable."

"Of course," Georgiana said. Alice paled. Poor Alice; ever since her mother died, she'd had a horror of sickrooms, but she couldn't possibly decline.

"He wants very much to meet you. We'd hoped to wait until he was feeling more himself. He doesn't like to be seen when he's so ill…" Her voice trailed off.

Before the Earl died, he wanted to approve his son's choice. Georgiana had believed being kissed by Reginald's brother was the worst experience, but this was far worse. What if the Earl assumed the courtship had progressed to an understanding? What if he said something leading, something about her becoming part of the family? How should she respond?

After arriving at the house, they didn't even pause to change clothes but went directly to the Earl's chamber. Georgiana and Alice waited in the corridor with Mama while Lady Iversley entered the room. It was a long wait.

After what seemed half an hour, the door opened, and Crispin's valet emerged. He gave them a small bow before slipping silently past. He was more than simply a valet, obviously, but why Crispin had some sort of medical man posing as his valet was beyond her. A delicate digestion was hardly cause for traveling with a personal physician.

The nurse opened the door and Lady Iversley invited them in. The Earl was in bed, sitting up, or rather, propped up with pillows. He was not the same handsome gentleman she had seen in the portrait gallery, or that she vaguely recollected from her childhood. This was a shrunken, elderly man who looked deathly ill. One side of his face sagged, and he wore an eyepatch. A sour odor of sickness permeated the room. She steeled herself not to react and hoped Alice was able to do the same. Lady Iversley beckoned them closer.

"This is Lady Georgiana," she said. "Lady Georgiana, the Earl of Iversley."

Georgiana approached the bedside and curtsied, head down. She murmured, "Good day, my lord."

His unpatched eye watered. He rasped, "Rare beauty." At least, that was what she thought he said. She prayed it wasn't something Jasper had said to him. She didn't want to picture Jasper describing her as his future wife.

"And this is Miss Fogbotham," Lady Iversley said, nudging a reluctant Alice closer.

"My lord," Alice gulped with a nod of her head, then stepped quickly back.

Georgiana realized she needn't fear an interview. The Earl was in no position to ask questions. And this was the Taverstons' *father*. It made her want to weep.

Lady Iversley said, "We've just come from church. The children will be returning soon."

"Brindle."

"Yes," she said. "Mr. Brindle gave the sermon."

The Earl tried to say something else but coughed. The cough turned into a fit. Lady Iversley rubbed and patted his shoulder while he attempted to regain his breath.

Mama said, "The girls and I will leave you for now."

"Yes," Lady Iversley said. "That's best. I think the Earl should sleep for a while."

THE DAY GREW even drearier. The carriage returned with all the siblings except Jasper, whose presence was required at some meeting or other with one of the local farmers. The rest filed into the dining room, bedraggled and tired.

Lady Iversley had absent-mindedly ordered a cold buffet to be served: assorted meats, cheeses, breads, and pickles. Georgiana saw a fleeting look of dismay on Crispin's face. His hand hovered a moment over the cheeses before he recovered and put only a small pile of pickles on his plate.

Table conversation suffered as they tried ignoring the Earl's decline and the miserable weather. Lady Iversley grumbled about the church service. Although the prayers and hymns were comforting, she could not make heads nor tales out of Mr. Brindle's sermon. That unleashed several minutes of unenthusiastic speculation and half-hearted argument until Reginald gave a succinct and meaningful summary of what the man had been *trying* to say—which was, boiled down, simply that separation from God was painful, and could be avoided through the renunciation of sin.

Georgiana was floored, though Crispin and Olivia merely smirked.

"Well, why didn't he just say so," Lady Iversley said, miffed. "Instead of muddling about."

"He should have used Malachi for his text instead of Job. Malachi is more direct. Job is always a muddle."

Reginald's offhand remark made Crispin snort and mutter, "Oh, yes, well, Malachi."

The conversation shifted to things the villagers had said and potential activities for the morrow. The meal did not last long. Afterward, everyone parted either to rest or to visit with the Earl if he was awake. Georgiana slipped off to the library.

The Principles of Analytical Calculation called to her, much as the ancient Greek manuscript must call to Reginald. But, like him, she wouldn't let herself be distracted. She had work to do. Propping *The Italian* on the edge of the desk, then closing the curtain halfway, she arranged the ledgers in the order she had decided upon and opened the one on the top.

She spent an hour checking figures and noted a few oddities. Was Cambridge tuition truly nearly twice that of Oxford? And what was this 'Binnings property' purchased four years ago? But she was just being nosy. She was supposed to be looking for what was missing, not what was there. And then she heard footsteps and the door to the library opened wider. Georgiana shoved the ledgers aside and stuck her nose in the novel.

"What do you think of Father Schedoni?" It was Reginald. Georgiana set down the book.

"What should I think? What does Olivia think?"

He came into the room. "It's chilly in here. You should have had someone light the brazier."

"I honestly didn't notice." She had felt damp rather than cold.

He went to drag the second chair closer to the desk, close to her. He sat down. Now she felt warm.

"Have you found anything?"

"Maybe. Nothing I can make anything of." She tapped her finger on the table, then asked, "Do you keep—you and your brothers—keep your own accounts?"

"I do." For a moment, he looked awkward. Then he shrugged and said, "Mine aren't very complicated. I couldn't speak for Crispin or Jasper. Why?"

"Would your father have kept his own? Before he became Earl?"

"If he did, I don't know where the books would be. Why do you want to know? What are you thinking?"

"Nothing yet. It was just a thought, but it doesn't matter." If it was the Earl hiding something, rather than Bradwell embezzling, she might find a clue if he'd once kept his own books.

Reginald peered at her curiously but didn't press her further. He picked up the novel and said, "If you'll give me a sheet or two of paper from that pile and lend me back my pen, I'll write out that summary."

She passed him the paper and pen.

"How is your father?"

"Sleeping. Some draught Dr. Haraldsen gave him to stop the cough and put him to sleep. I'd rather..." he paused. "I'd rather think about something else."

She nodded. Quietly they both set to their tasks, Reginald scribbling away, Georgiana running her finger down long columns of numbers, tallying them in her head.

She hadn't been mistaken about there being oddities. In three of the years that she'd now checked—these evenly spaced across the years of the Earl's rule—there was not only a discrepancy of thirty pounds per quarter, but there was an additional sum missing in the second quarter of each year, averaging about five pounds. The disturbing thing about this was that Georgiana had also checked the first five years after the Earl had ascended to the title. For the first four years, the numbers added up correctly, but there was a regular item listed as *L.C. gift* in the second quarter of the first three years that was in the range of five pounds, and in the fourth year there was a *C.B. gift*. Beginning with the fifth year, no second quarter "gift" was listed. There was no entry, but the money nevertheless disappeared.

Correlating with this, the Earl and Lady Iversley were married when the Earl was thirty-four. The following year, the annual Christmas balls began. That required a regular large outflow of just under one hundred pounds per year. This was easy to segregate out because each year—so far as she had checked—there were several lines of expenses, grouped together, in a fine, feminine hand: musicians, extra servants, food and wine, winter bouquets. These were tallied separately in the same lady's hand. Georgiana could only assume that Lady Iversley took control of the ball from planning to execution. Reginald had said that ladies kept accounts. Perhaps he had been thinking of this in particular.

Well, it meant nothing yet. Except that there were no discrepancies—the numbers all added up—until the year of the first Christmas ball.

Georgiana paused, staring at the page, trying to think what it could mean. Her right hand lay lightly on the opened ledger, marking her place; her left was beside the book. She knew, without turning her head, that Reginald, too, had stopped to ponder. He set down the pen, then rested his hand, slightly curled, on the table a hair's breadth from her own. They both sat still, intentionally motionless, very aware of one another.

Then his little finger straightened and touched hers.

Her breath caught. Was it accidental or on purpose? They were not gloved and a current of warmth seemed to flow between them. She didn't dare move, fearing to break the connection. Every thought in her head, every conjecture, every calculation dissolved into nothingness. There was only this moment. She didn't want it ever to end.

Very gently, very slowly, his pinky caressed hers.

Georgiana felt a bolt of pure bliss.

What she was feeling, he must be feeling too.

He pulled his hand away and rose from his chair. She could tell nothing from his expression. He stepped away, to the smaller niche, and gazed out the window into the rain. After a moment, he cleared his throat.

"I didn't give away the ending. In case you do wish to read it."

Olivia picked up the summary he'd written. His handwriting was clear and bold. But it was peppered with heavy underlining and numerous, sometimes tripled, exclamation marks. After reading a few lines, she laughed. She feared her laughter was a little shaky, but she pretended it wasn't.

"I can hear Olivia's voice in my head."

He turned and smiled, but the smile looked more sad than amused.

"She'll do most of the talking. You only have to agree with whatever she says."

"Safer than challenging her, I suppose."

And then they were quiet. Awkwardly so. Until he said,

"Have you any more questions? About my family, I mean?"

"Maybe." She hesitated, then asked, "Do you know anyone with the initials L.C. or C.B?"

His brow wrinkled. Then he rubbed his nose and said, "Not that spring to mind. Why?"

"Probably nothing. I'm going to have to keep digging."

"I'm sorry to put you through this." His head drooped and he turned back to the window, one hand brushing back the curtain as if for a better view. "I never should have asked. It seems now…I don't know. Unimportant. Unless—"

"Unless?"

"Unless there are payments that should still be made. A creditor. Maybe, well, it's possible I suppose that the Earl made a bad investment. Do you see?" He spoke to his own reflection in the glass. "And he's been paying it off. But Bradwell became ill, and the payments stopped."

"Surely then there would be notices of some sort."

Georgiana heard Reginald sniff, and, from behind, saw him shrug.

"I don't suppose you could be concerned about blackmail," she said, mostly joking but about five percent concerned.

He turned slowly around to face her again. "Blackmail?" He looked faintly amused. "The Earl?"

"I don't know!" She smiled ruefully. "I'm reaching. But I feel as though I might be close."

He laughed. "Not if you're thinking of blackmail!" She couldn't tell if he was diverted or frustrated or annoyed.

"Give me a few more hours," she urged. She really did feel she was close. "I'll have a better theory. If you're worried there are outstanding bills that are hidden, I'll look more closely at the most recent five years. Maybe I'll see something there."

He chewed his lip, then shook out the folds of the curtain beside him. "Can I do anything to help?"

"No. I need to concen—" She halted. The word would be a confession of how distracting she found him. "Concentrate," she finished quietly.

He flushed. Then they both looked away.

"Well," he said, "then I suppose I will see you at tea."

CHAPTER TWENTY-ONE

THE DAY COULD not get any drearier. When Georgiana decided, by the clock on the wall, that it must be nearing teatime, she took herself to the ladies' parlor, hungry, tired, and hoping to find Reginald there. He was not. She was the first to arrive. She settled on the davenport, close to the fire, watching the flickering tongues behind the grate.

Finally, she had something to report. And she wanted very badly to give him good news. The discrepancies had ceased to occur about three to three-and-a-half years ago. It was impossible, of course, to be sure of anything in the last eight months; Reginald had only entered the bills and receipts he was given. But those were now tidied and tabulated, and he could, if he wished, hand those books over to the new steward without being embarrassed by them. If this new steward were to look back over the last three years, he would find nothing amiss.

She had learned something else, but it was not worth reporting. At least, she didn't think it was. In the earlier books, the servants were listed individually by name rather than by job performed. Later, they were lumped into categories and only the highest-ranking servants were named.

One early name had jumped out at her. Lucy Carter. There was no one with the initials C.B. After three years, Lucy disappeared and instead, C.B. appeared, no name, just initials, but only for a year. Just like the "gifts." Georgiana had no idea what it all meant, if anything. She was afraid Reginald would think she was mad, poring over the servants' entries. Servants came and went in large households. Likely that was why Bradwell gave up keeping track of them.

Yet something about it bothered her.

So. Did Reginald want her to keep looking? Perhaps he would rather remain ignorant of what they might find. Blackmail and bribery had been ironic hypotheticals. But what could the true explanation be? And did it matter? Reginald said it seemed unimportant now. Maybe it was.

Not Reginald but rather Crispin came striding into the room. His hair was damp and there was mud on his boots. He stripped off his gloves, warmed his hands before the fire, and then sprawled down next to her, laying soggy gloves on the arm of the davenport.

"Good afternoon," she said, aware that her voice held a note of disapproval. "You are wet."

He grinned at her. "I took my chances with the weather, but it didn't work. Here you still are. Where is everyone else?"

"I don't know. But you needn't worry. I won't ask any impertinent questions."

His eyebrows flew up. "Are you referring to the thing to which you are not allowed to refer?" His indignation seemed more mocking than sincere, but she was not in the mood for teasing, so she made no answer. He sat up straighter and drew his knees together. "I have found that drilling my men in foul weather is better for morale than letting them huddle in the wet, complaining. It works for officers as well."

That was an interesting insight into Crispin's character. The man had more layers than an onion. "Are you a hard taskmaster?"

"Yes." He drummed his hands restlessly on his knees. "After tea, I will march you all out into the rain."

"Even Jasper?" she asked, smiling now, because she was teasing even if he was not. "Does he take orders from you?"

"Jasper has not yet returned. I went out to the stables to sing to my horse—"

"To what?"

"Mercury is high-strung. He doesn't like heavy rain. While I was there, I saw that one of the grooms had taken a horse into the village for Jasper to ride back. The horse is still gone."

Georgiana shook her head. "Will you march us all out to the stables to sing after tea?"

Now a smile did spread over his face. "Mercury would love to hear you sing. Will you?"

"I can never tell if you are joking."

"It takes practice. But I think not the stables. I think we should all go out to the folly. It was built to mimic the ruins of an abbey. Rain improves the atmosphere of decay."

"Still can't tell." She was never bored talking with *him*. Probably because he was not courting her.

"The last bit was all serious. Except that Mother would not approve of such an outing, so I don't really think we should go. Now, you tell me: how did you spend this wearisome afternoon?"

"Reading." That was close to the truth.

"Ah, did you? You found something worthwhile in our library?" His nose wrinkled skeptically. But she had a sudden idea.

"No, it was a book I'd brought from home. A novel." She blinked and looked down at her hands. She hoped she was blushing at least a little. She meant to appear a little silly and embarrassed to be so. "I'm...to be honest, I'm a little lost."

"I think authors do that intentionally."

"But maybe you can help." She went on quickly before she lost her nerve. If he knew anything about the old servants, perhaps she could surprise an answer from him. "There is a rather shadowy figure in the novel. The men refer to her only by her initials: C.B.. Do those initials mean anything to you?"

He bit his cheek. A gleam came into his eyes. "I suspect they are referring to Miss Blanche."

"Miss Blanche?"

"*Carte* Blanche."

Her expression, once she caught his meaning, must have been appalled because he burst out laughing. "Good Lord, Georgiana. What kind of books does the Duchess allow you to read?"

"I'm sure that's not it," she said, her heated blush scalding now. But she was sure it was. C.B. was the Earl's mistress. Lucy Carter may have been so as well. Or they were one and the same. Her heart sank. When the Earl and Lady Iversley married, Bradwell hid Lucy's name, and then—*Good Heavens!* Oh, she was too, too certain. Because when Lady Iversley began putting her own entries into the account books, all evidence of C.B. disappeared. Lest the Countess stumble upon it.

Oh. Her heart sank even further. The payments had continued.

She needed to have another look at the books. Had they been continuous throughout the Earl's marriage? Could there have been more than one woman?

Did anyone besides Bradwell know?

"Georgiana, I am so sorry." Crispin sounded concerned. "I didn't mean to embarrass you. What an oaf I am! Certainly, that is not what the initials mean in your novel. That is too scandalous. Please forgive me."

"You needn't apologize." Her voice wavered. "There is assuredly another explanation in my book. But I'm not so priggish that you embarrassed me."

"I didn't mean that you are priggish. Only innocent."

"Let us change the subject, if you please."

She had gone from hot to chilled to hot again. She stood and moved away from the fire, unable to bear Crispin's gaze. She wracked her brain for something to divert him. Suddenly, she recalled what Alice had said, and she turned back to look at him. "Is your valet a spy?" She forced a wry smile. "Alice thinks so."

"Does she?" One eyebrow rose. Then fell. He cleared his throat, accepting the abrupt change in topic. "She's in good company. But he is not."

"Excuse me?" Now *she* was diverted.

"Not a spy. Merely a do-gooder who likes patching up bleeding men, no matter their nationality."

"You don't mean…Frenchmen?" *Napoleon's soldiers?*

At that moment, Reginald and Olivia entered the parlor and Crispin stood up. Olivia had been crying. Reginald merely looked morose.

"Were you with Father?" Crispin asked.

Reginald nodded. "He isn't any worse. Just no better. He's going to crack a rib with that cough."

Crispin muttered, "I hate that he's suffering."

"Mother is not coming down for tea. She suggested we go ahead and ring for it. Olivia can pour. Alice and the Duchess are on their way down." Poor Reginald was forcing the words from his mouth. Georgiana made up her mind. She would not tell him anything except that the most recent three years were sound. Even if her suspicions were right, they were not important now.

TEA HAD BEEN dismal. Dinner, with Jasper returned, was even worse. Georgiana thought he looked worn down. He was grim and barely communicative. He did make one announcement, which was that Dr. Haraldsen would be around later in the evening, not only to check on the Earl but also to see if it was feasible to have Jeremy and Jeffrey removed to their home in the morning. If so, he asked Crispin to escort them. He could, if he wished, take Adam along.

It was not tactfully stated, sounding less like a request than a command. Georgiana half expected a snide reply from Crispin, but he merely nodded and answered: *of course.*

After dinner, the Taverstons all slunk away. Mama shepherded Georgiana and Alice into the ladies' parlor to sit with their embroidery and not bother anyone. Georgiana only did needlework for show and had been embroidering the same pillow slip for two years. But she had no heart to return to the library to confirm her suspicions. In fact, she'd had another inkling of something even worse and truly did not want to know.

They settled into the parlor's armchairs and one of the maid-servants lit the lamps for them. Embers still glowed in the fireplace, so Mama told the girl she needn't rebuild the fire. Then they were alone.

At first, while they sewed, Mama read excerpts from a letter she'd received from Charles. Alice made appropriate noises in response, but Georgiana barely listened. Her brother was a dutiful but unenthusiastic correspondent. He listed for Mama and Father his recent activities, but not whether he enjoyed them. He named what he was studying but gave no indication of what caught his interest and what did not. It bothered Mama, but Father always laughed and said men of Charles' age were naturally sparing with details when writing to their mothers.

Thinking of this now did not make Georgiana smile. Would Charles take a mistress? Had Father ever had one? She was certain he was faithful to Mama, but…

What about Jasper? Did he intend to follow in his father's footsteps? Would Crispin? She felt a sharp ache in her chest. Would Reginald?

Mama laid the letter down. She, too, looked tired, heavy-lidded, with frown lines around her mouth. There was even a smudge of ink on her fingers.

"I have been wondering," she said, "if we ought not to depart for home in the morning. Georgiana? How would you feel if we left the Taverstons to wait upon the Earl without having to worry about entertaining us? Especially with Christmas next week…'"

"I think that might be for the best," she answered, but the thought of leaving Reginald gave her a tight feeling in her throat.

"Is there anything I should know?" Mama peered at her close-ly. "Has Lord Taverston put anything into words? I know it has only been a few days, difficult days for the family, but you have spent some time with him. Has he…"

"He has not indicated that he will offer for me." Georgiana decided that the kiss and its aftermath had canceled each other out.

Her mother's brow furrowed with consternation. "He will, surely. But now I think it would have been better had we waited for him to return to London. It will be awkward for us to go back, with nothing having been said, and everyone at home assuming we've come to announce a betrothal."

"How can anyone assume that?" Georgiana exclaimed, annoyed.

"Dear, we all expect it. You two make a very handsome couple. And you do seem to enjoy one another's company."

"I enjoy Lieutenant Taverston's company," she said with a huff, avoiding Reginald's name. "Do you expect me to receive an offer from him as well?"

"Don't be rude, Georgiana." Then she softened. "And don't be concerned. There is no need for Lord Taverston to rush. I suppose I'm just fretting because they are sending the twins home. I expect the Earl will not linger much longer. And the timing is so poor." She grimaced. "That isn't what I mean, of course. It's only that Lord Taverston has so much on his mind right now. I don't think you should worry that he isn't interested."

"Mama, that is the least of my worries."

Her mother gave her an odd look. "What is that supposed to mean?"

"Nothing," she said quickly. Then, because she didn't want to continue giving the wrong impression about her own intentions, she said, "I'm just not certain I'd want to accept an offer if he made one."

Mama sighed with clear irritation. "Georgiana, we've had this discussion, haven't we? I'm sure Lord Taverston is not sweeping you off your feet, but if you can't make allowances for his situation, then I don't know what we're going to do."

Georgiana's eyes stung.

Alice interceded, her hesitation to do so evidenced by the strain in her voice. "Lord Taverston has been distracted, but even so, he shows a decided preference for Georgiana's company. I'm sure back in London..." Her words trailed off. Lord Taverston would not return to London until after his father's death.

Mama picked up her letter and stood, shaking out her skirts.

"I'm going up to bed. I don't think you two should remain up much longer either." She walked to the door and then turned. "Georgiana, I'm sorry. I know you were reluctant to come here and now, I think you were correct. I shouldn't have pushed you. I didn't know quite how sick the Earl was."

She waited, but Georgiana had no answer to make.

"Your father and I want you to be happy, to have a good life, and I do think Lord Taverston is the correct gentleman for you. I know—" She held up a hand to forestall any protest. "I know that you are not head over heels in love with him. But love will come."

She took a few steps back into the room and spoke more quietly. "Sometimes a girl may feel a rather instantaneous attraction for a gentleman, or even for more than one gentleman, before she...before she understands what she is feeling. That isn't necessarily love." She gave Georgiana a searching look, then continued. "I was always rather relieved that you seemed so sensible. We never worried you would run off with a stableboy. Or have your head turned by an inheritance chaser. But I hope you aren't dead set on...on a spark. Sometimes a girl needs to admire and care for a man first and then that special attraction will follow. Give it a chance."

A sob welled up in Georgiana's breast and she couldn't speak without bursting into tears. She *had* felt the spark. How was she to explain to her mother that she felt it not for Lord Taverston, but for his younger brother? She could not marry Jasper and spend the rest of her life as a sister to the man she loved with all her soul.

How could anyone believe she and Jasper made a perfect match? Could they not sense the invisible cord drawing her and Reginald together?

But would Reginald ask for her? When the whole world believed she had already promised herself to his brother, how could he? And what would Jasper think? Or do? She feared Reginald would not, could not, alienate his brother. And she should not want that!

She had felt the love in this family. In all this horrible mess, that was one comfortable, wonderful thing she had noted. The love. The brothers rallied one another. And they adored Olivia. They were good to their mother. They were devastated by their father's illness. These lords of Iversley shared a bond.

And here she had come to Chaumbers, landing like a cannonball in their midst. Was she to spring upon the family the devastating news that the Earl had been unfaithful to his wife throughout the whole of their marriage? And then, was she to tear apart the brothers?

"Why don't we wait and see what tomorrow brings," Mama said.

CHAPTER TWENTY-TWO

THE MORNING DAWNED clear and warmer than it had been. It promised to be a beautiful day. Reginald thought they sorely deserved one after yesterday's dreariness.

He was not early down to breakfast; he'd gone to bed late and slept like the dead. Jasper was seated in the breakfast parlor with a newspaper spread open before him. He looked more himself. The hollows beneath his eyes were less sunken. He must have gotten some sleep as well.

"Has anyone else been down?" Reginald asked, setting down his plate and sitting a few seats away so as to not crowd Jasper's paper.

"Crispin and Jeffrey. They've already gone to take Jeremy home. Dr. Haraldsen approved. I suspect the Squire will be glad to have them both back."

"I'm glad it was not any worse than it was."

Jasper grunted and bit into his toast. After a sip of coffee, he added, "Father was still sleeping when I peeked in. I think I woke Mother. She shouldn't sleep in that chair."

"I know. But I doubt she'll leave him even for a moment now."

Jasper shook his head. Then he let out a groan. "This is so difficult, Reg. I want one day not to have to think. I want to lie in bed and do nothing but stare at the ceiling for a full twenty-four hours."

"You've been shouldering the lion's share. But you know Crispin and I will help any way we can." The words sounded empty. He added, "If we can."

"Yesterday Crenshaw had the gall—the gall—to drag me all the way out to his farm, complaining all the while that Willie Jepson had stolen one of his piglets. I didn't need to see the damn pigs to know one was missing. We could have handled it there in the churchyard."

"Oh, the devil!" Reginald swore. "Is he still picking on that poor boy? Willie hasn't got the sense of a two-year-old. He wouldn't know how to steal a pig."

"Well, he did steal it. But not to fatten it up for slaughter. He made a pet of it. Crenshaw demanded it back and was cruel enough to say he meant to grind it up for sausages. Willie started bawling. It was asinine."

"What did you do?"

"I tried to make Crenshaw see reason, but he's a mean-spirited, spiteful old fart. So I bought the damn pig. For far more than it's worth."

"I'm sure Crenshaw was thrilled. Did it satisfy Willie?"

"It should. I hired him to be our new pig boy. Tollerson will have to put up with Willie for a while until he loses interest." Jasper grimaced. "Then I suppose we'll grind it up for some very pricey sausage."

Reginald snorted.

"The thing is," Jasper said, looking down at his hands and then up again, "the thing is, I don't know what the Earl would have done. There are so many things I just don't know."

"You did fine. It's just a—"

"I know it was just a pig. But that was this time. Next time it won't be a pig. And I still won't know—"

"And you don't want to hear me say you'll do fine. Jasper, it's certain you'll make a few mistakes. But I'm sure Father did too. And you should not discount the possibility that you may do some things better than Father did."

"I just wish there was more time."

Reginald's throat closed. "So do I."

He never had the talk with Father that Crispin had urged him to have. He never told him he wanted to work for the university instead of the church. He never said that he bore Mr. Tibury no grudge. He would never know how Father really felt about any of his youngest son's decisions. Father would not live long enough to see those decisions carried out.

Jasper closed the newspaper he had probably not really been reading.

"I've been neglecting our house guests shamefully these last couple of days. I'm worried they will pack up and leave."

"I'm sure they understand."

"It was a mistake inviting them. But I expected I'd be here for the whole Season. And Georgiana would be snatched up by someone else. Then I'd have to start searching with no idea where to start. But this is absurd. I've gone about it all wrong. Hell, I'm not even sure she *likes* me."

Reginald knew he was supposed to say *of course she does*. Instead, he said, "But you do like her?"

"Everything about her." He rubbed a hand through his hair. "It's only, she isn't Vanessa. You understand? And I handled that badly too."

He needed to say something. But he had no idea what. That Jasper didn't deserve Georgiana if he was still tied by the heartstrings to his mistress? That Jasper could not wed Georgiana because *he* was desperately in love with her?

"Well," he said slowly, "what are you planning to do?"

"I can't do anything this morning. I have a proposal to read over that I should have gotten to a month ago. One of Lord Billings' projects. He's stopping here today on his way to Plimpton. I'd forgotten I invited him. Thank God Peters reminded me."

"Billings?" One of the Earl's good friends. "Will he want to see Father?"

"He may want to, but he won't. This is not how the Earl would want to be remembered. I mean to spare him that. So I suppose we'll have a dinner for Billings. Set up the targets and do some shooting. That'll amuse him. Then I'll have to give him an hour to try to convince me to support his theater censorship bill."

"Well, at least you know what the Earl would do with that."

"Ha! Yes. That I do know. And that Father always aimed just a hair off the mark, then served his finest brandy, so that Billings would trot off well pleased with himself regardless." The faintest smile crossed Jasper's face. "Can I trust you not to humiliate the man if I let you shoot with us?"

"I haven't shot a gun in over a year."

"I don't think that matters. Aim to the side."

Reginald laughed. "If that's all you require of me—"

"Oh, well, no. There's more. I've got to play host to Billings which means I'm going to neglect Georgiana yet again. I hate to ask, but can you and Olivia entertain her this morning? And Alice, of course. And the Duchess unless she chooses to sit with Mother."

He felt the request like a physical blow. "Entertain them how?" He knew what would interest Georgiana, but they couldn't drag Alice to the library to thumb through accounts.

"Fortunately, it looks to be a fine day. I had wanted to take Georgiana out to see the folly if the sun ever came out. The walk out there is pleasant and it's an amusing pretend ruin."

"Crispin will be sorry he missed it. The folly is his favorite part of Chaumbers."

"Well, if he gets back in time, he can join you. You don't mind, do you?"

"No. I don't mind." And that was the truth. It was almost too perfect. Olivia and Alice were thick as thieves. It would be no trouble to find a spot for a private talk with Georgiana. She'd said she felt close to figuring out where the money had gone. If she had, then they were done with all this. If she hadn't, well, perhaps they were done anyway. Once Bradwell and Father were both dead, what did a few hundred missing pounds matter?

The important thing was they needed to talk. He'd touched her hand. Stroked it. It had been such a tiny gesture. Insignificant on the vast scale of possible ways for humans to touch. But it hadn't felt insignificant. It felt monumental. Intimate. It had been the most utterly wrong thing to do. He owed her an abject apology. But the truth was, he did not regret it at all.

SUNSHINE STREAMED THROUGH the windows. Georgiana did not see a cloud in the sky. Everything that was wrong was still wrong; nevertheless, her spirits lifted.

She waited for Alice to wake and dress, and then they both went downstairs together. Mama must not have announced any decision to leave, because Reginald and Olivia awaited them in the breakfast parlor with plans for the morning.

"We thought we'd walk out to the folly," Olivia said. "It'll be good to stretch our limbs. It'll be just the four of us unless Crispin returns soon. Jasper is obliged to meet with Lord Billings."

"Oh," Georgiana smiled. "Is he coming here? Mama will enjoy seeing him."

"Evidently," Reginald said. "And my mother appreciated the Duchess volunteering to act as hostess for the dinner. She's with Cook now, going over the menu. While Jasper is reading through whatever hare-brained proposal Billings wants him to support."

They ate a quick light breakfast, then gathered their wraps and bonnets and set off. The path across the meadow was wide enough for the girls to walk three abreast. Reginald trailed behind. He was so quiet that Georgiana glanced over her shoulder a few times to assure herself he was there. His brow was clouded. She didn't think he was even listening to their talk.

Olivia served as guide, pointing out the various landmarks.

The village was behind them, the lake off to the left. Across the lake, though of course they could not see it, was the neighboring village of Crofton, where Jeremy and Jeffrey had their home. And beyond that, was the town of Ipswich, where one could find a surprisingly good milliner, Olivia's bonnet being proof.

It was a hefty walk up a long, gradual incline. Georgiana was beginning to feel it in her legs when the gradient increased abruptly to an actual climb. They reached a plateau and Olivia halted and bid them turn around. Reginald came up to stand beside them, a wicked grin on his face.

"Oh," Georgiana said, looking back at Chaumbers. From this perspective, one was able to truly form an impression of the whole of the house. She tried forcing a smile.

Alice giggled, then guffawed. "I do apologize," she said, drawing breath. "I'm sure your grandfather was a lovely man, but..."

"He was no architect," Reginald allowed.

Georgiana knew that many gentlemen's country homes had been built in stages, with each new owner adding a little something of his own. As styles changed, there could be incongruities. But this home had no such excuse. It had been conceived as a whole. To look like this.

Olivia laughed. "I'll tell you a story. A few years ago, my father hired a young painter to be my tutor. I had no particular talent in that direction, but I liked painting and Mama was eager to encourage anything that got me off of a horse. The man was engaged for six months."

"Can you imagine the boon?" Reginald put in. "He was required to spend only a couple hours a day with Olivia, yet was paid a salary, provided with all the paint and canvas he required, and given a room and board. Jasper said the man put on at least a stone."

"You didn't like him?" Georgiana asked.

"I never met him. I was away at school. Jasper did not like him."

"What was wrong with him?" Alice asked.

"He was very superior," Olivia said. "Of course, I thought that meant he was a very good painter. All artists, I thought, were superior."

"And he was young and handsome," Reginald said.

"He was not. He had frog eyes."

It was wonderful to see the two of them teasing one another. Georgiana realized it was not only the boys who rallied one another.

Olivia said, "He was not handsome, but he was young. And there was my dangerous impressionability to fear." She made a face. "We were only to meet in the small parlor, door open, and every ten minutes someone would pass by. It was very distracting, but I persevered. We tried portraits first, but I soon showed myself a miserable portraitist. I had no desire to paint fruit in bowls. So we moved onto landscapes."

Olivia looked at Reginald, as though daring him to say something, but he kept his lips clamped.

"We were permitted to take the easels out onto the lawn or the terraces, and I did paint some decent views, but there simply was not that much to inspire me. So we went back to the small parlor, and I made some sketches of better views from memory. I sketched this." She swept out her hand.

Reginald laughed, knowing where she was headed, but did not interrupt.

"Well, the dim man made me sketch it again and again and kept pointing out what was wrong. It infuriated me. Finally, I said I was going to do the painting. And I did. It was a very good painting, if I do say so, but he mocked it."

"And Olivia started to cry." Apparently, Reginald's silence had limits.

"I was angry. It must have been Jasper's turn to lurk nearby because he stormed into the parlor looking ready to strangle poor Master John. I showed no signs of having been—I don't know what, accosted, I suppose—so Jasper merely demanded to know what was wrong. I sobbed 'He hates my painting!' or something to the effect. Jasper looked at it and said, 'What's wrong with it?' And in his oh-so-superior way, Master John scolded Jasper and said, 'She will never improve if you patronize her.'"

They all laughed. Olivia could mimic a supercilious painting master to a T. But she was not finished with her story.

"Now *Jasper* was infuriated. He put Master John on a horse, which pleased neither John nor the horse, and hauled him here. The view offended all his artistic sensibilities. He said he couldn't be expected to anticipate Chaumbers' architect had been an imbecile. To which Jasper replied, 'You are referring to the previous Earl of Iversley.'"

"And," Reginald interjected, "no painting master can out-superior Jasper. John saw his salary and meals evaporating before his eyes."

"It was awful!" Olivia exclaimed. "Poor Master John spent the next two weeks abasing himself. If I dropped a splatter of paint on the floor it was a masterpiece. I finally told Father to send him away." She pouted. "My painting career was over."

They laughed with her. She obviously had no regrets.

"Ah, but if only you had painted the folly instead of the house. Shall we?" Reginald indicated the way forward. The ground now slanted down. In the distance, Georgiana could make out an irregular outline of stacked brick and stones.

Olivia linked her arm through Alice's and led. Reginald and Georgiana followed, though he did not offer his arm to her. That seemed an admission of the discomfort they both felt. She could hear Olivia continuing to chatter.

"Crispin used to bring us out here to get us out from underfoot. Me and Reginald. We would hide and he would look for us. I used to think we were so clever and that there were thousands of places in the ruins where he would never find us. But of course, there are only four or five rather obvious spots, and we hid there over and over. You wouldn't think Crispin would be so patient, would you? But he was."

Oh! This family! They broke Georgiana's heart. They were so

close. All of them. That was such a rarity. She couldn't say anything, *do* anything, that might disrupt this. Especially not now when they needed each other so much.

Georgiana didn't hear Alice's response and couldn't make out what Olivia said next. She and Reginald were walking quite slowly. They had fallen behind. He touched her arm.

"Georgiana, we should talk."

CHAPTER TWENTY-THREE

GEORGIANA HEARD LAUGHTER. Looking ahead, she saw Olivia and Alice had broken into a run.

"Not here. Not now," she said, shaking off Reginald's hand. "Come. We shouldn't be dawdling."

He looked relieved rather than disappointed. They hurried after the others, but walking, not running. It made Georgiana feel old. She hadn't run since she'd left Marbury, and even then, the last time she remembered doing so was chasing after a puppy that had been digging in the garden. She couldn't recall the last time she'd run sheerly out of exuberance.

The folly had been built in two main parts, separated by forty or fifty yards, with a low, broken wall of bricks connecting them.

"This is supposed to be the ruin of the cloister," Olivia said, standing beside the larger structure with Alice as Reginald and Georgiana drew near.

Georgiana could imagine that it had once been an abbey's cloister, a small one; there was a squarish outline, a few standing pillars and several more broken ones, and a single, rather substantial brick wall.

"We'd hide back there," Reginald said, gesturing to the wall. "Behind it, there are a few niches that we claimed were the nuns' cells. Olivia believed it for the longest time."

"And that over there," Olivia pointed to the other structure.

"That was the kitchen and refectory. There's a hearth there. It's safe to build a fire in it, though we haven't done that in ages. We used to have picnics here. Come see. Come see."

Alice followed readily, but Reginald said, "Go on. Georgiana and I will look around here first."

The girls scampered away. Reginald waited until they reached the other structure and disappeared beyond its archway. He led her into the "cloister," to sit on a brick bench cut into the wall. She sat very still. He did also.

Reginald cleared his throat. "Did you reach any conclusions?"

"The last three or three-and-a-half years are fine. Whatever the expense was, it seems to have been resolved." She knew her speech was stilted, but she was having trouble speaking at all. She didn't want to do this. She wanted to be back in the library. With him. Suspended in time. "I don't think you need have any qualms giving a new steward the ledgers."

"But you have no idea what those expenses were?"

She hesitated a little too long before shaking her head.

"Huh." He looked toward the ground. "It worries me more that you won't tell me what you found."

She didn't want to lie to him. "Please don't be worried. I think that what matters is not what I might have found buried in the past, but what you all have now. You and your family."

His brow furrowed. "And what you discovered will hurt my family?"

"No!" She wished she had never stuck her nose where it didn't belong. "No, it shouldn't. But why take the chance?"

He gave her a long look as if debating whether to press her. She shook her head. "It's done with, Reginald."

He drew back, startled, or wounded. Then asked haltingly, "Done with?" He put his head in his hands, rubbed his temples, then looked at her again. "We should not risk the chance."

She felt it again. That jolt. That love. That desire.

He must have seen it in her face because he reached for her. With both hands. He grasped her by the shoulders and pulled her close. Then he kissed her.

Georgiana dissolved into his arms.

They kissed and they kissed and they kissed. She didn't think she would know what to do, but it was the most natural thing in the world. She kissed not only his lips but his chin, his cheeks, his eyelids, the way he kissed hers. He parted her lips with his and they kissed as if trying to meld themselves into one. He pulled her closer, until her leg draped halfway across his lap. And then she was on his lap. And his hand slid from the back of her neck to her shoulder to her breast.

She made a noise. An involuntary noise. It was surprise, not protest, but Reginald stiffened and pulled back. He shifted her from his lap onto the bench and stood up.

"We should not—*I* should not—I won't, don't worry, I would never say anything to Jasper."

"Jasper?" For a moment, the name meant nothing to her. Then it meant everything. Of course, Reginald would not tell his brother about this. But to think that *that* was what worried her? He'd say nothing for *her* sake?

"He means to ask for you. To have you for his countess." His voice shook. "Of course, you know that."

Yes, she did know that. But she did not appreciate having Jasper's intentions thrown into her face. She stood up as well.

He went on, sounding wild. "We can't chance his finding out. We won't meet again. The books don't matter. I can't be near you, Georgiana. You must think, God, you must think the worst things of me. I'm not that kind of man. He's my *brother!*"

He couldn't be *near* her? Was she a temptress then? Turning him into the type of man he was not?

She didn't trust her voice. Which didn't matter since she had nothing to say. She gestured for him to step aside. Then walked past him. To join Alice and Olivia and put this miserable scene, this whole horrendous week behind her.

Did Reginald honestly imagine she would ever marry Jasper?

That hurt. More than she ever thought she could be hurt.

❯❯❯❯❮❮❮❮

REGINALD WATCHED GEORGIANA walk away. He was wretched. Wretched.

He'd intended to apologize for caressing her little finger. Instead, he assaulted her. Good God! What had he done?

Jasper must never find out. He wouldn't bother shooting Reginald, he'd have him committed, straightaway, to an asylum. Because Reginald was evidently mad. And if not yet, he would be. If Jasper married her.

But Jasper surely wouldn't marry her if he ever found out. He'd be horrified. He thought she was such an innocent. Georgiana's kisses had not been innocent. Moreover, there was what Crispin mockingly called their unwritten, unspoken rule— they would never pursue the same woman. That had never been an issue. Not for him. Perhaps it had been some time in the past for Jasper and Crispin. They were closer in age. But Reginald doubted they'd ever given his interests any thought. Certainly not as any threat to Jasper's.

Jasper must never find out.

As Georgiana reached the archway, Reginald turned abruptly, unable to watch her disappear beyond it. He turned and saw Crispin regarding him coldly from the far edge of the wall. His stomach plummeted even as bile rose in his throat.

"And here I thought you were the intelligent one," Crispin jeered.

"God!" Reginald exploded. "Where did you come from? Were you spying on me?"

"Spying?" Crispin laughed, sauntering forward through the soggy patches of grass. "That's a lark. Believe me, I had no desire to hear any of that. I stopped here on my way back from the Squire's. I sent Adam ahead on the road to take back the carriage and I came here. For a respite, I thought. Mercury is grazing out back." He gestured toward the wall and halted beside Reginald. "I had no idea my sanctuary was going to be invaded."

"You might have shown yourself." How much had he heard?

"If there had been any moment during any of that where showing myself would have been appropriate, believe me, I would have leaped out. Bloody hell. First—you had Lady Georgiana looking for your stray missing bits in the ledgers? What the devil? That alone set my head spinning. And she *found* them? That nearly brought me shouting from behind the wall. But I was brought up short. Christ! Reginald. You were kissing her!"

"You could not see that." He was sweating. Panicked.

Crispin laughed, a disbelieving, mocking, appalled laugh. "I did not have to see. I have ears. I was afraid to poke my head around and see you two rolling about on the ground."

Reginald hit him squarely on the jaw.

Crispin's head was flung back, and one foot moved for balance, but he didn't fall. He rubbed his chin and shook himself, scowling. Then he regarded his brother with an appreciative gleam in his eye.

"Not bad. Now tell me what the hell is going on."

There was no point denying it. Crispin would not say anything to Jasper, though he was likely to insist that Reginald confess. "I'm an idiot is what. I'm in love with her."

"I know *that*." Crispin regarded him as if he'd said something amusing. "And she feels the same. And Jasper bores her to tears. And he will always and forever be in love with Vanessa. I am a simple, casual observer, yet this has all been evident to me now for days."

Evident for *days*? Reginald felt almost faint. Evident to everyone? Surely not. "Jasper still intends to ask for her."

"Then he is the idiot, not you. Jasper attempted some sort of chaste kiss, and she clocked him. I didn't see what you were doing to her, but it didn't sound as if she minded."

"Shut up." Heat rose up his neck to his ears. *Damn it.* His obvious mortification would be more ammunition for his brother's pistol-quick sarcasm.

"What I don't understand is why you insulted that delightful young lady—"

"I lost control. Crispin, I don't go around grabbing women—"

"That wasn't what I meant. I meant why did you accuse her of leading you on while she's dangling after Jasper?"

"I did not accuse her of any such thing!"

"Reg, I heard you. And if that is what *I* heard, you can believe that's what she heard too."

"She came to Chaumbers to be courted by Jasper!"

"Which makes Jasper one of at least sixteen fellows to throw his hat into the ring. She won't accept him."

"He is going to be an earl. And he's *Jasper*."

"That is incredibly offensive. If I was not now leery of your right paw, I would throw a punch on her behalf. She won't marry Jasper. She may end up marrying someone else, someday, but it will never be Jasper. Now you can go tell him to shove aside because you are going to woo her, or you can let her go. But whichever you decide, you owe her an apology. Not for kissing her, but for *thinking* she would let you kiss her like that if she had any intention of encouraging Jasper."

Reginald stood still, breathing unsteadily. There was some sense in what Crispin said. It made him feel worse, but at the same time, left open the door to a glimmer of hope. Just the faintest glimmer. He was bound to do something that would slam that door shut.

"Think it over," Crispin said more gently.

"I don't have to think it over. I won't simply let her go. But I'm not like you. I can't just barrel into fraught conversations." He studied his brother. "How do you do it?"

Crispin's face changed. Rather than sardonic, he simply looked tired.

"Reg, I will say this, but you are not permitted to reply. All right?" He paused, and when Reginald said nothing, he went on, "I have lived most of my life with one foot in the grave. I don't procrastinate. Which includes not putting off necessary conversations." He smiled wryly. "I rather enjoy them. The discomfort reminds me that I'm still alive."

"You do avoid some conversations."

"*Upt!*" Crispin held up his hand. "No response, remember? I avoid *one* topic. Now we move on to the next. Why was Georgiana going through Bradwell's books? And what did she find that she refuses to tell?"

Reginald balked. He could not reveal Georgiana's secret, her gift, because that would be a betrayal, even though Crispin would find it as remarkable as he had himself.

"There is nothing worthwhile in our library. She was bored."

"She has that novel from home."

"*The Italian?* That's Mother's. Or Olivia's."

"No, something else. About a courtesan."

"What?"

"It doesn't matter," Crispin said. "She was bored. So you gave her a ledger to read? Were you drunk again?"

God. He could not lie to save his life.

"Not to read. I just asked her to skim a few of the ledgers and note a few things."

"What things? What did you have her looking for?"

His neck felt hot. "I can't say—"

"You can't say because this is a fudge. I'll ask her."

"Crispin, drop it. I don't know what Georgiana found, but she says it doesn't matter and I trust her."

"It may not matter to you. Or to her. But I have a nagging suspicion of my own and if it's the same one, what she found does matter to someone. Very much so."

"You can't ask her, or she'll know you were listening behind the wall."

Crispin laughed. "Didn't we just establish that I *live* for embarrassing conversations?"

"Crispin—"

"Don't look so terrified. I'm not going to interrogate her

now, in front of Olivia. We'll tell them all I just arrived. I came this way from the Squire's. You'd better let me do the talking. Now, come on, gudgeon. We have to get back to the house. And you'll have to face her sometime. Let's get it over with."

CHAPTER TWENTY-FOUR

GEORGIANA WAS GRATEFUL that Crispin had finally joined them. He walked back with them too, allowing Olivia to return with his horse. Olivia had been speechless. Apparently, riding Mercury was an honor he granted to no one. After she sped off—skirts hitched up, straddling the horse, leaving Georgiana and Alice gaping—Crispin entertained them with a laughing description of the warrior's welcome Jeremy received at his homecoming, so it was not too noticeable that Georgiana and Reginald scarcely spoke at all.

Lord Billings had already arrived by the time they returned. Georgiana and Alice scrambled to their chamber to wash their faces and change their clothes.

As Jeanette tied her ribbons, Alice asked, "Georgiana, did you and Reginald quarrel?"

"Quarrel?" she laughed stiffly. "Why would you think that?"

Alice shrugged. "You both seemed a bit peeved."

"No. We did not quarrel. I suppose we simply ran out of conversation."

"Maybe he's just tired of being in company all the time. Olivia says he's not very sociable."

"Why were you discussing Reginald with Olivia?" She felt a twinge of irritation.

"Her brothers are her favorite topic of conversation." Alice spoke teasingly, but not without a touch of wistfulness.

Georgiana didn't want to discuss the Taverstons anymore. The *coup de grâce* would be Alice confiding an interest in Reginald.

"*Voilà*," Jeanette said. "You are both presentable."

"Very good, thank you," Georgiana said, then tentatively shared a smile with Alice. "That walk made me hungry. I hope I don't astonish Lord Billings with my appetite."

Alice giggled. "I'm sure he'll be too puzzled by what Crispin doesn't eat to notice what you do."

They went down. The men were waiting in the drawing room, all except Crispin, who would be joining the Earl and the Countess instead. Georgiana and Alice exchanged glances but were not so rude as to laugh.

Mama had arranged the seating, placing Georgiana between Jasper and Lord Billings. Georgiana liked Lord Billings even though he had a high opinion of himself and tended to dominate conversations. He talked over Jasper with the condescension of an old dog batting aside a pup. For the most part, Jasper took this in stride, but when Billings tried insisting he would pay just a short visit to the Earl after dinner, because "surely a visit would do the old fellow good," Jasper answered with a firm no. "The Earl must not be disturbed."

Lord Billings appeared put out, but only for a moment. Then he returned to telling them what they were missing in London. "And the first official match of the Season has been announced: Lord Dunstun and Miss Blakemore." He paused, smiling with satisfaction at the sly way he had delivered the word "official." Georgiana felt a blush rise on her neck. Was everyone in London awaiting an announcement from Chaumbers?

Mama responded, "How delightful. I'm sure they will be very happy. Lord Billings, have you seen the Duke recently? He had a cough when we left and although he assures me it is gone, he would, of course, say that."

"I did see him at White's. He wasn't coughing. However, he was drinking some sort of toddy." Lord Billings laughed. "But don't worry. He looked very hearty."

He rattled on. Georgiana relaxed and began to enjoy his various bits of unimportant news. As the dessert course was being served, Crispin entered the room. He sat down next to Olivia but waved aside the servant who offered him macaroons.

"Father is sleeping," he said, tactfully assuring his brothers there had been no change. "Mother suggested I come down."

Lord Billings paused for breath during the interruption but then turned to focus on Georgiana.

"And you, dear lady! I remember you with your hair down in ribbons. Now look at you. Good show! Though I daresay you left a trail of brokenhearted swains behind in London!"

Then he chucked her under the chin and, over her head, winked broadly at Jasper.

Georgiana reeled back, aghast, but knew of no appropriate response to something so vulgar. Jasper went rigid. She dared not look across the table to see Reginald's reaction, but slanting her gaze to his left, she saw Crispin's expression darken.

Mama rescued her once again. Her tone was sharp. "I believe Lord Taverston has an entertainment planned. Why don't you all gather again outside?" She stood, which meant the men all had to rise at once, putting an abrupt end to the meal.

Lord Billings looked startled, then puzzled, then embarrassed, all in the space of a few seconds. But he recovered enough to offer Georgiana his arm. He led her from the dining room. Georgiana tossed a glance behind her to see Alice and Olivia following, but the lords of Iversley had clustered together to exchange a few words. Whatever they had to say to one another did not take long.

Jasper came quickly forward, giving instructions to various servants. The party waited inside until a footman returned and murmured something to him. Then Jasper herded them outdoors.

A shooting range had been established on the front lawn. There were several wafers, bold circles painted on paper, wrapped around metal frames that had been hammered into the ground. They stood three in a row, with the rows placed about thirty to fifty paces away. There was a breeze, enough to set the targets rippling. Chairs were lined up at the edge of the drive for the ladies who would spectate. Servants stood at the ready with pistol boxes.

"Will you shoot first, Lord Billings?" Jasper asked. "Would you like to use the Earl's guns or your own?"

"Never use any but my own," Billings said. "And please. You do the honors."

Jasper nodded. "Very well. I will be using the Earl's."

Georgiana watched him take a pistol from a box, then move to a line that had been chalked on the grass. He aimed for the nearest target and blew a hole through it.

"Oh, very good!" Billings said. "You have been practicing."

Jasper nodded, teeth gritted. "I have."

Billings turned. "Lieutenant Taverston, you must be next."

Crispin smiled coolly. "I will not be shooting. As an officer of the King's Army, I should have unfair advantage. And, if I do not, I should not like anyone to know."

Billings laughed. He looked to Reginald. "You, young sir?"

"After you."

Billings cupped the second wafer. Then Reginald cupped the next. They moved to the second set of targets, a little farther away. Jasper missed. Billings hit his, but there was the distinct sound of metal being pinged and the frame tilted.

Billings frowned. "Not very clean, was it? But a hit is a hit."

"It was a hit," Jasper agreed.

Reginald said nothing. He stepped to the line, held up his gun, then lowered it.

"It is a bit out of the usual range," Billings said, with more than a hint of condescension.

"No, it's fine," Reginald said. He took his spectacles from his pocket and donned them. Then he took aim and fired, tearing a hole through the middle of the target.

Billings looked disturbed. "Very nice."

"I'm out," Jasper said. "The next is too far. They should not have set them that far. Shall we call it quits or have them brought closer?"

"Nonsense," Billings said, clenching his jaw.

He stepped to the line, aimed, and missed. He moved aside. Reginald took his place. He hit it clean.

"Bit of luck there," Billings said with forced humor. "Once more?"

Georgiana felt nastily pleased to watch him struggle. Billings missed again. Reginald, after tapping his spectacles into place, did not.

"Let's move our lines up ten paces or so and shoot from closer," Jasper suggested. "The targets should not have been placed so far. Not in this wind."

"No!" Billings thundered. "I'm just now warmed up. I'll take my shot."

He missed.

Reginald stepped to the line, but Crispin stopped him. "Let Lord Billings try again." He said it in a tone so gentle it was cutting.

Furious now, Lord Billings came back to the line while Reginald was still moving aside. He glared at the target and took a long time to steady his gun. He fired. The wafer split along its side. A hit—but barely.

The contestants stood silent, but Olivia applauded and shouted, "Oh, very good!" capping the Taverstons' triumph by perfectly miming Billings' patronizing tone.

Billings stomped over to where his man waited and shoved his pistol back into its box. There was a moment of awkwardness. Georgiana could no longer feel angry with him. He seemed rather to be pitied. A man would not wish to find himself with the Taverston siblings arrayed against him.

Jasper went to him and said, "The wind has picked up. It's not worth the bother to reset the wafers. Why don't we go have a brandy and discuss this bill you sent me?"

PERHAPS IT HAD been a childish sort of vengeance, embarrassing him as he had embarrassed her, but Georgiana now understood the satisfaction such pranks afforded the Taverstons. After all, no one was hurt. Jasper would smooth things over with brandy. But they had put Billings in his place.

Reginald had put Billings in his place.

When they went inside, Jasper took Lord Billings off to his study. Reginald and Olivia went upstairs to sit with the Earl. Crispin announced he was going to the music room to learn a new piece, so he'd appreciate it if everyone else avoided that wing of the house.

Georgiana flinched inwardly, thinking he must be speaking to her, warning her out of the library. But by the way, the others laughed and groaned, it seemed it was not an uncommon request—his talent was not effortless, for all he might like it to appear so. Besides, he couldn't know how much time she had been spending there. Moreover, she would not be going there now, or ever again. Instead, she followed Alice back to their chamber because it had been a strenuous morning and, after such, ladies were supposed to rest.

The list of what ladies were supposed to do was exhaustive.

The list of what they could not do was infinite.

THE EARL AWAKENED briefly but remained in some sort of delirium. He took a bit of broth from Mother's spoon and a few sips of tea laden with honey and rum from the cup she held to his lips, then murmured a thank you, calling Mother "Lucy." After that, he lapsed back into a sleep racked with alternating shivers and sweats.

"Lucy?" Olivia whispered. "Who is that? He called me that once before."

Mother sighed. She looked terribly weary. "I believe his nursemaid, when he was very young, was called Lucy."

That wasn't right. Reginald remembered stories. "Wasn't that Lilian?"

"What does it matter, Reginald? Maybe there were two." She sounded snappish. Of course, she did. It was an annoying habit of his to seize on details that no one else considered important.

He sat, watching his father suffer, then staring at the window, then watching his father. All the while, he attempted to put thoughts of Georgiana out of his head. It didn't seem possible for him to have felt so many intense emotions in one day. And the day was but half over. *Bloody hell.* Now he felt drained.

At one point, he heard a carriage in the drive and went to the window to watch Lord Billings depart. He felt a little guilty for his part. The man was a blowhard, but generally harmless. He wouldn't have intentionally insulted Georgiana. The devil. If Billings had been correct in his assumption that Jasper had already secured Georgiana's hand, they would have more readily excused his choice of words and the crass wink. But Jasper had not.

And Jasper had been livid. Livid. If he had not been, he would never have humiliated a guest in his home. He certainly would not have enlisted Reginald's help to do so.

Seeing Jasper so livid was concerning.

Reginald returned to his chair, flexing his fingers, then tapping his feet, then staring, bleary-eyed, at his father. The room was beginning to darken when Mother started in her chair and looked quickly about. "Oh. I think I fell asleep."

"You should go to bed, Mama. I'll stay," Olivia urged.

"No, I'm awake now."

There was a rap on the door and Crispin entered. He focused on Mother and spoke very low. "How is he?"

"Still sleeping."

Crispin let out a long sigh. "If you'll excuse us, I need to borrow Reginald for a while. Jasper needs to speak with us."

"Of course. There's no need for us all to sit here. I'll send for you all if there's any change."

Reginald stood, feeling guiltily relieved for an excuse to escape the sickroom, and frightened by what Jasper might have to say. He hoped Billings' nudge had not led Jasper to rush his proposal. He left the room with Crispin. As they departed the west wing, Crispin headed for the main staircase.

"Where are we going? Not Jasper's study?"

"No. Jasper has not sent for us. I sent for him. And for Georgiana. We'll be congregating in the library."

Reginald stopped dead and grabbed his brother's arm. "What have you done? What did you tell Jasper?"

Crispin lifted away Reginald's hand. "Nothing. And nothing yet."

"Then why the library?"

"Because that is where I've been for the past two hours. I need to know what Georgiana found because…well, because I could not discover it." *Damn it!* Crispin meant to interrogate her. And in front of a witness. "Why bring Jasper into this?"

"Because he'll be the Earl. And we'll have to abide by what he decides to do."

"Do about *what*?" Crispin said he hadn't discovered anything! Oh, hell. Even if he *knew* nothing, he obviously *suspected* something. And the probability was high that it had to do with the same financial shenanigans Georgiana had been investigating. Crispin's digging risked exposing the family *and* Georgiana!

Crispin drew an irritated breath. "I need to know first that I'm right." He let the breath out with a resigned-sounding sigh. "I hope I'm not. God, I hope I'm not. If I'm wrong, I'll intercept Jasper and give you a chance to speak with Georgiana alone."

Reginald gave up. He was powerless to stop whatever Crispin had just set in motion.

"Do not embarrass her, Crispin. Don't press her. If she does tell you anything, don't ask her to explain how she knows."

Crispin looked at him oddly. "What is going on?"

"Just don't make this about her."

"The deuce, Reg! What is it? Witchcraft?"

"Don't be an arse."

"Well, don't be a pigwidgeon. I don't care how she knows. I just want to see *what* she knows. Now, come on. Unless you want Jasper to get there before us and embarrass her with a proposal."

Bloody hell! Reginald hurried down the stairs, terrified and furious, swearing at Crispin the whole time.

They met Georgiana at the foot of the stairway leading from the guest chambers. She looked worriedly from Reginald to Crispin. "Is it your father?"

"No," Reginald said. "His condition is unchanged."

Then she paled. Her eyes grew huge as she continued to search Reginald's face for an explanation. He wanted to flatten Crispin, but even Crispin appeared disturbed by the magnitude of her fear.

"Georgiana," Crispin spoke very quietly. "Please, let's go to the library. I want to show you something and ask you something."

"No. No, I don't think you do," she said, shaking her head as she lowered it.

"If you'd prefer," Crispin said, taking her hand and raising it toward his chest, drawing her gaze back to his face, "we can leave Reg here, and he can keep Jasper away."

"Jasper's coming too?" Now she swiveled her gaze back and forth between them, chin trembling. "This is wrong. I can't."

"He won't be here for another fifteen minutes at least. Georgiana, would you rather speak with me alone?"

"The devil, Crispin!" Reginald swore. "Not alone. I won't let you bully her."

Crispin said, "Georgiana?"

"Oh, all right!" she cried. "Reginald, you may as well come too." She ground out through clenched teeth, "I cannot *believe* you told him."

"I didn't. Georgiana, I didn't say anything. And he is not going to interrogate you or, by God, I'll—"

"Yes, that's enough," Crispin said, grabbing him and Georgiana each by their elbows to steer them to the library. He nudged the door open with his foot, pulled them inside, and shut the door with a gentle kick. While they huddled close to the exit, Crispin let go of their arms and strode to the desk to pick up a stack of ledgers that he then brought to the nearest corner table. He dropped them on its surface and gestured to the leather chair. "Sit," he ordered in a way that reminded Reginald that his annoying brother was now an officer in the King's Army—and no doubt a very effective one.

Georgiana sat. Crispin knelt on the floor in front of her, picked up a ledger, and opened it to a page marked with a slip of paper. Reginald came to stand next to the chair, peering down at the book in Crispin's hand.

"This is odd. Don't you think?" Crispin set the open book on Georgiana's knee, then opened another and displayed that also.

Georgiana glanced down, then back at Crispin. "Yes," she admitted. "I thought so."

"What?" Reginald asked.

"Your Cambridge tuition is twice that of Oxford's," Crispin said.

He started and leaned to look at the figure. That made no sense. "That can't be—"

"Wait," Crispin said. He removed those ledgers, set them on the floor, then opened four more and stacked them, open, on Georgiana's lap. "Did you notice this as well?" He shuffled the books, pointing at something. Reginald tried to see what he indicated, but Crispin moved the ledger too quickly.

But Georgiana had seen it. She exhaled, closed her eyes, her expression pained, and nodded. "I could not make sense of that. I didn't...have time." Her voice was small.

"To correlate all the changes in tuition costs at Harrow with the irregular salaries for tutors? I'll help. Look. I had to leave school *here*."

She opened her eyes and then nodded. He flipped to another book. "And here. Father hired tutors for me for six months first, and then for a year."

Georgiana's eyes widened. Reginald recognized the look that came into them. Excited. Challenged. He felt a warm rush of *communion*. However strong her fear of violating society's norms, it was evidently no match for her drive to pursue her passion— just as he was driven to abandon a perfectly respectable profession as a clergyman to translate long-lost Greek philosophies. She pulled the book from Crispin's hand and scanned it. "Give me the other again."

He handed her the ledger and she scanned that too. Then she looked at the pile on the table beside Crispin and pointed to the spine of one. They were marked by year. Crispin passed it to her. She turned several pages rapidly, then paused, then looked up at Crispin and nodded.

"What?" Reginald said. What did they see that he didn't?

"Your Harrow tuition was also about twice the cost of mine and Jasper's."

"That's nonsense. Why would it be?"

"Because he was sponsoring another student," Crispin said. "And Bradwell was hiding it." He was still looking at Georgiana rather than Reginald. Then he asked, "Do you know what I am asking? Do you have proof?"

"Of the student?" Georgiana asked.

Crispin shook his head. "I know who he was. And frankly, his mother does not interest me. But his father?"

Georgiana tightened her grip on the books, then nodded.

"The Earl?" Reginald said. *Loudly. Too loudly.* "You can't mean the Earl. *Our* father? Crispin! You're saying he had a son? Another son? I don't believe you. That isn't true. That *can't* be true. He may have sponsored a boy's education, but that doesn't mean anything."

Crispin asked quietly, "Have you proof? In case Jasper wants proof."

"Bloody hell!" Reginald shouted. His entire world was crashing down on his head. "*I* want proof!"

Georgiana answered Crispin in a soft voice, but one that was matter-of-fact, without any polite ladylike apology. "It isn't proof. It's conjecture."

Reginald saw how Crispin had not once removed his focus from Georgiana. While *he* had been having quite reasonable-under-the-circumstances fits, Crispin had maintained a steady, calm demeanor while coaxing her along. *By God.* Reginald could picture him cooly organizing his regiment while under fire—and just as cooly sending his men to their deaths.

"Will you show me?" Crispin asked, with an almost soothing deference. "Only if Reginald wishes it too." A tiny bit of steel entered her tone. She would not allow Crispin to lead *her* like a lamb to the slaughter.

Crispin looked at him. "Reg?"

No. This could not hinge upon him. It was not his role to decide the fate of the Taverstons, to destroy their belief in the *rightness* of their familial bonds. I don't know why you are digging—"

"Because he's our brother."

"Who?" *For God's sake! Who?*

"Tibury, goddamnit! He's our brother, and we never knew it, and he never knew us! Except that we are 'the lords of Iversley' and he is not. And we have all this! And Olivia. And each other! And he gets the worst of the two benefices and has to thank Father, then slink out while *we* are all gathered to support each other through a deathbed vigil. Can you live with that? Can you? Because I cannot!"

Reginald stared. His mind was a scramble. All he could manage was, "Tibury?"

"I read the recommendations. He's a good man, our brother. But it wasn't simply that his friends were putting him forward.

Father had evidently written *first*. He must have *asked* the rector, *asked* the elders, *asked* Tibury's ordination examiners—he wanted to know. He wanted to know more about his son than he did." Crispin put his face in his hands, then shook his head and murmured, "At least he must have been proud of him, from what he read."

"'I've good boys. *All* of them,'" Reginald said, remembering. He swallowed hard. His head swam. "Father said that the other day. I thought he meant *us*."

Crispin laughed hoarsely. "I don't think Reg or I need any more proof," he told Georgiana. "But Jasper might. He's not going to do anything that will upset Mother. Not that I would wish to. Especially not now. But I want to reach out to Tibury. I have to."

"Because it is one of those conversations that you live for?" Reginald realized aloud.

Crispin sniffed. "Yes. Exactly."

Reginald said, "The proof that Jasper may need is that there are about one hundred and twenty pounds missing, unaccounted for, every year since…" He looked to Georgiana.

"Since the Earl married Lady Iversley." Georgiana bit her lip. "Before that, it was accounted for. Buried in with the servants' salaries. After the marriage, the expenses were hidden, but they are there."

"Expenses?" Crispin asked.

"I don't know how it works." Georgiana blushed. "Thirty pounds a quarter, fairly regular gifts each spring, small amounts here and there. And the tuitions."

"He may not have been visiting her—whoever she was—the entire time," Reginald said as a thought struck him. "He may have given her a pension."

"It may have been on again, off again," Crispin said dryly. "But the sad fact remains that you and Tibury are nearly the same age. There is a slight family resemblance. I'd wager Tibury got sent to Eton to be certain your paths never crossed."

"And that was why Father agreed so readily to Cambridge for me. He could send Tibury to Oxford like a true Taverston." Reginald felt hollowed out but forced himself to laugh.

Georgiana stood up abruptly. The ledgers fell from her lap to the floor.

"How can you laugh? Are all men…are all *Taverston* men…so wicked? So heartless? Have you all mistresses? Children that you won't acknowledge? That your wives will have to pretend don't exist? Is this *funny* to you?" Her voice cracked. Reginald was horrified by the way she fled from them, pushing past Crispin to reach the library door. There she collided with Jasper, who stood in the doorway, wooden-faced. Reginald had no idea how long he had been standing there.

"I won't marry you!" Georgiana said, shoving Jasper aside. "Don't you dare ask for me! Don't you dare!"

She ran out. Her footsteps faded down the hall.

Crispin said, "Jasp? How much did you hear?"

"Enough."

"Will you permit me to reach out to Tibury?"

"What do we say to Mother?"

"Merely that we know." Crispin stood. Then he threw up his hands. "She knows, Jasper. Mother is no fool. I'm convinced she knows."

"God," Jasper said. "What a bloody mess. Yes, I should think Mother knows. And once she is no longer protecting us, she'll probably insist that reaching out to Tibury is the decent thing to do. Mother is a rock. But how the devil did Georgiana become involved? How am I to continue to court her when she's disgusted with us?"

Reginald tensed, but Crispin said, "I don't think that's the important question."

"Then what is?"

"What do you intend to do about Vanessa? Or is this to be an intergenerational curse?"

Jasper slammed his hand against the wall before he turned

and walked out.

Crispin and Reginald stood a few moments in silence. Reginald could not absorb all of what had just occurred. All he knew was that he hurt. Everything he had ever believed about his father was a lie. And worse, their family's dirty truths had been vomited out before the woman he loved. For God's sake—the woman he loved had uncovered them!

Worst of all, Jasper evidently still meant to pursue her.

Crispin bent to pick up the ledgers, stacked them on his arm, and carted them back to the desk. He set them down and stared at them for a moment. Then he looked up.

"She was tallying it all in her head. And not just what I pointed to, but things she remembered. She calculated the Harrow tuitions and my tutors and the difference—my God, I could see it in her eyes. The numbers clicked instantaneously."

Reginald said nothing. There was nothing he *could* say.

Crispin shook his head. "If you don't marry her, Reg, I wash my hands of you."

CHAPTER TWENTY-FIVE

ALICE WAS SEATED at the writing table focused on the letter she was composing when Georgiana flung open the door.

"Is it suppertime?" Alice asked, head down. "I'm just finishing."

Georgiana dropped flat on her back onto the bed, shaking uncontrollably. Alice looked up.

"Georgiana! What's wrong? Did—did the Earl—?"

"No." Everything *else* was wrong. So very wrong that she could not possibly explain. She never should have offered to help Reginald. It was an inexcusable violation of the Taverstons' privacy. And she had acted like such a child, erupting over the Earl's infidelity. What was it to her? What did she care if the lords of Iversley were all rakes?

"Then what is it?" Alice pressed, coming to sit beside Georgiana on the bed.

She had to give some sort of answer. Fortunately, there was one thing she could—in fact, that she had to—confess. "I—I refused Lord Taverston."

"He finally asked you? And you *refused?*" Alice stiffened, horrified. Georgiana knew everyone in London would react the same. *What on earth was wrong with Lady Georgiana?*

"He didn't ask me. I preemptively told him no." She gulped back her tears. What had she done? But what *could* she have done? "Mama will be so disappointed with me, but I don't want to marry him. I can't!"

Alice stared without comprehension. "You rejected him before he even asked?"

"It has been torture. Going through the motions." She turned her face away, looking upward. The ceiling swam in front of her eyes. "Like a chain around my neck that kept getting heavier. Mama says I will grow to love him, but I won't. I just won't."

"But you seemed to like him. You two are so pleasant to each other—"

"I tried!" She couldn't tell Alice why marriage to Jasper was impossible. Reginald had made it clear that he would never ask for her. He wasn't "that kind of man." And she was furious with him for being angry with her. Did he blame her for not loving Jasper as she should? "Oh, Alice. I've tried. I don't dislike him. But I can't love him."

"You're certain?" Alice sounded peeved, and if Alice was peeved, Mama would be incensed. "What could you possibly have against him?"

Why must she have something against him? Why could she simply not want to spend the rest of her life with him? She flopped onto her side and, blinking away her tears, regarded her disapproving cousin.

"If you must, he is uninteresting."

"Uninteresting?" Alice looked startled. Then she laughed with high-pitched disbelief. "Jasper Taverston? Not interesting? Who *is* interesting then? Can any such person exist?"

"Of course! Hazard is interesting. Crispin is interesting." She hesitated for a moment before adding, "Reginald is interesting."

"But you wouldn't *marry* any of them!" When Georgiana did not respond, Alice's eyes widened. "Would you?" She put her hand on Georgiana's arm. "Would you?"

She jerked away and sat up. "None of them are asking me."

"Georgiana!" Alice gaped. "Are you interested in *Crispin*?"

"Oh, for Heaven's sake. No."

Why not Reginald? Was that so unfathomable? Georgiana rubbed her eyes, got control of herself, and stood. "I should never have agreed to come here. People are going to talk. They'll say I'm a coquette, collecting suitors like trophies. But Alice, is *that* a reason to marry Jasper? Because people will talk if I don't?"

"Of course not," Alice said, getting back to her feet also, but her expression was not sympathetic. "You're not a coquette. But honestly, Georgiana, it isn't good of you to reject all these wonderful gentlemen out of hand. It isn't—" She twisted her hands together. "It isn't fair. It's capricious. And I'm sorry. I promised myself I would not be jealous of you. That I would keep my expectations realistic. I'll likely marry Mr. Gamby, Georgiana. Mr. Gamby! While you toss Jasper Taverston aside because he isn't *interesting* enough for you."

Georgiana found herself at a loss for words. Alice was frustrated with her own coming out, disappointed with her own suitors, *and* she'd had to follow Georgiana to Chaumbers and take a back seat once more. Then Georgiana rejected the perfectly fine gentleman she had come here to pursue. Of course, Alice was irritated with her.

"Oh, Alice, I'm sorry. I've been so callous. This should be your Season. I had my chance last year and this year, we should be focusing on you. We will. When we go back to London, we'll plan your coming out ball and I'll stay in the background."

A small enough sacrifice. After this fiasco, she would rather stay out of society altogether.

"That's not what I meant. I want to enjoy this time *with* you. I know you can look higher than I can. That's simply the way things are. But I'm worried about you. And so is the Duchess. Because there is no gentleman more eligible than Jasper. If you turn him down, who is there left to accept?"

Georgiana bit her lip, then looked down at the floor. "I'm not capricious. And I don't think that I was being unreasonable, waiting for the right man to love. Not anymore."

"Not anymore?"

"The thing is…" she sighed. She had always shared her secrets with Alice. It was only this one she had been too fearful to share. "It's Reginald. I've fallen in love with Reginald." *There.* She said it aloud.

Alice looked stunned, not as though disbelieving but as though she wanted to argue. "Reginald Taverston? But, when? Georgiana, *why?*"

Why? How could anyone ask that? How could anyone spend five minutes with the two brothers and not see that Reginald was *the one?* "Because he's brilliant."

This should not need explaining. Yet, she supposed Alice had not spent time alone with him. How would she know? "He's translating a manuscript from the ancient Greek that has never been translated before! And you heard the way he reinterpreted Mr. Brindle's incomprehensible sermon. And—"

Alice laughed as though tickled by Georgiana's brimming enthusiasm. Still, once unleashed, her excitement brimmed over. "He studied mathematics at Cambridge. He has *Principia* in his collection and *The Principles of Analytical Calculation, and* he said he would read them with me," Georgiana finished breathlessly.

"Be still, your heart!" Alice teased, fluttering her hand before her face. "He's good-looking too, if you haven't noticed."

"Oh, please don't make fun. You know how odd I am." Her enthusiasm died as quickly as it had kindled. "I've been so unhappy. Pretending all the time. But I don't have to pretend around Reginald. He doesn't care that I'm odd."

"So he feels the same?"

"No. He brushed me aside and said I belonged to Jasper."

Alice's face fell. "I'm afraid that is what everyone thinks. Lord Billings certainly did." She gestured to the writing desk. "Even my father is asking when the announcement will appear."

Georgiana groaned. "This was such a mistake. We shouldn't have come. Or we should have left as soon as the Earl's condition worsened."

She would not have uncovered the Earl's mistress and his

natural son. She would not have displayed her freakish talent before the lords of Iversley, all of whom she had now insulted. And she would not have had her heart broken.

"But then you wouldn't have met Reginald."

"It doesn't matter. He doesn't want me. He apparently thinks he is betraying his brother if he does. And of course, I wouldn't want them to fall out over me!"

Alice took her arm. "I don't think Jasper is that thin-skinned, but I admit I don't know him well. And maybe he is no more in love with you than you are with him. I didn't want to say anything, but he spends a great deal of time on 'correspondence,' don't you think? For a man who's supposed to be courting the lady in front of him?" Alice paused to let that sink in. "This may sort out, given time. Why don't we take a walk in the garden? We should compose ourselves before dinner. Your mother said it will be potluck, taken on the terrace."

"Don't you want to finish your letter?"

Alice smiled a little ruefully. "Not that one. I imagined things were going according to plan. I'm going to have to tear it up and start again."

THE GARDEN WALK was soothing. They did not discuss Georgiana's dilemma but rather her Uncle James' news from home. The ton was all agog over Lord Haslet's sudden interest in Lady Andini and more so over the fact that she had apparently permitted him to call.

"Would you have welcomed his attentions?" Georgiana asked, wondering now if she had wronged Alice by steering him away.

Alice shrugged. "I suppose not. I may not be very romantic, but I am more romantic than that."

They talked of other things until a servant approached to inform them that the Duchess was on the terrace and wished them to come up.

A few small tables had been placed close together, surrounded by chairs. Lamps had been lit strategically around the perimeter. A larger table held an assortment of hot and cold dishes from which they could serve themselves. Mama was talking with Olivia. Reginald and Jasper stood to the side, near a set of steps that led down to an orangery. They were deep in conversation and didn't appear to notice Georgiana and Alice approaching.

Mama did. "There you are! We are supping very informally. Lieutenant Taverston and Lady Iversley are with the Earl."

"And Adam," Olivia said, her voice low and raspy as if she had been crying.

"Has the Earl taken another turn?" Alice asked.

Olivia nodded, then said, "Oh, I don't know." She looked a bit desperate. "He's breathing very oddly, and it has been hours since he has waked even a little."

Jasper stepped over to her and took hold of her elbow. "Come have something to eat, Livvy. Don't make yourself sick."

Olivia appeared ready to protest, but then she nodded and let herself be led to the buffet. Georgiana dared a peek at Reginald, but he looked grim and did not glance her way. Mama gestured for them all to start. Jasper was very solicitous, seeing Olivia seated with her plate, then beckoning for Georgiana and Alice to join her. He pulled out a chair for Georgiana and asked if he could bring her a glass of ratafia. One would never have guessed that an hour ago, she had flung a refusal in his face to a proposal he had not even made.

Mama also joined them at the table, but Reginald and Jasper did not. They put food on their plates and returned to their corner of the terrace to talk in subdued tones. Georgiana shuddered to think what they were discussing.

Alice shared the gossip about Lord Haslet, and Mama responded with a small, disinterested smile. Then Alice tried to explain to Olivia that Lord Haslet was well-known for avoiding a leg shackle.

"Oh, I know Hazard," Olivia said, trying to hold her end of the conversation. "He has come here to hunt several times. He's one of the kindest men I've ever met. If Lady Andini has any sense, she'll grab hold of him."

Footsteps, urgent ones, came clacking out onto the terrace, and they all turned to see Crispin's valet, a serious, sympathetic expression on his round face.

"My lords, Lady Olivia, you should come quickly."

ONE MOMENT HE was breathing. The next, he was not. Reginald stared long at his father, looking for a change, watching for evidence of the soul leaving for wherever it was that souls went. But all he heard was silence. All he saw was stillness.

Until his mother started to weep. Then Olivia. Jasper next. Crispin moved to the window and stared out, then his shoulders started to shake. Reginald, dry-eyed, felt broken. Memories of his childhood, of his father's laughter, of the one ridiculous time his father had caned him, gently enough—for disobedience, downright insurrection!—of his father teaching him how to play piquet, the proper way to mount a horse, the way to shoot a gun. So many memories. How proud his father had always shown himself to be, of all of them. How Reginald had admired the man. How much he had loved his father.

He felt as though he didn't know what was true anymore. He felt lost. He didn't know what he was going to do.

But he knew what Mother would want. What she expected. What his father would have expected of him. So he moved to the bedside, knelt on the floor, and prayed aloud the words he would be expected to say. One by one, his sister, mother, and then his brothers joined him. Alongside them, he didn't feel quite so broken.

CHAPTER TWENTY-SIX

THEY LEFT THE terrace without finishing dinner. Georgiana, Alice, and Mama retired to the ladies' parlor.

"Although I hate to abandon the Taverstons, it would be the height of ill manners for us to stay," Mama fretted. "Georgiana, I worry it will be awkward for you back in London, unless, well, I wouldn't be surprised if Lord Taverston speaks to you before we go."

Georgiana thought *she* would be surprised. But she said only, "Mama, maybe I should go to Marbury for a few weeks. I'll come to London for Alice's ball but stay out of view until then."

Mama pursed her lips. "Maybe. That might be better, but I can't think right now. We'll see."

If she had not planned three steps ahead, this was bad.

Mama went to speak with Peters about sending a messenger to London to have the Duke's carriage brought back. They would leave as soon as feasible the following day.

The lamps were too low for needlework or reading, but Georgiana and Alice did not bother to light more. They were too saddened, too worried, to converse. They simply sat, lost in their own thoughts, waiting for word. An hour or more passed before Olivia came to speak with them. She looked pale and tired and very, very young.

Georgiana and Alice both jumped from their chairs and

rushed to embrace her, offering condolences. Olivia let them hug her but then stepped back. She seemed to be trying hard not to cry again.

"Your mother spoke with mine. I understand you're leaving in the morning. You're to use the Earl's carriage as that will be more convenient." She sniffled. "I'm so sorry you must go, but it's for the best. I-I hope you will write to me."

They both assured her they would, telling her how much they would miss her, and how they hoped to see her again soon. Georgiana's heart hurt for her, but it seemed their sincere words were distressing her more.

"I hope so too," Olivia said. "But I won't be in London this year." Then she squared her shoulders. "I'm to make my brothers' excuses. Jasper has retired to—oh, he has so many people he must write to. Poor Jasper. I think this is the hardest for him. Reg is riding out with Adam to bring back Mr. Brindle and Dr. Haraldsen. Crispin is sitting with Mother. And I have been commanded to go to bed." She sniffled again. "They have all taken it upon themselves to coddle me."

Alice said, "It's very good of you to let them."

Olivia gave a faint laugh. "Yes, well, it is all they will let me do." She took another step back. "Good night. I hope I will see you in the morning before you go."

When they were alone again, Georgiana said, "I suppose we may as well go to bed also. We'll have a long day of travel tomorrow, and Mama will want to leave as early as we can."

"Should you not wait to see if Jasper comes to speak with you?"

"I doubt he will."

"Or Reginald?"

Georgiana shook her head. "I'm sure he won't."

IN THE MORNING, the Taverston siblings came down early to send off the Duchess, Georgiana, and Alice. Lady Iversley had retired to begin her mourning and they would not disturb her. It was a dour parting. Exhausted and grieving, the Taverstons were rigidly polite, but only Olivia appeared sorry to see them go. Jasper was distracted, Crispin quietly mournful, and Reginald kept his reddened eyes fixed on the ground. Georgina's heart broke for him, and she wished she could comfort him. But she did not, of course. Instead, she made her goodbyes and turned to the carriage.

Once settled in the coach, Mama turned to Georgiana. "In your father's last letter, he wrote that there is a good deal of rumor circling and a bit of what he calls 'good-natured wagering' amongst the gentlemen of the ton as to whether you have accepted Lord Taverston or sent him to join the ranks of 'The Disappointed.'" Mama looked appalled. "I don't know why people must be so vulgar."

"Oh, Mama." Georgiana could actually feel the blood draining from her face. "What should I do?"

"He says that as he has not received a letter or request for an audience, he can only assume Lord Taverston has the good sense and breeding not to rush his courtship while the Earl lies dying." Mama gave her a sympathetic look. "Which is my impression exactly. But I've decided the best course may be for you to spend a few weeks at Marbury, rather than to return to London and brazen it out."

Well, that was something anyway. Relief swept over her. "Yes, I'd rather go to Marbury."

"I've told the driver we will go there first. We'll spend a day or two, then Alice and I will return to London for the Christmas festivities. Alice, dear," she turned to face her, "I'm afraid you may find yourself besieged by the curious."

"They will find me entirely ignorant of the matter," Alice said. She squeezed Georgiana's hand. "I'm sure it will be sorted out."

THE EARL'S FUNERAL, held in the ancient church in Iversley, was small by design, and attended only by villagers, family, and a few of the Earl's closest friends. Lord Billings came. Viscount Haslet came. The Duke and Duchess of Hovington did not, but their association with the Earl of Iversley had been a tenuous one until recently, and had they come, it would have caused more talk.

Christmas came and went without notice.

Reginald went about in a haze of grief. He supported his mother and his siblings with whatever they needed, but he was unable to think. He did not look at the Greek manuscript. He didn't touch the account books. In fact, he avoided the library altogether. He didn't *want* to think. Or feel. He needed to be numb for a good long time until the pain could be dealt with.

Jasper disappeared into the role of Earl. He had no choice; Reginald understood that. There were things that had to be done. He also understood that Jasper used busyness as a distraction the way Reginald was using inertia.

Crispin chose the opposite path, attacking grief and disappointment headlong as though throwing his battalion into the breach. Before Father was even cold, Crispin had spoken to Mother about Tibury. It wasn't how Reginald would have done it or Jasper, but Crispin did not procrastinate.

Crispin told them afterward that she was aware. She did not want to discuss it but seemed relieved that they knew about their brother since it was a secret that was bound to come out. And it was, after all, none of the poor boy's fault. She gave him permission to tell Olivia, after the funeral, because it would not be fair for her to be the only one who did not know.

The day after Father died, Crispin rode to Ipswich. When he returned, he repeated that their brother, Giles Tibury, was a good man. Giles would not come to the funeral out of consideration for Lady Iversley. Nor would he attend the reading of the will.

But he would pay a call in a month or so. He said he did not expect them to open their arms to him, and, in fact, he did not wish to be openly acknowledged as he *had* a father, who, though long deceased, he had no wish to disavow. Nor did he wish to be known as the old earl's by-blow. Even so, he would like to know his brothers and sister.

Crispin, Jasper, and Reginald discussed this once, and then they did not discuss it again.

The reading of the will took place on the last day of the year, a fact that felt as if it should hold some significance, but of course, did not. It was solemn and sad. There were only two surprises. A month ago, Reginald would have been shocked if there had been any. Now, he was relieved there were only two.

The first was that the will included no mention of the livings. Father had not had the chance to make the change. Reginald thought it fortunate that Jasper had been in the room during Tibury's visit, or it would appear that the lords of Iversley had simply discounted the Earl's wishes.

The second surprise was that Father had repurchased the family's lakeside cottage in Binnings and restored it to Crispin's inheritance. This was an unentailed property where the family had spent many summer months swimming, fishing, hunting, and picnicking. It had been deeded to Crispin upon his majority just as the great-aunts' townhouse in Bath had been deeded to Reginald upon his.

When Crispin had announced he would join the army, Father had said no. Crispin's health was far too tenuous. He refused to purchase a commission for him. The ensuing argument had seemed to Reginald to be cataclysmic. Crispin left home. After three days, word came from Father's banker that Crispin had sold the Binnings cottage and bought his own commission. Crispin returned to Chaumbers to pack his bags and politely take his leave. He never spoke of the argument; he went off to war as though it never happened.

Yet Father had repurchased the cottage and re-deeded it to

Crispin. Apparently, Father was the one with regrets.

After the reading of the will, the brothers gathered in the Earl's study. Reginald had another surprise.

"That chair is new." The design was similar, but it was brown rather than black and the arms squarish rather than round.

Jasper shrugged. "I ordered it when you asked me to. It took a while to arrive from London. The old one is in the library. Haven't you noticed?"

"I haven't been in the library."

Jasper narrowed his eyes, then shrugged again. "Crispin? Did you know about Binnings?"

"No." Crispin coughed as if to clear his throat. "No, Father never said anything to me. Perhaps he was afraid I would refuse it. Which, if you are wondering, Jasp, I most certainly won't."

They were quiet for a moment. Then Jasper poured two glasses of sherry and handed one to Reginald.

"The deuce," Crispin said. "One glass won't kill me. Pour another. I'll drink to the Earl."

They stood, glasses raised, and drank to their father. Then Crispin set his glass down.

"I have to get back to my regiment. I've already extended my leave once and my lieutenant colonel wants to lay eyes on Adam to ensure I haven't misplaced him."

"Haven't what? Misplaced your valet?" Jasper looked blank.

"Yes, I'm in charge of him. Didn't I explain? I thought I did."

Reginald knew Crispin thought no such thing. "What have you been hiding from us?"

"Not from you. From Mother." Crispin grinned, then rolled his eyes at their irritated expressions. "Oh, come now. Alice guessed. Surely you did, too."

Neither Reginald nor Jasper spoke. They refused to be baited.

"He's on parole. Idiotic, really. He is no more Boney's man than I am. But we caught him in a hovel tending to wounded crapauds. If I hadn't taken charge of him, they were going to shoot him for a spy."

Jasper muttered, "Here I thought your secret was that you'd finally, *finally*, hired yourself a personal physician."

"No." Crispin's grin turned to a grimace. "I don't need a physician."

"Adam fits the bill, though," Reginald pointed out. He'd been thinking pretty much the same, but of course, one could not put the question to Crispin.

"He is intellectually curious. I'm letting him experiment upon me. Now, remove your noses from my business."

They spent a moment absorbing the news that they had spent the last month in the company of a French prisoner of war.

"When are you going?" Jasper asked at last, settling back into his new chair, which had a creak rather than a squeak.

"Tomorrow."

"Tomorrow!" Jasper and Reginald both cried out.

"A little warning, Crisp," Jasper sputtered.

"I am giving warning," Crispin said. "It's not as though I'm heading out *now*."

Jasper shook his head, annoyed. "Yes, but I have to return to London at the end of the week. Parliament is open and I have to take my seat in the Lords. And there are…calls I have to pay."

"That leaves you, Reg, watching over Mother and Olivia," Crispin said, giving him a light punch on the shoulder. "If Giles hasn't come to visit in the next couple of weeks, will you ride over to Ipswich?"

Jasper grumbled, "You've already extended a hand to him. If he wants to know us, it's his turn."

Ignoring Jasper, Reginald said, "Yes. I'll go."

Crispin sat down. "Good man." He snickered a little. "Will you hint to him that Framingham will also be available sometime in the next few years?"

"Framingham is Reg's," Jasper said firmly. He drummed his fingers on his desk, looking as if he wished he had papers to shuffle.

"Reg?" Crispin said.

Reginald groaned. Crispin was making him think. Feel. He didn't want to have this conversation. Or any conversation.

"It's what Father wanted," he said.

"Bosh." Crispin leaned forward, pressing his hands into his knees. "It was his *suggestion*. He also suggested that I not go into the army but waste away in my bed."

"Reg has to do something," Jasper said. "He's suited to the church—"

"Stop talking in your 'earl' voice," Crispin mocked. "Reg, speak up. I am not fighting your battles for you."

"What battles?" Jasper sounded offended.

"I don't want Framingham," Reginald said, scowling at them both.

"You don't?" Jasper turned up his hands. "Well, the devil. I don't care. But what will you do? You can keep your allowance, naturally, it's just I don't see you idle."

"I don't need an allowance. I've been offered a fellowship with Bastion. It isn't much, but it's enough. The work will take several years."

Jasper stared at him as though he'd just sprouted horns.

Reginald continued stiffly, "I don't know why we need to discuss this now. Framingham has a rector."

"I'm just getting the ball rolling," Crispin said. "Is there anything else we should be discussing before I go?"

"No." Reginald made to stand.

"Ah. No?" Crispin said. Then he stood up, took Reginald by the shoulders, and pushed him back into the seat. It was idiotic, but if Reginald resisted, they would end up scuffling which would be even more childish. Crispin turned to Jasper. "What calls? What calls do you need to pay in London? Please tell me you need to see Vanessa."

Jasper's jaw set stubbornly. "Vanessa will not see me if I crawl to her on my hands and knees over broken glass. She asked one thing of me—that I tell her *first* when I decided I would court my countess."

"And you didn't?" Crispin's face fell. "Jasp—"

"She learned it from ton gossip. Damn it. It all happened too quickly. I know that's no excuse. I know it. I couldn't... But you're right. I'm not going to do as Father did. God. It's for the best. It's for the best."

"So you mean to pay a call on Georgiana?"

"I owe her that."

"She's already told you no."

"Can you blame her?" Jasper exclaimed. "Good God! I still don't understand why she was in the midst of that imbroglio. But I'll be honest with her. I'll tell her I did have a mistress but don't anymore. And that there are no children. If there had been, don't you think I would have married her? The hell with the ton?"

"I don't know," Crispin said, sneering. "You've never in your life said 'the hell with the ton.'"

Jasper glared at him.

Reginald wished to God he were elsewhere, but he inserted himself into their quarrel since it was what he did when they got like this. "And if she says no again?"

Jasper refocused on him, then shrugged. "Then I start looking elsewhere."

"So, your heart won't be broken," Crispin said. Reginald knew he was pushing the point home, but Jasper was clearly unaware there even was a point.

"I'll be miffed." Jasper tossed off the response as though it were of no consequence, then added, "I can't see that she'll say no. I don't think she has anything against me, really. And we were heading in the right direction until that last ugly scene."

Crispin caught back a laugh. "Can you truly be so overconfident? And so blasé? Is it enough for you that she has nothing against you?"

"You know what I meant. And it's not overconfidence. We're well-matched. She must see that. Why would she refuse?"

The room fell silent. Reginald felt Crispin's eyes boring into him, but he couldn't bring himself to speak. He couldn't see

Georgiana accepting Jasper, but neither could he see himself challenging Jasper for her.

If he couldn't even do that, he didn't deserve her. Yet before he could say anything, Crispin spoke up in an exasperated tone. "Maybe she's in love with someone else."

Jasper's confusion was almost comical. But he thought it through quickly and dismissed the idea. "Why, then, would she have come here in the first place? She knew why she'd been invited. And, moreover, who could it possibly be? She's had offers from half the ton and turned them down. I grant she might be infatuated with someone ineligible, and the Duchess brought her here against her inclination. But she was not sullen, not behaving as though she had no wish to be courted."

"She slapped you," Crispin reminded him.

"I should not have tried kissing her."

Crispin fixed his gaze on Reginald, waiting. Reginald gulped and lowered his chin, trying to think what to say. But the devil. Georgiana could just as easily refuse *him*. And then Jasper would be furious that he'd backed away for no purpose.

"Right then," Crispin said, annoyed. "Don't go to London. Olivia says Georgiana has gone to Marbury."

"Marbury!" Jasper sniffed. "Of all the…I can't go to Marbury. Not for a fortnight at least. I have too much to do in London. She'll have to wait."

At that, Crispin laughed outright. "With bated breath, I'm sure. A fortnight? Aren't you worried someone will beat you to the punch?"

"Not unless you plan to ride to Marbury before you rejoin your regiment," Jasper joked weakly.

Reginald could take no more. "I will."

"What?" Jasper said, turning his head.

"I will ride out to Marbury. I—you can't marry her, Jasper. She isn't merely a 'perfect countess.' She's *Georgiana*. And *I'm* in love with her." Now it seemed he could not shut up.

"But—" Jasper looked startled. Or confused. "Crispin!" He

finally complained. "Is this where you have been pushing this conversation? To get Reg to confess?" He gave his youngest brother a condescending, gentle reproof. "Reg, that's all right. I'm not surprised you should have fallen for her. She's very beautiful. And, she sings."

"Christ," Crispin muttered. Jasper ignored him.

"Yes, well, but Reg," he went on in a voice as earnest and kind as if he were explaining something to Olivia, "the ton expects her to marry me. If you are determined to ask her, I certainly am not going to make her choose between us. But you should consider—"

"Oh, for God's sake," Crispin said. "Reginald, tell him he's an arse."

"I kissed her. She didn't slap *me*." It felt shamefully satisfying to throw that in Jasper's face. Of course, he immediately regretted it. Especially when Crispin hooted with laughter.

But Jasper didn't grow angry. The confusion faded from his face. And then he looked relieved. Simply relieved.

"Well, Reg," he said, getting up from behind his desk. "You should have told me. This is wonderful, really. I am not an idiot. I've had enough girls throwing themselves at me to recognize when one is not. I feared it would be a chilly marriage. But I couldn't *not* propose. I felt some sense of obligation to do the right thing." He laughed. "This will cast the ton into a frenzy. Do you suppose there will be rumors that I called you out?"

"No one who knows us thinks you that brave," Crispin scoffed.

"Well," Jasper said, looking from one to the other. He really looked shockingly relieved. "To hell with the ton."

CHAPTER TWENTY-SEVEN

GEORGIANA WAS RESTLESS. Hiding away in Marbury might be convenient, but it was only putting off the inevitable. Currently, the ton was diverted by Hazard squiring Alice about. Mama wrote that she had voiced some reservations about their scheme, but that Viscount Haslet's attention apparently benefitted Alice's prospects more than standing in Georgiana's shadow had. If that was meant to make her feel better, it didn't. And she knew she'd have to face down the gossip eventually—the ton wondering whether she had rejected yet another perfect suitor or that Lord Taverston had failed to come up to scratch.

People should have more important things to talk about.

There were numerous beautiful places to walk on the Marbury estate. The village was small and safe. The library was splendid, not as large as that at Sayles, but still, splendid. Even so, she was not satisfied to while away the hours in quiet, not the way she had been after her first failed Season. Now she knew what she wanted, and it was not this.

She had just spent an hour idly practicing the piano. But that made her think of Crispin's effortless playing which had not been effortless at all. She could not stop thinking of the Taverstons. She could not stop pining for Reginald.

She tried reading one of Father's astronomy books but could not concentrate. Disgusted with herself, she took a novel into the drawing room, curled up on the davenport, and read. It was not as fatuous as she'd expected. In fact, she was becoming rather engrossed when Fenton, their butler, appeared at the door.

"My lady, you have a caller." His face was rigid with disapproval. "A gentleman caller. A Lord Taverston."

Georgiana tensed. What was he doing here? She'd told him no. How did he even find her? Oh, good Heavens. Olivia must have told him where she was.

"I'm not receiving callers." She had a good reason, even if it was rude of her. "Lady Millicent is not at home."

Her father's widowed cousin had made her home in Marbury. She was a little batty and fairly deaf, but she served the purpose of chaperone very well, especially as no one called on Georgiana in Marbury except the elderly curate and his wife and a few ladies from the village. But Millicent had gone into town to shop for a new bonnet to add to her collection.

"Very well." Fenton evidently approved. He spun on his heel to send Jasper away.

Georgiana tried to read again, but the book had lost its appeal.

Fenton returned, carrying a package wrapped in brown paper.

"The gentleman asked me to bring you this. He said his sister wishes you to have it."

Wonderful. *The Italian* had followed her home. But it was kind of Olivia to think of her. She gestured and Fenton came and handed it to her. She untied the strings. Unwrapped the brown paper.

The Principles of Analytical Calculation.

Georgiana's heart stopped. She could barely speak, yet managed to murmur, "Has he gone away?"

"No." Fenton pursed his lips. "He is awaiting a response, I gather."

"Show him in."

The butler huffed loudly but went to fetch him.

Georgiana sat up straight and set the book on the table, wringing her hands. Decorum, she reminded herself. She knew how to behave. She did. She'd let him say his piece and decide from there.

The butler opened the door. "Lord Taverston," he announced.

"Mr. Taverston," Georgiana said, rising and going to greet him. He had that unshaven appearance again and his hair was windswept from his ride. She offered her hand. He bowed over it. She said, "Fenton, that will be all."

The moment he was gone, Georgiana shut the door. She turned the lock. And she threw herself into Reginald's arms.

"You came."

He answered with kisses. Flooding her with kisses. Backing her up against the door. They kissed as before, but Reginald was even more…insistent than he had been at the folly.

"Forgive me," he murmured against her throat.

"Yes." She would have said more, but he scooped her up and carried her to the davenport. He set her down, kissing her without ceasing. His hands roamed over her back, her shoulders, and then her breast. This time she wasn't startled. She made a noise, but it was more of a moan than a gasp, and it didn't prevent him from continuing. Somehow he loosened her gown by her shoulder and slid it down, down, then he began kissing her through the thin fabric of her chemisette. When his mouth tightened over her nipple she cried out.

"Stop?" he asked.

"No!"

He laid her down, crowding beside her, parting her thighs with his knee, while continuing to kiss her and be kissed by her. At the same time, breathing heavily and pushing his thigh close against hers, he also gathered up the folds of her skirts in one hand, pulling them up, exposing her legs. Then he slipped his hand under the material and caressed her skin.

"Tell me if you want me to stop," he said. His voice did not sound like his own. It sounded raw.

She said nothing. She definitely did not want him to stop.

He began stroking her thighs. Like tickling but nothing like tickling at all. And then he touched her between them, bringing his hand to the most private part of her. He kissed her mouth and her neck and her breasts while continuing the strokes. She gave up trying to suppress her moans and couldn't keep herself from moving, straining against his fingers. What he was doing felt so good. Until it was unbearably good. And then shattering.

Moments later she was still quivering even after he'd moved his hand softly to her side and his kisses had gentled.

"I'm going to London to speak with your father."

"Yes." She twined her arms about him, almost perfectly contented. "That will be interesting."

"Will he be very disappointed with me?"

"*What?*" Georgiana's cheeks heated.

"Oh, Georgiana, no!" He laughed. "I'm not telling him *this.*" He went on more earnestly. "I mean, will he be disappointed I'm not Jasper? Not an earl?"

Her poor father would be more confused than anything else. "At this point, I think both my parents will be thrilled if a gentleman asks for me and I say yes." Then she teased him. "You *are* asking me, aren't you? I don't remember hearing the words."

"Did you open your book?"

"Yes. Why?"

"Did you open the pages? I wrote the question on the flyleaf."

"I suppose I was too impatient to see you."

His eyes glowed. "Too impatient to look at Woodhouse's pages? I'm flattered beyond belief." He rolled aside and sat up. "I should go. I want to reach London tonight."

"Don't go yet." She didn't want him to leave. Surely they weren't finished. "There's more, isn't there?"

"More?" He shifted and put his hand on her thigh. "Were you disappointed?"

She heard a caress in his voice. This was a side of Reginald she did not know existed. It was seductive. Rakish, even. An urgent curiosity flushed through her.

She murmured, "I think you know what I mean."

"I do. Which is why I had better leave immediately."

"Please don't."

He swore under his breath then slid down beside her and began kissing her again. This time she tried to concentrate rather than losing her head. She kissed him back with more confidence. She listened to him, to the sounds he made. She felt the way his thigh pressed against her hip and realized he was as aroused as she was.

"What do I do?" she asked. "What would you like me to do?"

He groaned. "Say you will marry me. Soon."

"Yes, of course. You know I will."

He unbuttoned the fall of his trousers and pressed her hand inside them.

"Just…there. Like that. Like that."

He rocked against her. He started kissing her again, rocking harder, squeezing her breast, rocking faster. Georgiana was fascinated. She felt warm and melting and wished…everything. That they could do these things over and over and over. She wished she knew how to make him feel the way he had made her feel. It seemed that he was too much in charge and she was contributing very little.

He turned from her abruptly, with a sharp cry, shuddering. He faced away from her for a moment, then stuffed a handker-chief into his pocket and rebuttoned his fall. He got to his feet.

"Georgiana, I have to leave now. I have to go see your father. If I stay longer, if we do anything more, we risk an eight-month babe. We are giving the ton too much fodder already."

He did not sound seductive now. He sounded embarrassed. And Georgiana was embarrassed as well. She didn't like to be ignorant. And he obviously was not. Part of her was glad that he was better informed, but part of her…

"How do you know what to do?"

He flushed deep red. "It isn't calculus."

"I think you know what I'm asking. I'm sorry, Reginald, but I feel—vulnerable, I suppose. I don't want to be naive. Just tell me."

He didn't answer right away, but finally said, "If you are asking if I have a mistress, the answer is no. Did I ever have one? Yes. She dropped me over a month ago. She had a better offer. I was not unhappy about it. In fact, I had been inattentive for many months. Georgiana," he chewed his lip, then went on. "I am not…needy in that way. At least, I wasn't. I find myself quite desperately needy for you. It's nice, actually." He seemed to be musing to himself. "Reassuring."

"Reassuring? I don't understand."

He smiled, a little ruefully. "Good. You may forget I said that."

"Although maybe I do. Mother called it a *spark*. I hadn't ever felt it before I met you."

"No? Good. And that's exactly what I mean. No spark. But this—" He gestured to that invisible cord between them. "Is a conflagration."

"How soon can we be married?"

"Assuming your father says yes? That will depend upon you. If you'd like a big London wedding, we should wait at least three months. A year if we'd like my mother there, which I would, but I will not wait a year."

She shivered. "The last thing I want is a big ton wedding."

"Then the sooner the better. I'll get a special license. Crispin suggests we sneak over to Ipswich and ask the curate there to marry us. Quickly before Tibury leaves for his new post. But Jasper says that's asking too much of Mother and the church in Iversley will do very well."

Jasper says. Another wave of happiness swept over her. She asked the question she had been afraid to ask. "Jasper does not—he's not upset?"

Reginald smiled. "He was 'miffed.' For about thirty seconds.

But he is exceedingly happy for us. Truly."

"Oh, thank goodness." She had not caused a rift. She couldn't imagine things being more perfect. "Then let's get married in Iversley. As soon as you can get a license. Do you think a week?"

"You're delightfully impatient."

"I don't want to wait." Then she *could* imagine it being more perfect. She swirled her finger over the back of his hand. "We're going to have a very interesting honeymoon."

"Are we?" he asked huskily.

She nodded, laughing. "Remember? You promised to read Woodhouse with me."

TEN DAYS LATER, Reginald and Georgiana were married in a private ceremony officiated by Mr. Brindle. Only family was invited so that the bereaved Countess could attend. Their impatience to be wed surprised everyone, which Reginald found a little embarrassing, but at this point, having waded through the awkwardness of asking for her hand when the Duke was clearly expecting Jasper, Reginald was past caring. He wanted Georgiana now—in his life and in his bed. They had not seen each other since Marbury, and although they wrote to one another daily, it wasn't enough.

Jasper stood as best man, which was funny in a way that Crispin would not have hesitated to point out had he been there. Reginald wished he could have been. His absence was the only thing about the day that felt wrong. The *future* might be a little iffy, but the *day* was otherwise perfect. They even had sunshine.

When Georgiana appeared in the doorway of the church, in a simple dark blue dress with flowers woven into her hair, Reginald was overcome with what had to be joy. The smile on her face showed him she felt the same.

Mr. Brindle had been warned by Jasper to keep the service

short, so as not to tax Lady Iversley. They said their vows, exchanged their rings, kissed one another chastely before God and man, and then hurried out the door and into the waiting carriage. The carriage was for form's sake. Everyone else would walk the short distance home.

Reginald laid his hand on Georgiana's knee. "I thought today would never get here."

"Me, too. Everything has been taking so long! I don't remember Mr. Brindle speaking so slowly before."

Reginald laughed. As the carriage lurched to a start, he picked up her hand and kissed it. The closer their wedding night, the more impatient he had become.

"Just the wedding breakfast to go, then we can leave for Binnings."

Crispin had volunteered his cottage for their honeymoon. The caretaker would have everything ready for them. The next month would be bliss.

Georgiana smiled at him, tentatively, looking a little shy. He thought she was thinking of tonight. God knew he was. But she evidently had something else on her mind. Her chin tilted down and she looked at him from lowered lashes.

"Reginald, what is this about going to live in Bath?"

"Bath?" He cleared his throat. He'd mentioned this to her, hadn't he? "I have a house there."

"So you told my father. Your aunts live there?"

"Great aunts. The house is large enough to accommodate them, too, and they're lovely. You'll love them."

"I don't doubt that. But..." She sighed. "Tell *me* what your plans are. The whole of it. What you told the Duke. Honestly, this is something we should have discussed before you went to see him."

He flushed. He hadn't been thinking so far ahead when he saw her in Marbury, but he'd had to present his case to the Duke as a reasonable one. He wasn't a fortune hunter. And he wasn't some sort of apologetic offering the Taverstons were making to the Stewarts after Jasper changed his mind. Both those fears, the fear that the Duke might think either, had reared up on his journey to London to ask for her. He didn't think he'd overstated his case, but something about it had evidently bothered Georgiana—not enough to delay the wedding, but too much to discuss in a letter.

"I merely assured him that I can take care of you." He didn't know how he could be embarrassed talking about finances with her after all they'd gone through, but he was. "I don't have Jasper's resources, but I have a house for us, and Bastion will pay me a small stipend." Upon marrying, he would lose his university fellowship, but to his immense gratification, his mentor volunteered to pay him for the work. "It'll tide us over until the living in Framingham—"

"Stop. Stop there. That's what my father said. Reginald! What on earth? A *rector?*"

"Yes, well," he ducked his head. "It's a respectable position. I can work on my translation for a couple of years and then…" *Grow up?* The Duke had seemed more concerned about his youth than his lack of a title. Which had been somewhat amusing since most people who knew Reginald considered him an old soul, not a youth.

The carriage bounced over a rut and Georgiana clutched his arm, though perhaps the two things were not related. She was scowling in an exasperated way.

"That was a worst-case scenario. You don't want to be a clergyman."

"I need a profession. It's a pragmatic decision, the right decision."

"A decision we should make together. Here is *my* plan. After Binnings, we lease a house in Cambridge."

"I don't think I can afford that. It's all right. I can work from Bath. And I can't sell the place. It's my aunts' home."

"Of course, we won't displace your aunts! Honestly, Reginald. I'm allowed an opinion too. You needn't take on that 'lord and master' role just because you're my husband." She frowned, shaking her head. "We have my dowry. And don't you dare say you won't touch that because that's what it's for."

"I told your father we'd put that in trust for our children."

"We'll put some of it in a trust. Reginald, please listen. If you wanted to be a rector, I would support you wholeheartedly. That is what I've been reared to do. Support my husband. Run his household. As long as *you* are that husband, I'm content to follow wherever you lead. Except to a place you don't want to go."

He blinked. He wasn't marrying her to 'run his household.' He hadn't considered—how could it be that he hadn't considered her wishes? He'd been so concerned about *appearing* worthy of her that he was behaving in a manner unworthy of the gift she had given him: her love, her trust.

"Georgiana, I'm so sorry. I suppose I told the Duke what I thought he wanted to hear. I needed him to say yes."

"My parents have only ever wanted me to be happy and secure. I told my father you had the offer of the living, but that I didn't want you to take it. I said you're a brilliant scholar of classics and mathematics and you're going to read Woodhouse with me. Possibly *Fluxions* as well. And that one of these days, you'd be a Don."

"Lud," he groaned. "I'm surprised he didn't rescind his blessing."

"He laughed. He said knowing me that made a lot more sense than what you were saying. He offered to buy us a house in Cambridge, but I told him we'd lease for now. Who knows? We may end up in Oxford."

"Georgiana—"

"We're going to live near the university, and you will translate those manuscripts and maybe tutor a promising student or two in addition to reading with me. And we'll go to lectures, and hold dinner parties for your brilliant colleagues, and build ourselves a marvelous library. And then you will write your book."

"My…book?"

"Explaining those manuscripts to the rest of the world."

"To the six or seven people in the world who would care?"

She nodded, beaming at him, and he felt a bit of a weight lifting from his heart that he hadn't even realized was there.

"Come here," he murmured, pulling her onto his lap to kiss her, quickly, because the carriage was already pulling up to the entrance to Chaumbers. They were going to be very, very happy together. "You are much smarter than I am. So I think we should go with your plan."

About the Author

Carol Coventry is a born-and-bred Jersey Girl transplanted to Kentucky. A quarter of a century working in the medical field has taught her that, after any tough day, nothing soothes the spirit like a guaranteed happily-ever-after. Escaping to the Regency Era is like a mini-vacation. After spending so much time there, she felt like a native and began spinning her own tales of historical romance.

www.ingramcontent.com/pod-product-compliance
Lightning Source LLC
Chambersburg PA
CBHW060438310726
48977CB00001B/240